THE INTERN

The Intern
A Novel

by

DAVID LAING DAWSON

Macmillan Canada
A division of Canada Publishing Corporation
Toronto

Canadian Cataloguing in Publication Data

Dawson, David Laing
   The intern
ISBN 0-7715-7324-3

I. Title

PS8557.A87167   1996   C813'.54   C95-932863-7
PR9199.3.D38167   1996

Macmillan Canada wishes to thank the Canada Council, the Ontario Ministry of Culture and Communications and the Ontario Arts Council for supporting its publishing program.

Macmillan Canada
A Division of Canada Publishing Corporation
Toronto, Canada

Jacket illustration: Brian Deines
Jacket design: Concrete Design Communications Inc.
Text illustrations: David Laing Dawson
Text design and typesetting: Bird-in-Hand Productions

1 2 3 4 5   00 99 98 97 96
Printed in Canada

for my father

Chapter One

I look at the world and I notice it's turning
While my guitar gently weeps
With every mistake we must surely be learning
Still my guitar gently weeps

— George Harrison

Paul, six foot four, elegant in white lab coat: "The bullet must have gone in here, right below the occiput, severed the spinal cord, come out over here, just above the clavicle."

Benny, thin, stooped, Oriental: "No, no. Up here. Smashing the occipital bone, shoving bone fragments right through the medulla, exiting through the thyroid cartilage."

Charles, bespectacled, studious: "How do you explain the explosion through the frontal bone?"

Paul: "There could be deflection. It doesn't have to follow a straight line. Or two bullets. There could be two bullets."

Robert, not as tall as Paul, not as elegant: "Either way, one hell of a lot of damage. Jesus." He could imagine, somehow, the impact. Almost feel it. The tearing through. Steel missile destroying brain. Suddenly through the skull, into the soft seat of consciousness, tearing through white and gray matter, the very nucleus of being. "He must have been unconscious, though, I mean instantly."

Charles: "Not necessarily. Cortex might be intact."

Paul: "No. The trauma would do it. The impact."

Robert wondering what would be better: instant blackness, lights suddenly, unexpectedly out, instant nothingness, or a terrible moment of recognition, perhaps a long moment, for there was no reason to believe time continued at its usual pace. No longer marked by external events, but by the sequential dying of a million cells. "Shit. I'm going for a walk."

"What?"

"A walk. If Friedman comes around, tell him I'm studying bones or something."

THE DAY BEFORE, sun shining, dry, fresh breezes tickling the laboratory building, inside, Robert and Paul, Benny and Charles, hunched over Fred with dissecting tools in hand. Four students to a body, fifteen bodies. They had become accustomed to the sweet smell of human tissue saturated with formaldehyde, but not to the fact of flesh, the fact of death.

The word spread quickly, from table to table, and then somebody brought in a radio, tuned to CBC. In Dallas, John F. Kennedy had been shot.

They had already removed the skin, the subcutaneous tissue, the superficial muscles from Fred's neck—they were down to the constrictor pharyngis superior, the middle meningeal artery, the levator palati—and they listened, transfixed, to the news, and they looked at Fred's exposed cartilage, the back of his neck.

Maybe the bullet had passed through the occiput, penetrated the brain stem and exploded out the front of the neck below the thyroid cartilage. Through the cerebellum, the pons, the pyramid, the olive, the lentiform nucleus, the claustrum, the insula. Or the bullet had entered from the front and blown out the back of his head. Coming in at an angle, like so. Or ricocheting here, spreading and tacking up. They had no way of knowing their arguments over origin and trajectory would still be resonating thirty years later, as they retreated behind the arcane language of anatomy.

Fred's skin and organs showed evidence of a difficult life, although it was hard to tell how old he had been when he died. And without reflection they thought of him as having died a long time ago, an indeterminate time before, while in truth, it must have been a specific day, possibly in July or August of that same year. After death Fred had been drained of blood and his vessels filled with formaldehyde, and then stored to await the students' crude prodding, probing, skinning, dismembering, and now Robert Snow and his companions, compelled to add a further indignity, were using long instruments to trace the path of the bullet or bullets that were this very moment killing John Fitzgerald Kennedy. Benny looked ill at ease, but he always did, convinced from the very beginning that he would be one of the fifteen (the number predicted by their professors) who would fail the year. Charles wanted to get on with the lesson of the day, find the ligaments, muscles, arteries, identify the bones and their notches and holes, their foramen, their tubercles, canals and fossa, isolate them, name them, commit them to memory, regurgitate them on exams, get a degree, set up an office. Paul was restless, determined to find a way for a bullet to pass through the middle of the back of the neck and do little damage.

But it must have gone right through the medulla oblongata, right through the brain stem, the reticular system, the thalamus, the substantia nigra, the John F. Kennedy brain stem. All afternoon as they cut and probed Fred the radio reported on Kennedy's condition in a hospital in Dallas. The associations to some simple words were changing forever: book depository, grassy knoll. Robert knew he was dead. You can't pass an inch of steel through that part of the brain and get off scot-free.

Fred, it seemed, had died a less traumatic death, but none of them really knew anything about their cadavers, these amateur pathologists. The size of Fred's liver indicated a major drinking problem during his undoubtedly troubled life.

But their brain stems would be the same, Kennedy's and Fred's, maybe no difference at all, unless Fred had lost some cells from alcohol poisoning and some of Kennedy's confidence, charm and oratory had resided in his brain stem. Unlikely. Rats have brain stems. Pigs have brain stems.

The body here before them, gristle, sinew, slippery fat, stench. There was no getting away from the nauseating sweet greasy stench of this thing that had contained a life and meant nothing to them now, something to be cut up into smaller bits, examined, tagged and put out with the garbage. They couldn't let it mean much to them, to be like them, and still hack and hew at it.

Kennedy had been, was, electronic reproductions, photographs, TV images, words on paper, now being killed two thousand miles away. The bullet, right here, see this, passed through, exploded out the front, and took with it all the dreams and hope, dreams and hope they had projected into the fractals on the television screen.

Robert Snow felt an ungodly excitement listening to the news reports coming in that afternoon. We should go home, he suggested, and watch this happening on television. This is history, man. This is history, he said, and then felt shamed by his own excitement, bewildered, frightened.

The small anatomy professor, the one who entered each laboratory session after all sixty students were seated at their respective stainless-steel containers, entered with his entourage devoutly following, including his successor-to-be and his wife-assistant, and then humiliated a group of students with names from A to L or L to W with a cruel spot quiz

(Robert Snow was given to prayer, bargaining with God and making pacts with the devil that he might start at the beginning of the alphabet)—this little man had frowned in cadaverous silence when Snow suggested calling the day off because, what the hell, cutting up Fred could wait another day but this thing happening in Dallas, coming in now on radio announcements, on television, this thing was the beginning or the end of something big, yeah, not happening here but happening here thanks to CBC, NBC and ABC and happening in that big fucked-up mess south of the border.

Much later Robert learned that Johnson had sent, at his first opportunity, a note to the Pentagon to disregard the previous note, the previous note being the one Kennedy had sent suggesting they start pulling the troops out of that sad crescent country, oh, yeah, sure, and what a fucked-up mess they are in down there in the U.S. of A., and we, Snow was thinking, don't know whether to shit or get off the pot. Love them, hate them, let them run our pathetic lives, they sure as hell were interfering with a perfectly nice November day in the lab with Fred.

Benny had a shiny steel probe sticking all the way through Fred's neck, back to front, getting the angle just right, and Snow was beginning to understand his excitement as a generic animation, arousal, his own brain stem functioning, lighting up, nothing specific, and when it was clear Kennedy was dead he felt like crying or bursting free of something, hitting something, exploding through the roof, screaming.

5

Chapter Two

I will bring you incense owls by night,
by candlelight by jewel light if only you will stay
— Joni Mitchell

F ROM THE BEGINNING Robert Snow had disliked medical
school. It had few redeeming features. You sat in lectures half the day and worked in labs the other half,
took home twenty pounds of books and notes each night, piled
them on the desk, stared at them until you had thought up
a compelling reason to drink beer, play cards or visit Ann
in her tiny bed-sitter down the street. Hearts had been the
game they played, something they could play interminably for
pennies.

There was, come to think of it, when Robert happened to
think of it, one redeeming feature, and that was the phrase,
"I'm in medical school," which could be trotted out when
asked, "What do you do?" or "What are you taking?" He always
spoke the phrase with a somewhat indefinite cadence, uncertainty, along with a touch of pride followed by embarrassment
(his father had always been clear on the matter: an expression
of pride should be followed by embarrassment lest it be taken
for arrogance)—uncertainty because Snow knew, and his professors regularly reminded him and the others, that fifteen to
twenty of them wouldn't be coming back next year. That's fifteen out of sixty. Undoubtedly it was a statistic quoted to

inspire them. What it had inspired was fierce, mean-spirited competition. And, of course, anxiety.

After a night spent avoiding studying, of wasting time, of building a temple of regrets, Snow would wake in the morning and argue with Paul, who slept in the same room in the upstairs flat they shared with Tony, about whose turn it was to get to the first lecture and take notes for both of them. Tony was a graduate student. He didn't have to get up. There were times Tony shared his bed with another graduate student and didn't emerge for twenty-four hours. And then sheepishly, for this was 1963, and everything was done, but done with the appropriate balm of shame and guilt. Paul, tall, slim, straight black hair, polite, clear of voice, of conservative opinion. Tony, much shorter, unkempt, thick unruly face hair, glasses, shuffling, smoking, blinking, taken to mumbling obscene poetry.

When Robert spent the night with Ann in her tiny bed-sitter, with only its thin sliding doors separating them from the accusing eyes of her landlord, he might get a call in the early morning, from Paul or Tony. "Your father phoned. He's dropping over. He's in Vancouver for some reason. I told him you were still in bed. You've got about ten minutes." Robert dressing quickly, saying sorry about this, running down the street, wondering why the hell his father was in Vancouver, answering the door in the appropriately tousled fashion. His father saying he was trying to catch the eleven o'clock ferry to the island, but maybe they had time for coffee. Robert showing him the apartment, his bed unmade from the previous night, small living room, tiny kitchen, balcony. His father commenting on the untidiness, the dust, the barren kitchen. Asking what they were eating, did they cook proper meals. But with bemusement. Then quickly off to drive to the ferry.

They, Tony, Paul and Robert, shared the second floor of an old house on First Avenue, a house owned by Mrs. Bacony, a woman in her seventies living alone on the first floor. Tony and Robert thought the place was just fine, cool, with its balcony off the small living room overlooking, between the trees and houses on the other side of the road, a glimpse of Jericho beach and the mountains of the North Shore. Paul, who had grown up in the suburbs, wrinkled his nose at the old plumbing fixtures, loose wood flooring, heavily painted wallpaper, flat mauve latex in the living room, flat green everywhere else, naked light bulbs in the hallway, the general, come to think of it, gloom of the place on a cold, watery day.

They pinned a large poster of the Kreb cycle to the wall above the kitchen table, the citric acid cycle, this mosaic of enzymes, coenzymes, catalysts, agents, metabolites, products and byproducts telling them what happens to a piece of toast and strawberry jam ingested on Sunday morning, its fecal remnants excreted, perhaps, Monday morning. Beside it they nailed a particularly large, dark, hard, inedible pancake one of them had griddled after saying, "There can't be much to making pancakes." At the time it had seemed as dry as Mrs. Bacony, but several months later was noted to be oozing down the wall. It was allowed, after discussion, to seek its own destiny.

Paul and Robert attended medical school by day ostensibly learning about health and, with Tony, ate Kraft dinner by night. One box might feed the three of them and could be found on sale, at times, for seventeen cents. Paul, having grown up in a wealthier home, insisted they add meat to their diet at least once a week, and they set out to find something they could afford. It was Robert who discovered neck bones in the back of the meat cabinets of several grocery stores. The exact animal was never identified on these packages, but they sold for less than ten cents a pound and could be made to taste something like pork ribs. Robert and Paul, like medical students everywhere, took perverse delight in identifying the various parts, though they were never sure of their origin, their living host. They speculated on species when they had one of their girlfriends over for dinner.

They could name the nobs and spines, facets, wings and holes of the neck bones because they were studying anatomy, and dissecting, at the time, a cadaver they had named Fred.

This humanistic profession, this brotherhood of healing arts, this medicine, asks that its acolytes respect people, experience empathy, think of their patients as wholly human, as complex, worthy, psychological, social, biological, spiritual beings, and then gives them a body to cut up. Robert sensed there was something at least paradoxical in this. Before being allowed to open Fred's stainless-steel casket they were reminded of the sanctity of the body within, the dignity—that was the word—with which it must be treated. It was still absolutely necessary, imperative, in fact, that some male in the class, a month or two later, hold over the head of a female student a freshly severed scrotum, dangling from its epididymis.

ANN DID CRY the day Kennedy was killed, and later, as well. She wasn't dissecting cadavers at the time. She was selling large cinnamon buns to law students in the UBC cafeteria. She didn't think much of law students. To them, she would explain angrily, she was merely a waitress. They think they can get away with anything because I'm just a member of the serving class. Arrogant pricks, she would say. They're so disgusting.

She couldn't afford to be a student that year or the next. She was smart enough and ambitious enough but oh so female-confused about her dreams, ambitions, duties, rights. And had no money; that came into it, too. She had lived in Britain, South Africa, Canada, New Zealand, and had come back to Canada because of Robert Snow, for which he felt grateful, pleased, proud, guilty, apprehensive. He knew he could not be worthy of such devotion. How could anyone?

Robert dreamed of being committed, stable, settled. He hankered after it, but never could make it. At times he carried an image in his head of his future, the kindly country doctor, selflessly, contentedly plying his trade. In this image the doctor (Robert Snow, tired, rumpled, soft-spoken, wise) is loved by one and all. But the truth was Robert was in medical school because, well, you couldn't just be an undergraduate, you had to be *pre*-something, and his course counselor, who was also his Philosophy 202 professor, a rather anal-retentive logician, having noted Robert Snow's lack of diligence, discipline, his tendency to be thinking about something other than the problem at hand, advised him to consider anything, perhaps teaching English, anything but medicine. In medicine, he suggested, one had to apply oneself, to study, to memorize, to—dare he say it—to work.

Snow, challenged, filled out his application the next day. He mentioned this in his twice weekly letters to Ann in New Zealand, written on silk-thin blue aerograms. Perhaps because the paper was so fragile, they added weight and substance with words and expressions of the absolute and the permanent. His writing was clear but uneven, slanting this way and that, sometimes big, sometimes small, ragged. Hers was consistent and schooled, feminine.

He had trouble putting words to what he felt about medical school. It was confining and defining him at the very time in his life he wished to dissipate, to run amok. When he was nineteen and had dropped out of university to hitchhike through Europe, his principal goal had been to get laid in Pigalle. A noble goal, but not one that he had shared with his parents, who were already concerned that he was running off like his uncle Tom, his mother's brother. The one, to that date, acknowledged black sheep of the family, who had been lured from his studies by the big bands, by swing. Before Robert boarded the bus to cross the continent his father had taken him aside and cautioned him against excessive drinking. His mother, perhaps intuiting his preoccupations and always a more realistic judge of human behavior, asked that he not bring back any diseases. His friend and one of his traveling companions, Jim, Jimmy, had confessed to wanting to experience a night so drunk he would spend it rolling, puking, pissing, wetting, cursing in the gutters of London streets, preferably near Soho. Either they had been reading different novels at the time or the same one, their fantasies differently excited. Their list of targeted experiences also included the Louvre, the Prado, the British Museum.

Robert, looking back, could admit how uptight they really were, coming from middle-class Victoria. Sharing a seventy-cent room in Paris one night, a trifle world-weary, they decided to spend the evening at a Brigitte Bardot movie, improving their French. Robert claimed to feel too tired, hung over, headache, etc., and begged off. When his two friends had left for their movie he took himself to Pigalle and got laid, achieved his goal. The equivalent of three Canadian dollars it cost him, the exact amount they had each budgeted, per day, for everything. Europe on three dollars a day. A *petite putain*, *putain petite*, a little sparrow, of indeterminate age under a streetlight, older in the headlights, older still in the room, fulfilling his Edith Piaf fantasies, but saying such disconcerting things as, "So, Charley, you vant a fuck or a suck?" In her small room—walk up and pay the madam at the counter first—dimly yellow-lit, sink in the corner, purple-spreaded metal bed, lying on her back, receiving, thin legs fanned, skirt up, heels on, his cock, which at that age often sprung to life with or without a moment's notice, limped out. But she was a pro and got him through it without excess humiliation.

On the Metro back to their three-and-a-half-new-franc hotel with regurgitating bidet on the West Bank across the Seine he swore off Henry Miller. And never told his friends where he had been. Besides, they made fun of him when he was smitten in Copenhagen, smitten in Berlin, Dublin, on the boat between continents. "You're like a dog with his tongue hanging out," Bryan had told him. "You lose your frigging brain." It was true. He'd left a girl back home with the longest prettiest legs and moaned about this until the plump big-breasted Dublin redhead with dancing eyes told him, "I guess it's okay. Some Protestants are as good as Catholics," and smothered him with damp kisses. She had assumed he was Protestant, there being perhaps only two possibilities in her mind. Much more than her warm soft body wet lips lying with him between the bulwarks on the pitching and yawing scow between Dublin and Liverpool, he remembered clearly her strange rationalization, her ditheistic sexual consideration.

AT TWENTY-THREE HE had, he felt, much more amok to run, getting laid in Pigalle not really being that satisfying, fulfilling. Not that enlightening. Certainly not transcendental. Medical school required clean fingernails, short hair, well razored chins, white shirts and ties, punctuality, decorum. No room for Henry Miller or Jack Kerouac. Vancouver had a large discount store, called the Army and Navy for obscure historical reasons, which happened to sell white shirts labeled Doctor, not Arrow or Armani, but Doctor, made in Korea, for one dollar each. Robert wore these with an innocuous thin tie. They didn't breathe or bend. Bleached parchment. (There didn't seem to be an equivalent dress code for the women in the class; it was assumed they would keep their fingernails clean.)

The anatomy professor actually did inspect their hands before allowing them to touch his cadavers. Those were clean hands and manicured nails holding the scrotum over Carolyn's head. At the time the boys had been gratified with a short but penetrating shriek.

The women in the class, almost to a one the oldest daughters of physicians, serious, studious, very young, sitting in the front row, taking copious notes, holding up their hands to answer questions—their brains obviously deficient in the nuclei, perhaps the red nucleus or the globus pallidus, the nuclei that housed the male attributes of cynicism, irony, detachment, of cool. On the other hand, when the class studied male and female parts, the women affected a noble detachment; these might just as well have been the reproductive features of white rats, mice. While the men, including Paul and Robert, experienced a very personal, even empathic relationship with these unattractive bits of anatomy. And groaned when their scalpels sliced through the vas deferens.

Robert fell into a depression in late November, through December, January, into February. He walked through routines during the day, fell asleep in lectures, procrastinated, worried, imagined other lives, careers, considered packing a typewriter and paper in his rucksack, perhaps easel and canvas, and going back to Paris, giving Henry Miller another chance. On small black-and-white televisions they had watched Martin Luther King at the Lincoln Memorial, and then over and over and over the Magruder film, the funeral procession, and Oswald coming out, surrounded by deputies dressed as in the fifties, enter Ruby, gunshots. Perhaps half the world became melancholic after November twenty-second, but Robert attributed much of his depression to the grind, the expectations, the lifeless, the uncreative, the constrictive, ponderous onslaught of his classes and labs, the very weight of medical texts on his shoulders, the helpless, powerless trivia.

In their physiology lab they anesthetized a dog and found

out what happens when you inject this into it, or surgically remove that, until the poor dark wiry tongue-lolling mongrel had as many organs out of it as left in it and couldn't be put back together.

On the weekend Robert, Tony and Paul found a mouse in their upstairs apartment. They chased it down the hall, into the kitchen, prodded it out from behind the old round-shouldered refrigerator, trapped it in a pan. They discussed its disposition, and not coming to immediate agreement, watched it scramble for a while in the empty bathtub. They decided to let it live and took it downstairs and dropped it out the front door. A few days later they found a second mouse, which after discussion they decided might be the first mouse, which meant they had mouse, rather than mice. They daubed red paint on its back while it lay bewildered in the porcelain tub and placed it on the porch. The next weekend they caught a third mouse, also with red paint on its back, an indication, they believed, if not proof, that they had mouse, rather than mice. It was possible, they argued through a case of Old Vienna, that someone else was coincidentally daubing red paint on the backs of mice. They took it several blocks from home and left it, alone, in the rain, and then discoursed, through a second case of Old Vienna, the ethics and morality of this action.

Ann's period was late arriving. The question every month, watched for, asked about with a raised eyebrow, an anxious glance. Triggering panic. Stress delays it, diet, exercise, are you sure about the dates, how many days now, let's go over those premenstrual signs again and again, how much would it cost, I hear they do it in Sweden, and Robert Snow actually found himself thinking about dilation and curettage, doing it himself, if she wanted, for Ann was as panicked as he was, drapes, a shroud, bleeding, stainless-steel instruments, the risk, but Jesus, what alternative, what else, attending a western medical school but asking what the Eskimo do, the Hopi, tribes on the plains of Siberia, Beduins, please God, isn't this bad enough already?

It finally arrived, the heaven-sent reprieve, the red message, and they celebrated. And a few weeks later, in the quiet night, a candle lit, he would be asking, whispering, "How safe do you think you are?"

"Pretty safe."

"How safe is pretty safe?"

"I'm due in maybe three days."

"If you're regular."

"What are you doing?"

"Seeing if your breasts are swollen."

"Robert. They're tender."

"Sorry."

"Would you stop being so clinical?"

"But I should pull out."

"Yes."

"Those little suckers seek it out, you know."

"Seek what out?"

"The mucous, the vagina, the right pH."

"I think I'll get some sleep."

"There're millions of them, millions."

And then, thank God or the pharmaceutical industry and the women of Puerto Rico, the pill was invented. Or rather, it had been invented, but doctors, those self-appointed guardians of public morality, had been futzing over the wisdom of prescribing it for unmarried women. And unmarried women, girls, at the time, weren't so comfortable asking for it. Ann went to a reasonable doctor Robert had met and got the pill.

THE DEAN ORGANIZED a special evening with all the students and faculty, a meal, drinks, speeches, discussion. It seemed socialized medicine, medicare, was on the horizon, and although they didn't want to influence their students one way or the other, information, informed decisions were important, and dialogue. And then, well-fed and watered, in the midst of heartwarming camaraderie, in the glow of welcome, acceptance into the brotherhood (and sisterhood), the students were informed of the evils of socialized medicine, and guided to vote against it.

Afterward, Robert wasn't sure if it had been his deep convictions, his strongly held beliefs or the two double Scotches that had forced him to speak out. For he had surprised himself and stood up and told the dean that medicare was inevitable, and that in his opinion the medical profession should be working with government to ensure a good system rather than fighting a losing battle. Robert sat down. The evening ended. Paul said, "That really wasn't very cool." They went home, drank some more and listened to Gil Evans and Miles Davis.

"He smiled when I said that, you know that."

"Who?"

"The dean."

"That was a scowl, a frown, a grimace."

"He smiled."

"If he smiled it was because he was thinking of feeding you to his Doberman."

"He's got a Doberman?"

"It was a metaphor, dipshit."

The word *metaphor* would arouse Tony, who might launch into a lecture on semiotics, linguistics, semantics, or quote an obscure poet in Middle English. As a graduate student, a thinker, an intellectual, Tony held this medical trade school, this guild, in both awe and contempt. He forever fretted that his own doctor might have done as badly in his studies as Paul and Robert seemed to be doing. On the other hand he believed there were larger worlds to understand than the deranged inner workings of a mitochondrion. Tony was bearded, thickly bearded, his black unruly hair falling over his checkered shirt, his glasses patched at times with masking tape. He could, at least, let his appearance run amok.

"After tonight, Snow, you're going to have to pick another career."

"Man, listen to that horn. Turn it up."

And then Paul would turn it up, and Mrs. Bacony would thump on her ceiling with the end of a broom and Paul would shout something about silly, senile old bitch, and turn it down, and they'd drink some more and wait for one of their girl-friends to arrive to fix them something to eat.

ROBERT, PAUL AND Tony came from Victoria, and on some long weekends they, with Ann, would pile into Robert's 1941 Plymouth, sacks of laundry in the trunk, and drive to the ferry. In that short trip through the Gulf Islands, in the slanting rains of January, or the cool warmth of April sunlight, Robert always felt at peace, that he was in the right place, finally, albeit moving quickly through a land and seascape both formidable and endless. Whistle-blowing through the pass, hard rock shores, the curl and rush of water parted, spilled, returned, confetti sea gulls trailing. Going home. Much better than being home, or being away. When the ferry arrived at Swartz Bay, Ann steered while Robert, Paul and Tony pushed the Plymouth up the ramp, to the impatience of the other passengers.

"That's it," said Paul. "That's the last time. It's embarrassing. Get a new battery for this thing."

"A new battery," said Robert, "is the equivalent of ten to fifteen cases of beer."

"Only by making a most inconvenient choice," said Tony, "can we be sure we are exercising free will."

"Will you shut the fuck up," said Paul, his feet slipping in a puddle, hands cold and wet on the back of the aging machine.

"When do I let the clutch out?" shouted Ann, who didn't have a license and couldn't drive.

Robert dropped Paul off in the suburbs, Tony in the city, Ann with a friend, and drove to the family home, a house even then that had lost its spirit. It seemed his father was there as little as possible, and when there working at something, his mother, on the phone to her mother, lost and anxious, angry. His younger brother, Michael, was home from wandering Europe and North Africa. And would probably be off again, somewhere, anywhere. They traded stories and looked at slides that night, his mother relaxing, blue eyes smiling over wisps of smoke, enjoying her boys, belatedly fretting about the evils and dangers to which they had each exposed themselves. His brother had outdone Robert, the highlight, as it were, of his trip being the feverish night he spent on a park bench in the rain in Istanbul puking and shitting his guts out.

The Wall was up when his brother traveled, blocking entry into East Berlin. Whereas Robert could tell the story of himself and his friends, Bryan and Jim, when they were nineteen, being told at the border to East Germany that only the Russians on the other side could give them visas to enter. The Russians, the Soviets on the other side of armed West German soldiers, American soldiers, East German soldiers, a hundred yards of quadruple guard posts. What the hell. They were Canadian. Lester Pearson had won the Nobel prize for Peace. Robert had led his friends in a run across the borders, waving their passports, shouting Canadian, Kanadier, Canadiensi and variations thereof, ignoring the returning shouts to halt, the waving of submachine guns, and then diving into the wooden hut, the Soviet command post, to stand before the stocky, ruddy commandant, again waving passports and saying,

Canadiensi, studenti, visa, visa. Goddamned if the commandant hadn't shaken his head in disbelief, then grinned and pasted a *durchreisen* visa in each passport. What the hell is *durchreisen*? asked Jim. *"Was ist das?"* translated Bryan.

"Travel, go, no stop, no buy."

Walking back to the West where they might resume their hitchhiking, they argued.

"Durchreisen, what the hell good is that? We can't stop, can't buy anything."

"Doesn't mean a thing. We can stop, buy food. They just have to do that. Official."

"Official? You're full of shit."

"They didn't shoot us, did they?"

"Do you realize what the fuck we just did?"

"We had to get there."

"What do you mean, had to. We could go to Paris, Rome, Athens. We don't have to go to Berlin."

"Greta."

"Oh, Christ. Don't tell me."

And Robert confessed that Greta, the German girl he'd met in Copenhagen, would be waiting for him at a certain time, in a couple of days, at the Brandenburg Tor.

"Jesus, shit," said Jimmy.

"That's Checkpoint Charley," said Bryan.

"Yeah, I guess so," said Robert, very pleased with the romance of it all.

She was standing there, waiting for him, under that massive gate, the west side of it, actually, because you couldn't quite get to it past the barbed wire, guard posts, American soldiers, boys with guns. A grand, dark, historic monument, become, with the ahistoric Americans, Checkpoint Charley. She stood alone, tall, thin, in a long brown coat, cold, January, 1961. They spent the evening necking in a jazz cellar, the Eierschelle, not,

19

for Robert, because it was such a wonderful thing to do, but because you sure as hell didn't do this kind of thing back home. After midnight he walked her home, through the dark streets of Berlin, some shattered, not yet rebuilt, from the American sector, through the British sector, to the French sector, stood in a cold doorway and made promises that could never be kept, and then walked back through the quiet furtive shadowed city to the youth hostel, maybe two, three in the morning, found an unlocked window and crawled in. She had told him of growing up in Berlin, during the war, and afterward, her father lost somewhere on the Eastern Front. He didn't know why she had waited for him at *der tor*, unless she had been ready to grasp at any future, no matter how unlikely.

Their *durchreisen* visas wouldn't get them past Checkpoint Charley into East Berlin, but in the confusion of the times they found they merely had to board the Underground in the West and get off in the East. They could buy East German marks in the West, but it was illegal to take them into the East. They bought East German marks, getting five for every one West German mark, and, having grown up in Canada, where they had worried about nothing more than getting busted for underage drinking at a beach party in Whitty's Lagoon or Cadbora Bay, they stuffed the small bills in their shoes and got on the U-Bahn. Somewhere underground the train ground to a halt and the Vopos boarded, army-green caps, jackets, boots, automatic weapons, short, expressionless. They questioned Robert and his friends, examined their *durchreisen* visas and moved on. They hauled a couple of protesting Germans off the train. Robert was greatly relieved but mildly insulted. He told his friends this. Bryan told him he was nuts and he sure as hell was not sweating through that again. Robert said the least they could have done was search them for weapons, contraband, messages for CIA operatives. Bryan told him he was out of his mind.

They wandered through the East Berlin of 1961, rubble being picked and swept by squat old women, shapeless dresses tented to the ground, drab kerchiefs, mutilated men on the street corners, mutilated buildings. Most would not speak to them, even to give directions. Most would not sell to them. On Stalin Allee, a yellow expanse of monumental facades, the weight and power and stolid puritanism of the Soviet occupation, the empty boulevard, they found they could buy a few things: chess sets, leather goods, approved books by Mark Twain, Ring Lardner, and *Let Us Live in Peace and Friendship* by Nikita Kruschev, shown on the cover shaking hands with Eisenhower. They found they could eat where the Party officials ate, arriving in Mercedes limos, although they never found out why they were given a table and served in the elegant dining room, red velvet wallpaper, oak trim, filled with well-fed men in bad suits who drank and looked at them and talked and laughed. Though the food—and this might well have been, for Robert, the deciding point against socialism— was as heavy and tasteless as Stalin Allee itself.

Robert always remembered well another moment, during his year hitchhiking, wandering, traveling: after arriving in the dark in a northern Italian city, alone, after the friendly men in the bar had walked him to a house in which he might have a room for the night, a room with a bed on the second floor, no lock on the door, in a house he afterward found was a bordello, in a city whose name he hadn't noticed in the dark, lying on a strange bed behind an unlocked door, he realized in the blackness that nobody, including himself, knew where he was. Panic, dissipation, infinite distances. Vulnerable, small, anonymous animal on a huge spinning planet. He purposely undressed to birth-nakedness and lay back on the bed, legs spread, arms outstretched, defenseless, receptive. He accepted, for that moment, his vulnerability, his aloneness, his total lack of control and power, the absence of the security of linkages, definitions, duties, familiarity, and then slept peacefully. And awoke with a new sense of freedom. He believed he had crossed a barrier in himself, one he would never have to confront again. Of course he had been wrong. Doubt, shame, fear rebuilding within a month, a year. Roots very deep.

WHEN THE WEEKEND was over they returned to Vancouver, savoring the last moments on the ferry, and once more had to push the Plymouth up the ramp, into the rain. His brother was going to live at home, work for a while and then attend university in Victoria.

IT WAS LATE March before Robert pulled himself out of his depression and found a motivation to study and perhaps pass first-year medicine. It wasn't the most enlightened or admirable of motivations. He decided one night, as he told Paul, that he wasn't going to let those bastards beat him. He wasn't going to let them get the better of him.

"What bastards?" asked Paul.

"All of them. The whole fucking shooting match. That ambidextrous little necrophiliac prick anatomist, our favorite should-have-won-the-Nobel physiologist, Dr. Benzene Rings, sturgeon surgeons, gynecologists who live with their mothers, all of those dick-weed bastards who tell us we're not good enough." He went on in this vein.

"This means?" asked Paul.

"This means we're going to study."

"Study?"

"And give up boozing, gambling and women."

"How about two out of three?"

"Two out of three it is."

"Holy shit," murmured Tony. He had been browsing through the twenty-sixth edition of Gray's *Anatomy*.

"What?"

"Have you seen this? Page thirteen eighty-eight. All through this book the drawings are cold, lifeless, anatomical, two-dimensional. But this one is magnificent. Wonderfully, lovingly rendered. Curling hairy arabesques, suspenseful chiaroscuro, three-dimensional modeling."

They looked over his shoulder. *Fig. 1266. —The external genital organs of the female. The labia have been drawn apart.*

"So now we know what Henry Gray was all about."

"You're saying he wrote fifteen hundred pages just to get this little graffiti in there."

"He was early Victorian. Repressed all to hell. Had to wade through layers and layers of petticoats and bone contraptions."

"Gotta admit I've never seen pubic hair that luxurious."

"You mind if I rip out this page?" asked Tony.

"What for?"

"I was going to take it to bed with me."

"Gimme the goddamn thing. We gotta study it."

"And learn it."

"Memorize all fifteen hundred pages."

"Starting tomorrow."

"Right. Starting tomorrow."

"First we'll go down and watch the fights."

There were hotels on Granville, Commercial, East Hastings, guaranteed entertainment. Voyeuristic, vicarious. An antidote to the mind-sucking goodness of dedication, mission, goals, ambition. Populated by men and women who might, sometime soon, die alone in back alleys, their broken earthly remains finding their way to the stainless-steel cabinets in the anatomy lab. Pickled once and pickled once again. Hard, enlarged livers like rubber paving stones, networks of swollen veins, shrunken cerebella, cavernous ventriculi. And every night there were fights. The trick was to find a corner, load the table with glasses, drink, talk, laugh and watch and be rewarded, eventually, when some discussion about trivial matters— the price of the cheapest rum, if Joe was Jocko's cousin, who bought the last round—would turn surly, antagonistic, then theatrical, a standoff, a hold-me-back-before-I-punch-his-fucking-lights-out moment, a lunge, a crash, the table overturned, the glasses smashing, the expletives running thick and hard, the burly bartender coming.

"Over there," said Paul.

"What?"

"The table in the far corner. Two guys, two women."

"That one?"

"Yeah. They're talking sex. Who's fucking who."

"Who's fucking whom," said Tony.

"What?"

"Fucking whom. You fuck a whom, not a who."

"I'll fuck a who if I want to fuck a who."

"Is that a who or a who're?"

"I give them five minutes they'll be into it."

"What the fuck you assholes staring at?"

"Gentlemen," announced Tony. "It is time to exit stage left. Posthaste. We must leave this battlefield anon."

They didn't actually want to be in a fight. Christ, no. Just close enough to bask in the heat of battle, the threat, the rush of adrenaline.

"Ah, shit."

"What?"

"He's coming this way."

And then, leaning over them, the beer-and-dirty-clothing stench, large bruised hands, the ugly mouth slurring, "What the fuck you college pricks looking at my woman for?"

"Thou art a cuckold, sir," says Tony, raising his glass in mock toast. "A collector of fine antlers."

"What the fuck is he calling me?"

"It's a compliment. He's a little drunk. Ask your woman. Cuckold. Not cocksucker. Cuckold. C-U-C-K-H-O-L-D."

"I will fucking ask her."

"Shit. He's asking her. Look."

"Don't look."

"She's laughing."

"Let's get the fuck outa here."

"There's no H."

"What?"

"There's no fucking H in cuckold."

AND THEY STUDIED, read, memorized, recited. There wasn't much left of Fred. Tag ends, greasy pieces, like the post-Christmas turkey tray, exposed drying bone, electric bone-saw cuts, brain in its own dish, layers of muscles teased apart, melding into one, purple bruises, thinning crimson dryness. Formaldehyde cheesecloth wrapping. Charts and formulas pinned to the wall of the small Formica and chrome kitchen tables, desks, books piled, lamps burning, pacing, reluctant industry.

"Ask me. Ask me anything about the brain."

"All right. The function of the pons."

"Get serious. We won't have to know that."

"The amygdala then. The hypothalamus."

"Right."

"Mine is fucked."

"Alcohol."

"Is that a question or an answer?"

"Alcohol poisoning damages the hypothalamus."

"Korsakoff or Wiernecke?"

25

"Herr Korsakoff is cute, Herr Wiernecke is long."

"I'll drink to that."

And their minds reeled with Latin and Greek derivatives, mnemonics, Every Good Boy Loves Jam. ABCD. I'll take the third part first, Mr. Van Doren, Cardiac. What the hell is D? You've added D. D is death, asshole. Got no A, got no B, got no C, you got D.

The sun shining, the waves sparkling, white sails racing off Jericho, they read and muttered in carrels, darkened rooms, bright balconies. They contracted the diseases they studied, they worried the loss of parts they dissected, they envied, hated Goldman, whose books lay open at his desk, highlighted, spotlighted, undisturbed, during the half hour he allowed himself for supper, the fifteen-minute break at nine, the two-hour leisure Saturday night, the other students who always seemed to have more source notes, summaries, charts than they had. Ann encouraging, understanding, bringing them coffee, biscuits.

THE LITTLE BELL rang, the students before Robert each moved to the next station, and Robert entered and sat at station one, the students behind reluctantly shifting closer to the door. To sit on a stool at a claustrophobic desk displaying a body part, a microscope, a petri dish, a specimen jar. One. Name the nerve that passes through the foramen indicated by the red pin. Two. Name the function of that nerve.

The red pin stuck in a piece of polished bone with a tiny wormhole in it, a bone, any bone, what bone, oriented how, part of what, white blurring, spinning, guessing, remembering Tony, once asked, on a fine arts exam, what is Tondo? answering, the Lone Ranger's Indian companion, deciding there would be no sense of humor in this medical school. We're in trouble here, Tondo.

The physiology professor, flanked by his fellows, asked,

"Who discovered calcitonin?"

"You did, sir," answered Robert Snow.

"And what is its function?"

Smaller than you had hoped, Robert didn't answer.

"What is the most common disease in the world?" asked the professor of public health.

"Slivers," said Robert, feeling, the thing coming over him unexpectedly, argumentative. Despite himself.

"Slivers?"

"Slivers, splinters, little pieces of wood that stick in your hands, under your nails."

"Are you being sarcastic?"

"No, sir. I know you want tooth decay, but I'm feeling compelled to point out how much it depends on definition and context."

After deliberation, they gave him, in Public Health, reluctantly Robert guessed, sixty percent, a pass.

Robert was sure medical school made you stupid. Studying made you stupid. The physiology lecturer, a diagram of heart, lungs, arteries, veins on the blackboard, had asked the class a question. Nobody knew the answer. They scanned their data banks, couldn't find it. Later it struck Robert that it was a simple enough question, you could figure it out, if you could figure anything out. He asked the question of Ann. Ann thought for a moment and then gave the right answer. You see, said Robert, I was right, they've made us stupid, cramming our brains with trivia, no room left for thinking.

"Nobody got the answer?" asked Ann, who was twenty years old and sold cinnamon buns to law students for a living.

"Nobody."

"I'm not surprised."

ROBERT TOOK UP hypnotism, wondered if he could do it, tried.

27

Entertainment Saturday night. No money left to go out. Robert, Paul, Tony, Ann, Paul's girlfriend, a physiotherapy student. Only Ann willing to be a subject. The posthypnotic suggestion: when you awaken you won't remember any of this but you will have a compelling, irresistible urge to bring us food and drinks.

She did. They feigned disinterest. She tried again. Then off to the kitchen to make them something. Told later. Still willing to be the subject.

This time she was told her hands would stick together when she woke up, she wouldn't be able to pull them apart. Ann, talking with her hands, puzzled when the left followed the right, confused, then frightened when she could not make them go separate ways.

Robert stopped playing with hypnotism. Glimpsing something he would have to think about. On the other hand he had an idea for Tony, Tony who went on and on about that Swedish actress crawling across the big screen, tits hanging into the first row. Robert offered to hypnotize him into believing she was spending the night with him, in his bed, think about it. Tony declined. He feared they would watch. No, never, they told him. Trust us. Tony declined.

But one night, in the car, parked, dark, with twenty-three-year-old John Lennon "I Want To Hold Your Hand" on the radio, she let him hypnotize her once more, and then he slipped a small Birks ring onto her third finger, woke her up, drove off, waited for her to discover it.

It was, he thought afterward, kinda cute, but oblique, doing it, not doing it. Reluctantly conventional.

AT THE END OF that year Robert married Ann. 1964. He didn't like the idea of a wedding, marriage, but still in the trajectory of the fifties, telling himself it would make little difference to their relationship but please numerous relatives. Her father came from New Zealand to give her away. He took Robert aside and, with remnants of a parsimonious Scots accent, told him that Ann had a tendency to be strong-willed, erratic, playful, disorganized. She would need his steadying influence. Robert listened politely but was puzzled. He had felt the union might provide the opposite vectors. She would be the mooring on his life, the anchor who might prevent him from floating away. The Ann he knew was surefooted, confident, going back to school next year no matter what it took. But maybe Daddy was talking about his eight- , his twelve-year-old Ann, and he saw Robert in a way that Robert didn't see himself.

Robert bought a suit, his first, for the wedding. Eaton's, dark green, ninety dollars. When the United Church minister asked him at the couple's mandatory interview if he planned to raise their children as Christians he answered no. He would only take convention so far. Ann gave him a shin kick. He figured the minister wouldn't really know what to do with that answer, which proved to be the case, except perhaps expand his lecture, his homily. The minister, one of those United, sweet-smiling-angelic-but-still-one-of-the-boys types, got in the last word on the subject, taking advantage a week later when Robert stood before the altar with a beautiful, radiant Ann, aunts, uncles, cousins, school friends, family in the pews, mother on the Valium of the occasion, schoolteacher father mustache-trimmed, brother dressed as best man. The minister looked Robert square in the eye and held forth on the importance of a good and moral household in which to raise God's children. His eyes said got ya.

THEY FOUND A basement apartment, furnished it with Salvation Army, moved in, worked all summer and still had to borrow as much as they could. Student loans. They walked the beaches of Vancouver, paid ninety cents for a plate of goulash at the corner of Fourth and McDonald.

On a visit to Victoria, they took Robert's grandmother to see *A Hard Day's Night*. They had paid a mandatory visit on their way to the movies, Grandmother having given them five hundred dollars as a wedding present, to everybody's surprise. As they tried to take their leave she had said she hadn't been getting out much lately, and Ann, quick of tongue and generous, had asked her along. Helping her from the car, paying seniors' rates, the Odeon full of popcorn Pepsi teens, Grandmother's broad glutei fitting snugly. She enjoyed it, she laughed, she chuckled, she smiled at the repeated line, "Clean old man." Robert was not surprised. She had made a career of shocking her own children, of being more modern than they. Reading Freud, being agnostic, Unitarian, independent, an early yet coquettish feminist, a suffragette. The story was: Robert's uncle, the musician, the relative Robert's parents feared he most closely resembled, had dropped out of university, taken his saxophone and crooning voice to join Moxey Whitney for the summer's engagement at the Banff Springs Hotel before moving on to the Royal York. In 1936. Robert's unconventional and recently widowed grandmother then booked in for the season at the Banff Springs, with a table by the stage.

Now living alone in a big Victorian house on Yates, looking more and more like the statue of Queen Victoria on the lawn of the Parliament buildings, in purple floral dress, imperious, timeless (though Robert had seen sepia prints of his grandmother as a young and stunning Gibson Girl). Maybe she would come for dinner, maybe not, depending on her health, her previous invitations, the manner in which she had been invited and then, at the last minute, slowly driving her ancient Dodge up the center of the road, into the driveway, requiring the car door to be opened, an escort provided, once in the house shedding her coat regally, and then, and then, ensconced in a suitable chair-throne, dominating all before her, talking incessantly, stories from then and now, counseling all her grandchildren, including Robert, to live together for two years at least before marrying, approving all the latest fads and fashions, advising on all matters, but her stories, as Robert came to know, having listened to them for years, always, while entertaining, informative, always demonstrated his grandmother's courage, ethics, righteousness. If you were her daughter (or her son) there was no room to breath. His mother, he saw, was trapped, her mood swings being alternating episodes of resignation and flight.

ROBERT AND ANN returned to their basement apartment for which they paid seventy-five dollars a month, found rugs, utensils, caught mice (and one rat before they closed the open drain), made beer, made love, made sand candles, tie-dyed T-shirts, made plans, watched the sun coming up, dreamed. Set up study areas for the coming year. Cast nets in the surf at sunset for smelts, oolachans, diamond threshing, water spreading fire, island silhouettes, lemon sky, iodine wind. In the morning dredged in cracker crumbs, fried in bacon fat. Good coffee dripped. Breezes, warm air, two-dollar wine.

He didn't know what she thought of his grandmother, the enveloping force, or his mother, enveloped, preoccupied. The tension between his father and mother. She did say, while walking in a park above the beach, reaching to touch a branch and turning in the sea wind, she was very happy, and afraid.

Chapter Three

Something happening here,
What it is ain't exactly clear,
There's a man with a gun over there
Tellin' me I got to beware
Stop children, what's that sound?
Everybody look what's goin' down
— Stephen Stills

"You never could spell," Tony had said before leaving for the University of Western Ontario. "Cuckold with an H."

"It should have one," said Robert.

"And raucous, you know how to spell raucous yet?"

"It was a bad word, I should have used something else. Besides, you read the note."

"I didn't proofread the note. I just read it for content."

The note they had sent two years before to the *Times* and the *Colonist* revealing themselves as the anonymous perpetrators of the local best-of-the-year college prank, for which they would be awarded the Pisspot Trophy—had it not itself been stolen—for boldly boosting, in broad daylight, the large celebratory sign bolted to the stone face twenty feet above the steps into City Hall. A pickup truck, two ladders, ropes, wrenches, overalls, gall. Robert had written the note, his misspelling of *raucous* allowing the president of Victoria University to deny the possibility any students were involved. His students could spell.

At the time Robert argued, "Raucous doesn't need the *o* in it. It's *us* not *ous*. Rock-*owse*, ridicule-*owse*. You said yourself language evolves, it lives."

"You're right," said Tony. "The Latin version has no *o*. It was added two hundred years ago."

"Fuck."

"Now there's a word that never changes."

"Write occasionally."

"Sure."

PAUL PASSED HIS first year, as well, and returned in September after a summer surveying in the north. Robert and Ann joined the ranks of the married students, a few. Ann, who had one year of university, signed up for a second. Robert would always remember the numbers. They had two thousand borrowed dollars to get them through the year. They packed the freezer with polyethylene bags of oolachans.

Slight improvement in medical school. Robert still had to endure pathology, microbiology, pharmacology, but they were now introduced to clinical subjects, taken on the wards, preludes to internal medicine, surgery, obstetrics, pediatrics, psychiatry. Somehow there was life here, problems to be solved, figured out, stories, people with stories to tell, glimpses of pain, suffering, hope, healing, recovery. Little white jackets and stethoscopes.

His 1941 Plymouth held out until a drunk driving a Volkswagen plowed into it while it was parked and empty. Its rusted frame, pitted axles collapsed. The insurance company offered him two hundred and fifty dollars and a waiver to sign, and he took it. Bought a 1946 Plymouth for a hundred and twenty dollars. All in all a good transaction. A more streamlined vehicle, the beginning postwar ornamentation.

A bottle of Mateus Rosé to parties, the Beatles, a new group called the Rolling Stones, "The Ed Sullivan Show," everybody learning guitar, singing folk songs, as yet protesting and grieving events of the past, John Henry, steel-driving man, dancing, jiving, Johnson beats Goldwater, some hope returning, Martin Luther King awarded the Nobel Peace Prize.

Robert on the bus for a weekend retreat up the north shore highway, above the Pacific, arguing with the professor of pharmacology, as rock faces flash by, the ethics of the American involvement in Vietnam, still there as advisers, encouragers. Robert arguing that the great clash of ideologies had to be played out somewhere, better it be the jungles of southeast Asia than in the air over Moscow and New York. The professor saying wrong is wrong, pain is pain, death is death. The whole thing, he said, is predicated on foolish notions, wrongheaded values, and beneath that the war industry, racism, money, power. It can't be justified.

Robert twenty-four at the time, the professor, maybe forty-four. It did not escape Robert that the professor in mid-life was an idealist, and he, without much conviction, was merely clever. The professor, kindly, wise, understanding, but resolute in his convictions, was an American, run out by McCarthyism, came to Canada to avoid testifying against his friends, his colleagues. Later, Robert meant to tell him, then to write him, that their conversation had remained with him, had rattled around in his head, sunk home. Not the details. The fact of this man in mid-life uncompromised. Robert decided he should return to youthful idealism; there would be plenty of time later to compromise, grow cynical, worldly.

Ann had no problem with that, being by nature quick to judge, optimistic, easily brought to tears by someone else's pain.

Ann studied for a year, the next year taking a job working

with disturbed children, coming home crying about the abused ones, and the year after that teaching elementary school. Robert surprised himself, astounded his teachers, by getting top marks in the clinical subjects. He knew it wouldn't last. So far it was just stuff you could figure out, from first principles.

ANN WAS OFF campus now, teaching, and Robert, in the cocoon of a professional school, had only the vaguest of notions about things happening among other students, beyond the radicalism of the school paper, the engineers announcing each year that Engineers Have Two Balls. These things sneak up on you. They heard about draft card burnings, some guy named Savio, the leader of the Free Speech Movement at Berkeley, Marines landing in Vietnam, napalm, burning glue (denied), five days of riots in Watts, fifty thousand troops in Vietnam, a hundred thousand troops, Dr. Che Guevara leaves Cuba to foment revolution in Central America, murderous Sukarno, burning Buddhist monks, Mao's Little Red Book passed around campus, sit-down strikes, walkouts at graduation in New York, bombing North Vietnam, miniskirts, hippies, be-ins, long hair.

Radicalism, it was thought, creeps up the west coast, a seaside contagion. The university rallied the medical and law students, brought them together. Unaware, it seemed, that most of them were unaware. Their message was plain. They counted on the support of the professional students in any major student-administration confrontation, sit-ins, occupations, walkouts. Graduation depended on it. Careers depended on it. They all got the point, simmered about it, talked about it, white shirts and ties all week, bell-bottom jeans and guitars on the weekends. Day-Glo paint. L-O-V-E. Free speech, but not on company time.

Robert endured medical school, studied hard enough to pass all his subjects. Ann thought the school system sucked, told her principal that, thought it hampered creativity in both students and teachers, worked to make the lessons relevant, a word now popular. They made a home of their basement apartment, survived the Vancouver rains, visited Victoria. Robert's brother was traveling again, had taken off for Australia, Samoa, Hawaii.

As a clinical clerk Robert saw things he would long remember: the robust sixteen-year-old hockey player, neck broken in last night's game, now quadraplegic, the surgeon with the paraplegic woodsman, lumberjack, saying to the man, "Got hit by the old widow maker, eh?", the emaciated man attached to multiple tubes, almost all his internal organs removed in an heroic attempt to quell the pancreatic cancer, the surgeon saying, outside the door, wistfully, "Funny thing, though, our pathologist didn't find any cancer cells." But through this, as with the war on television, Robert remained, could remain, an observer.

THE YEAR OF internship looming, catapulted from studenthood. Ann said she would go wherever he wanted.

"Are you sure?"

"Yes, I'm sure."

"Boise, Idaho."

"There are limits."

"Okay, Montreal, Toronto, Hawaii?"

"Hawaii?"

"Probably not. There are credentialing problems."

"Montreal'd be nice."

"It's a crapshoot anyway. I gotta put down three choices, go where they take me."

IN THE MONTH between final exams and graduation Robert grew a beard, let his hair reach his collar, burned his tie in a brief ceremony. On the podium, gowned and capped, he received his diploma from the dean, once again smiling enigmatically, maybe knowingly.

They learned they were going to Toronto. He had to be there July 1, 1967. He would go a week early, by train, find an apartment for them, she would finish her year's teaching, pack up, sell the car for scrap, join him. He has a photograph of himself on the lawn of the campus, capped and gowned, bearded, diploma in hand, Ann on his arm, flanked by his mother and father, mother proud and lost, shrinking, father a little distant, puzzled, dreaming, making comments about the beard.

CHAPTER FOUR

I know there's no such thing
as hell or heaven
I know it's 1967
— LEONARD COHEN

Lost in a Roman Wilderness of pain,
And all the children are insane;
All the children are insane;
Waiting for the summer rain
— THE DOORS

ORONTO. THE ROYAL York, where his uncle played saxophone years before, years before the alcohol washed him down to cruise ships and hotels in Bermuda. (His uncle had once told him, on a visit to Victoria, that in his day it took either talent or luck to break in. Today, he said, it takes both. His parents may have put his uncle up to telling him that, but they needn't have worried, Robert knew that though he might have the dreams, he didn't have the talent, and he wasn't about to base his life on luck alone.) And then Yonge Street, his grandmother born at Yonge and Bloor in 1880, Irish family, her father working the CN. His grandmother taking the train across the continent at the turn of the century, age nineteen, alone, settling in Victoria, working at David

Spencers, later bought by Eaton's, making dresses, running a department. His grandmother, who must have had all the courage and confidence in the world until her second child was lost to diphtheria.

He found the hospital down Bathurst Street, seven-story red brick rising from the street. He circled it, stayed outside, located it in his mind, willed it to be familiar and then went back on the trolley to the subway and out to Mount Pleasant where his friend and old roommate, Tony, now married and teaching, still shuffling and bearded, had an apartment. The hospital waiting for him, all too firmly located in his mind.

He had four days to find digs, or, as they were calling it now, a pad, modestly furnish it on credit, survive, breathe, wait, shave off his beard.

ON THE FIRST day of his internship, arriving on time by trolley, anxiously worried he might miss the stop, surrounded by short Italians, Portuguese, Hungarians, Snow taller, a misfit, thinking belatedly his course counselor, the logician, had been right. Early morning, humid. No salt air, no breezes. Alone.

Followed the signs to the main auditorium, an amphitheater, past reception, white lab coats, curious glances, nurses giggling, for introductions, welcoming addresses, information, instructions, assignments, too anxious to listen, then hearing a strange note, warnings about property damage, responsibility. Following the crowd to the basement laundry for a sack of whites, keys. Then into a courtyard, overnight case in one hand, laundry bag in the other, shyly entering the squat brick interns' residence behind the main part of the hospital, the single small door in the bottom right corner, climbed one flight of stairs to the main floor and the lounge, past exiting residents and interns lugging suitcases, boxes, garbage bags out, the outgoing group, looking at one another as they passed but not saying anything, like rival teams entering and leaving a stadium. The first floor was unexpectedly damp, sticky, wet, and then Snow saw the broken glass and shattered furniture, the unwound fire hose, overturned tables, bottles and more broken glass, the place trashed and destroyed and broken, the warning a few minutes before now making sense. He picked his way to the second floor and discovered the same destruction and passed more drawn, tired faces, gathering, leaving, and found his assigned tiny cubicle on the second floor with its small hard bed and the ever-present telephone lying in wait.

He changed into his newly issued whites, the tight-collared barber's shirt, cotton slacks, jacket. Notebook and pens in the breast pocket, stethoscope stuffed in the side pocket, Merck's Manual in the other, pins in lapel, rubber hammer in pants pocket, no room for the ophthalmoscope, otoscope. Should he carry them in hand? Buy a little doctor's bag? Looking in the mirror in the shared washroom, getting more and more anxious, trying different pockets, different arrangements. Wishing he had studied harder, paid closer attention, feeling overwhelmed, inadequate, and at the same time wishing the clock to freeze before he must begin his one-year sentence. Rubber-soled canvas shoes, for walking, standing in comfort.

He lay back on the bed, closed his eyes, pictured Ann arriving soon, pictured rushing her off to a bed, pictured her kneeling above him taking off her sweater and then her brassiere, and then stretching to wriggle out of her panties, imagined her naked right leg catching the moonlight slanting in the window of their new apartment. Paused for a second. The only light that would come in that window was incandescent, from the next apartment building. Imagined a flickering candle instead, flickering on her thigh as her breasts fell close to his mouth. His watch told him it was time to check himself one last time in the mirror, open the door, walk himself across the quadrangle and up to the ward.

JULY ROTATION ON the general medical ward with forty beds, twenty of them his and twenty of them belonging to the other intern, a short intense young man with a quick mind and suspicious eyes. Appropriately named Sandy. A thousand grains of silicon. His hair Naples yellow, boyish. Twenty cases to learn quickly amidst the haze of nurses and documents and forms, instruments, curtains and bodies. To learn each well enough to not appear unduly foolish in front of the head of service, introduced to him by Harvey Ryan, the chief resident. She, the head, Dr. Dolanski, a solid short angry-looking woman, eyes scanning, permanent exasperation, not at all motherly or feminine but very female in that shoulders, heels, hips and fingernail way.

"Dr. Snow," she said, the *doctor* inflected with intimidating sarcasm. "Listen to this chest and tell me what you hear." Ryan stepping back to watch.

She led them to the first patient in the first bed and pulled the man's pajama shirt apart as he lay on his back on a bed in the dormitory, the curtains partially drawn, his eyes like those of a deer caught in headlights. Snow knew the routine: there'd be a murmur and a double sound where there should have been only one, and the chances of him hearing exactly what she thought he should hear were about a thousand to one against and so he had the choices of telling her he couldn't hear fuck all, or a gentler version of that, or trying to tell her what he actually heard through his nice gray Littman stethoscope, or faking it. It wouldn't matter a hell of a lot, the exercise being meant for humiliation as he had learned often enough before in medical school, and if he actually hit on the right combination and location of murmurs and clicks she still would let him know, and the students, the other intern, Sandy, Harvey the chief resident, the nurse pushing the chart rack, let them all know it was dumb luck and he was still just an ass-hole intern, antecedent to slime mold on the food chain. Or maybe not. Maybe now that he was a real doctor he would be treated with consideration, if not respect. And there was another difference. What he heard or didn't hear in his stetho-scope was suddenly important, or would be tomorrow, could decide someone's fate. This time around, his first interpreta-tion proved correct.

At the next bedside Dolanski expressed surprise the patient had not gone for radiation treatment of her breast cancer. Robert looked at and felt this woman's breasts, the left larger and harder than the right, and glanced at her drawn, depressed face, a face that was still elegantly framed with straight black hair pulled back. They had not been introduced, this woman and Robert Snow, and his hand itched with the shame of touching a sacred part of her and finding sickness there, finding hard lumps of cells invading her very being. Dr. Dolanski said, "They must have found metastases in her bones and canceled the treatments."

The woman said something like, *"Per qué? Per qué?"* but her voice trailed off and her frightened eyes turned away. They moved on to the next. Snow looked back at her handsome face, wanting to apologize with a smile, but couldn't catch her eye. That was all. She was not his patient. He never spoke with her. A very brief encounter. But he would always remember her face, her eyes, her black hair, and imagine the life she had and what was now in store for her, and how coldly they had treated her.

THAT NIGHT, THE first of his nights on call, he stood by an open window on the ward as a thunderstorm enveloped the city. There was sickness and death in the forty beds behind him, and the air around them was still and heavy. Oppressive, close, timeless, crowded and alone, a delegation of misery. With the first flash of lightning across the power lines and rooftops and the first splash of rain against the sill, a cool breeze blew around him, touched his face and went on to stir the nearest bedside curtain.

SHE WAS TOUSLED, tired, flushed, had been sitting through the night sleepless, when she stepped down from the coach at Union Station, struggling with bags and boxes, suitcases. Robert also sleepless, coming directly from an overnight on call at the hospital. Wondered about his grandmother crossing the other way sixty-seven years before, smoke belching coal burning, wooden benches, sleeping compartments. She had stayed behind, finished her year, packed, cleaned, shipped, stored, sold, while he reclined, fantasized, worked, subdued, quelled panic and fear. He held her, kissed her, wondered briefly if his hands had been contaminated, hands that for two weeks had touched cancers, infection, putrefaction, sores, wounds, skin of varying shades and cleanliness. Antiseptic smells, hospital soap.

"That is the last time," she said, "absolutely the last time I travel by train without a compartment."

"At least the Rockies must have been something…"

"First of all we went through at night. Then there was always some drunk coming on to me, and I don't think I slept more than five minutes at a time the whole way. I've just been layering on deodorant. I need a four-hour bath. It's so hot and muggy here. I don't believe this heat." Coming from the west coast.

"I have to warn you about the apartment," he told her. "It isn't much, but it's all I could find. I mean available right away."

"As long as it's got a bath."

"Well, down the hall a piece. We share with a couple of families."

"What?"

"I'm just kidding. There's a bathroom, hot water."

He wrestled with the bags and boxes, avoided the eyes and entreaties of redcaps, didn't want to do it, couldn't imagine an older man, maybe an older black man, carrying his burdens, then waiting hand outstretched for a tip, which he'd fumble, know was too small, also feeling foolish banging into people, doorways, when they could have been strolling behind a temporary servant with luggage trolley.

There was too much baggage for a subway and walking three blocks. They went to the head of the line on Front Street and chose a taxi, two dollars extra for bags.

Their driver was Haitian—Ann in her easy way learned this quickly, and that he'd lived in Toronto two years, wife, couple of kids, very bad in Haiti, Papa Doc and the Tontons Macoutes, the Americans in the Dominican protecting the Western Hemisphere from Communism. Robert listening but worrying he wouldn't have enough cash to pay him. Windows rolled down, she sat back and told Robert about some of her battles with postal, hydro and telephone authorities and then, relaxing a little, turned her amber eyes his way and asked, "So, how is the hospital?"

He began to tell her and then realized the hospital would always provide too much, too many experiences, posing the same problem in two weeks as writing a letter to a friend after a five-year absence. So he didn't tell her about the elegant Spanish woman with breast cancer and the quick, silent cardiac arrest, the frightening head of service, the diabetic with no circulation in her legs, the smoker with two legs amputated still bumming cigarettes from his wheelchair, holding them in the stubble of his fingers, the endless mind-numbing work, the nights sleeping fitfully, waiting for his mistakes to catch up to him, the phone ringing, jangling him awake with bad news, questions he couldn't answer, things forgotten in the daytime, small and large disasters. Instead he told her about sending a poor slob home on a meatless diet, his first discharge, the chief resident asking him a few days later why the hell he'd done this and Robert replying that he had just copied the diet orders on the chart from the man's inpatient stay, and the chief resident, Harvey Ryan, a nice enough forgiving man, saying his name's Steinberg, you asshole, he's kosher, he can eat whatever the hell he wants when he gets home, as long as the rabbi approves. Ann smiled slightly. Maybe you had to be there, he said.

He showed her the apartment he had found in this expensive city and her eyes betrayed some disappointment with the small barren place on the seventh floor, up a single gunmetal elevator, and its one-window view of the side of another building maybe twenty feet away. He also told her about the little room he had at the hospital where he'd be staying every second night and every other weekend.

"Every second night?"

"More, sometimes."

She stopped unpacking and looked around and he could see from her face that she was suddenly aware of herself living alone in this barren apartment in a new, indifferent city.

"Every second weekend?"

He'd bought a box spring and mattress for them and little else. Sitting on the floor eating crackers and cheese they decided the first evening he had off they'd find a department store that would sell them a sofa, a kitchen table and chairs and one chest of drawers on credit. The cost of his room in the residence and the frequent laundering of his white uniforms was deducted directly from his paycheck, leaving less than enough for the rent of this aging apartment a couple of blocks north of the stadium and a subway trip along Bloor followed by a trolley ride down Bathurst to the hospital. He told her it would be all right, they'd make it somehow, but his mind was already slipping back to the wards, anticipating. They lit candles on saucers and made love that first night on the new mattress, glasses of Mateus, white walls, moving shadows, breezes from the high window, forgetting for the moment they were no longer living by the sea. He got up afterward, and while she slept, wrote a poem. Embracing, unfolding, comforting images up to the last line, which came out, wrote itself, "And a cough brought the world upon his soul."

A few nights later when he read it to her she asked about the last line.

"Well," he said to her. "I don't know. That's how it came out. I just wrote it that way."

"It's very beautiful," she told him. "Up to the last line. Why can't you just leave it off?" This from a woman, he thought, a girl who came home crying about the abused children she took care of, played with, schooled, wanting to return to the fathers who abused them, the alcoholic mothers who neglected them, Ann, who cried much more easily than he did. "Even so, I love it," she said, and kissed him quickly on the cheek.

HER THREE BROTHERS brought Elsa to the emergency department. It had taken them a long time to convince her to come. They all lived together in the old family home, the brothers working, with Elsa, the oldest, staying home to do the cooking, washing, cleaning, looking after her younger brothers. All in their late fifties and early sixties. She had been able to do less and less over the past couple of months and was now short of breath just getting up from a chair.

"She wouldn't come before, doctor. We had a heck of a time persuading her."

"I'll die in here, Harry, please don't leave me here. This is a dying place."

Through his stethoscope Snow heard the gurgling of brooks in the base of her lungs, crepitations, rumbles, rales and rhonchi. Sloppy wetness, compromised passages. A tired, frightened woman, stubborn. Clutching the sheet to cover her breasts. Clinging to her brothers, their lives unchanged for years, passing through life in the same family home, avoiding danger, change. Her body a scrubbed floor and a sink full of dishes. She was short of breath, easily fatigued. The chest X ray showed scattered opacities in the base of her lungs. The fluid seeping up from heart failure or the inflamed cellular spillage of pneumonia. But with pneumonia she should have a fever and her white scavenger cells mobilized, mounting an offensive. She had neither.

Dr. Snow talked her into staying in hospital. She would have nothing of it at first. "I'll die in here," she told him. "This is a dying place." In the summer heat Snow felt a chill wind blowing. He promised they would help her, take care of her, make her feel much better. Her brothers promised her they would eat properly and do the housework themselves, take care of themselves, visit every day, and then, nervously, they left her.

Robert ordered a diuretic for the ankle edema and the apparent heart failure, went off to the Friday night party in the residents' lounge, stayed on call all night, up four times, did rounds in the morning, handed over to Sandy and caught the trolley at noon for a weekend off. One and a half days to sleep, buy furniture, walk with Ann on Yonge Street, Yorkville.

When he arrived on the ward early Monday morning and joined the group doing rounds, Sandy, on call all weekend, was looking sheepish, Harvey's mouth locked in anger, and Snow wondered who had screwed up this time. Harvey told him. Because of the way Snow had written the order for diuretic

Friday night Elsa had been given double dosage, the order carried out in the emergency department and once again when she arrived on the ward. All right, a little dangerous, but not enough to produce the look of disgust on Harvey Ryan's face. Ah, but there's more, said Ryan. Over the weekend her breathing had worsened, her ankles remained swollen and Sandy had given her two more injections of diuretic.

"Two more, for Christ's sake," said Harvey. "Jesus, Joseph and Mary. Four shots in what, thirty-six, forty-eight hours? It's a wonder you haven't killed her. Christ. Her potassium's in the toilet, she's semicomatose, we'll be lucky to get her through the day." Moments when you hold your breath, breathe shallowly all day. Robert thankful it wasn't entirely his fault, and then feeling worse for having such a self-centered concern.

In the afternoon Robert, breathing a little more easily, walking through an admission to another ward, taking the history, asking after all bodily functions, heard the cardiac arrest code on the overhead. His own ward was identified. He walked slowly to the other wing through the dormitory to Elsa's room, all the way picturing in his mind what he'd find there, all the way hoping he was wrong and some other patient would be this very minute jumping under the paddles.

The arrest team was already there, an array of white jackets and green scrubs, machines, poles, bottles, carts, tubing—someone bagging her, someone getting a drip in, someone organizing the wires of a cardiogram, someone sliding a board under her and someone up on the bed, heel of hand to sternum thumping up and down calling out one, two, three, four, breathe, and Harvey Ryan standing off to one side watching, Snow taking it in, a moment frozen in time. And in that long minute Dolanski, standing at the foot of the bed, her back to Snow, swung around, her lab coat flying open over her red wide-shouldered suit, her stethoscope swinging with her, and her eyes now directly scanning, recognizing Snow in the doorway, in the background shouts of one, two, three, ten c.c.'s bicarb, *now*, get it in, everybody back, on the count of one, and as the paddles of the cardioverter clamped on Elsa's chest and jumped as she jumped, arching up and falling back, the sound of a heavy fist hitting a chest, Dolanski opened her crimson mouth and screamed at Snow, "Look what you've done. You've killed her."

THE NEXT SATURDAY, after working two days and two nights straight through, thirty minutes sleep snatched here and there, white on white, red on white, feet aching, hot, he handed over to Sandy, a Sandy momentarily chastened by the Elsa events, but not talking about it, Christ no, still, it seemed to Snow, watching him the way Liston watched Clay, or Clay watched Liston, competing with him for some invisible trophy, for what? The year's fewest fuckups, editorial praise from the head of service, their wicked stepmother. Got off by eleven, changed into civvies, hair on his collar, sideburns lengthening, wire-framed glasses, tinted.

Up Bathurst to Bloor, along Bloor to the stadium, up St. George to the apartment. The jangled noon hour after a sleepless night, bright lights flickering in his peripheral vision, the wind in the wires whistling eerily, momentarily mimicking the overhead speakers calling his name. Ann fed him, kept him moving, back to the subway, over to Yonge, up to Mount Pleasant to visit Tony and Beth in their neat small apartment in a complex with a swimming pool. Air-conditioner hum in the courtyard haze. In the midday heat they decided to swim, hang around the pool. Ann, Tony and Beth got changed quickly. Robert told them to go ahead, he'd follow. He went into the bedroom with swimsuit in hand. Sat on the queen-size bed, soft, luxurious, curtained window, got shoes and pants off with a struggle, lay back for a moment and fell unconscious. He dreamed of being on the ward hunting through a chart, unable to find the pages he was looking for, falling away, scattering, the pages with answers, as someone nearby bled to death. Later, they discovered him asleep on the bed, half undressed, still clutching his swimsuit, legs dangling over the edge, twitching.

Candlelight dinner, shelves of books, tablecloth, four-dollar red wine, Medoc, Dansk cookware, wedding-present apartment. Tony and Beth now young teachers at a nearby college, Beth small and quick and neat, Tony smoking, thinking, wry, young professionals having a dinner party. Talking of books and students and fellow teachers. Tony had roomed with a student pathologist at Western, could tell gruesome stories. Ann bright and vivacious, but not quite herself, Robert could see, unemployed, alone in the city. Robert, still exhausted, was unable to find the right tone in which to tell his stories about shit and piss and blood and pain and death and sorrow. They weren't secondhand stories anymore. He tried to focus on Ann's life, its equal meaning, its frustrations, sorrows, worries, concerns, hopes, on Tony and Beth's new life, career, pedagogical concerns, but he was overwhelmed with his own experiences, the intense swirl of accidents and tragedies and mind-numbing work. And always thinking about what hell tomorrow might bring.

In the subway station, waiting for a last train down Yonge, Ann quiet, holding his arm, worried about him, listening to a long-haired boy, sitting on a sack, playing guitar, pupils dilated, dreamy, playing badly: We all live in a yellow submarine, a yellow submarine, a yellow submarine.

ELSA'S HEART RHYTHM sputtered back to normal, sinus rhythm they called it, and she came partially around, moaned, opened her eyes, muttered incoherently. Snow was amazed how quickly someone who had been vertical, pink-cheeked, clear of eyes, articulated, could become someone horizontal, white, sallow, aged ten years, eyes half-dead, and reduced to monosyllabic muttering. Harvey Ryan, still struggling to figure out what had been wrong with her in the first place, before they knocked hell out of her potassium, causing various muscles including the heart muscle to throw in the towel, put her on antibiotics in case the stuff in her chest was bacterial infection, septic fluids, and not heart failure after all. The next morning Dolanski gave him shit for this, pointing out that he had no proof of infection, white count still being normal and nothing having been found in the sputum—blue-suited today, fingernails prominent, impatient, *evidence* being the word she used, what is your evidence?—all of them, Harvey, Robert, Sandy, standing at the bedside with Elsa lying before them, breathing badly, and now, as they say (indicating a level of consciousness rather than an observation on the meaning of life), responding only to pain. The oxygen mask had been replaced by a green tube, a nasal catheter running from her nose to the tap on the wall. A transparent tube dripped salt water and glucose into her vein, a brown tube ran over her leg under the sheet to trickle urine into a bag. Altogether three tubes, two for in and one for out. There are times, said Harvey, in an aside to Snow, falling behind the head of service as they left the room, tired, rueful, there are times I think we should listen to our patients.

Elsa's breathing worsened the next couple of days while they adjusted this and that and measured the contents of each and every body fluid. The oxygen catheter was no longer adequate. They would have to breathe for her, put her on a machine to breathe, but she was too awake and responsive to pain to leave her with a fat tube in her mouth and down her pharynx, so Dolanski sent her over to the ear nose and throat guys to do a tracheotomy. The ENT boys. She came back with a new fat tube coming out of her neck just below the larynx attached at the other end to a breathing machine plugged into the wall. Jesus Christ, said Harvey, looking through the chart, I don't believe this shit. They cut her goddamn esophagus doing the trache.

She was Snow's case, and he did maintenance work as required, but things seemed to stumble around her, just happening, everybody getting in on it, consultations, opinions, discussions, drugs, and everybody screwing up and then screwing off, it seemed to Snow. He injected cortisone into her IV drip every two hours as treatment for the cut esophagus. Someone had ordered it. Left alone in her room, he checked and recorded her fading heart beat, her inadequate blood pressure. The only sound she made was through the breathing machine, known as the BIRD, the slow rhythmical wheezing of air being forced into her lungs and then sucked out again relieved of some of its oxygen.

The BIRD was a small apparatus attached to a shining, clean steel pole with silver rods and connectors, a small white-boxed electric motor, transparent green plastic tubes and a glass chamber housing black bellows and a little black ball that jumped up and down making a popping sound at the end of each wheeze. On its single steel pole it looked something like, unless this was simply Snow's private whimsy, a mechanical flamingo. For a long time he sat watching Elsa and the black bellows filling and deflating and the little black ball popping, and listened to their wheeze-pop, wheeze-pop, wheeze-pop, in the otherwise silent, lonely room.

The BIRD was a pretty machine, simple, elegant, reliable. Elsa was overall gray with mottled bruising patches of dirty yellow and purple. Her skin sagged loosely from her face, her neck, her arms. Her dry white hair spread randomly out from her skull.

At the autopsy they found multiple abscesses in her lungs, which meant even the esteemed head of service had contributed to her death when she stopped the antibiotics. Harvey took the chest X rays back to the radiologist who reluctantly put them up on the box and said, "You sure these are the same ones? Yeah, well, Christ. Abscesses. Don't know how I missed 'em."

Standing out on Bathurst, clearing his head, getting a lung full of cinder-tainted air, facing the cupolaed orthodox church across the street, with its gold archways and frescoes of a tortured Jesus, glitter on a circus clown, next to the car radio shop on one side, a small crummy variety store and a poorly tended house with its furniture spilling into the front yard on the other side, Snow wondered who the hell you could tell this story to—forgive me Father for we have sinned, we know not what we do—and felt silence descending.

CHAPTER FIVE

Slow down, you move too fast
You got to make the morning last
　　　　　　　　　— PAUL SIMON

Before you slip into unconsciousness
I'd like to have another kiss
　　　　　　　　　— THE DOORS

IN THE LOUNGE and cafeteria the Jewish interns and residents were all talking about visiting the reunited Jerusalem. They spoke excitedly about the sudden complete victory, Moshe Dayan's tactics. Snow thought he had a better understanding of how the Arabs must feel, having started something that unleashed an unexpected fury of uncontrollable events, and loss, and defeat, in roughly the same amount of time.

HE WASN'T FEELING too good about himself that Friday when he finished his work at nine in the evening and wandered over to join the regular party in the lounge planning not to drink more than one beer, maybe two, because he was still on duty until Saturday morning. There was a spread of food at one end, a sound system at the other, bodies milling about, dancing, grouping, shouting above the music. Whites and greens and civvies, and nurses drifting in as they came off duty, the place filling up. Mad dancing on the grave site, no rules, no consequences, temporary escape. There were some interns there he had come to know who partied all night the nights they weren't working all night. Life being much too short for sleep. Sandy wasn't there, probably in the library, nose buried in a journal.

He danced with a student nurse whose eyes were glassy and who breathed rye in his face. She was compliant enough, leaning into him when he out of habit and feeling like shit anyway and feeling a need to grab anything to hold onto suggested (shouted in her ear) they go for a walk downstairs to a smaller lounge with a pool table and sofa to sit and talk. She said okay and went with him out into the stronger light of the hallway where she didn't seem nearly so attractive and her eyes looked even worse. They went downstairs to the pool room and because another couple were entwined on the sofa stood uneasily for a few minutes by the table and then the girl leaned against the wall, the wall being a bilious yellow stucco, scuffed and dirty. He pressed against the wall around her, encircling her, facing her, and knew what he really wanted to do was get to his bed and sleep or drink himself into oblivion or get the hell out of the hospital and walk in the air, which he couldn't do because they'd probably call him anytime, but what he did do was lean in to kiss her in a search for some touch of living kindly flesh, a response, a return, something to fill the emptiness in his chest, and just as his lips brushed hers she turned green, pulled aside and said, excuse me, I think I'm gonna puke.

Saved from himself, saved in the nick of time from a pathetic romance and its emotional hangover, released, he climbed the stairs to his cubicle, lay on the small hard bed and called Ann. They talked of what they might do tomorrow afternoon and evening. He asked after her job interviews. He couldn't tell her they had killed an old woman while trying to help her, a long story, complicated. He couldn't tell her it made him feel very small, empty. He couldn't tell her of the cruelty of the hospital.

There was a pounding on his door, someone shouting, Snow, they're paging you. Answer the fucking page.

"Ah, shit," he said. "Gotta go. I'll get there around noon. Have some coffee ready."

Dialing the operator he realized he had avoided saying *home*, as in I'll get home around noon. Half-empty shit apartment, hot noisy city.

The operator said Seven West has been trying to reach you, your line's been busy. He told himself to stop feeling sorry for himself, splashed cold water on his face, slipped on his canvas shoes, headed back to the hospital.

THE SUMMER WAS hot and there was rioting in the cities on the other side of the Great Lakes. Detroit, said the mayor of Detroit, according to the *Globe and Mail*, looks like Berlin in 1945. Jimi Hendrix made his guitar cry in California. Robert said, "Look at that. They're burning, looting and killing all across the U.S. of A. Here we're discussing a possible street closure." A little more than that, Ann pointed out. The hippies had barricaded Yorkville Avenue between Avenue Road and Bay, trying to force the city to close it off to cars.

Ann, loose flower-print dress, blond wig, sandals, and Robert, bell-bottoms, sandals, longish hair, self-consciously a peace medallion around his neck, strolled through Yorkville, suddenly become a counterculture community, a Haight-Ashbury North. Runaways, young beggars with a new demeanor, like enthusiastic amateurs, street kids, peace lovers, very long hair, all tattered, patterned, swishing, bell-bottoms, paisley-print dresses, the sweet smell of smoldering marijuana in the air. Incense shops, sand-molded candles, the new notorious sex shop, lubricants, scented oils, rubber vaginas, multicolored penises, peace medallions.

THEY FOUND LE Trou Normand, decided they could afford it one night, seated in a quiet corner, transported to a village in France, Ann across the table in candlelight, Robert relaxed, grateful they didn't have an intimidating waiter. Hippies outside, flowers in their hair, the hospital miles away and temporarily locked in the closet in the back of his mind, he began to feel whole again, where he could be, with whom he should be, and not forcing and shaping himself into a white-coated human technician, a body-organ engineer, a body-fluid attendant, not yearning for the life of the tune-in, drop-out, make-love-not-war hippies, not envious of the focused committed students marching and protesting the war in Vietnam, not envious in some perverse way of the racists and bigots and hawks and capitalists who lived with certainties. Finding a small path through the perilous extremes. Ann lightened up, too, in this recess from living alone in their barren apartment looking for a job each day and waiting for those evenings when he might get home and not fall semicomatose on top of their bed.

He might get through the year without killing too many people, he might get to like being a doctor, they might travel together, they might get back to the west coast, they might try some of this marijuana. He ordered in French, the words lingering on his palate, in English reminding him of Fred: brains fried in butter. She ordered in French with a much better accent. French requires flirtation, movement of eyes and shoulders.

They played a game of guessing the occupations, stories, secrets of the other patrons. There was one he was sure of: a young doctor from Winnipeg, he told her, probably a resident in internal medicine, earnest expression, curly hair, sincere, probably Jewish, not quite Toronto, not west coast. At the end of their meal she asked, interrupting with a charming smile. Robert had been right on all counts. A resident at Toronto General.

Walking home arm in arm she said, "You knew him, didn't you? It wasn't a guess."

"No. Honestly. I'd never seen him before. It was written all over him, young doctor from Winnipeg."

"What a liar."

"Honestly."

"Okay."

He had not seen the man before, but now he wondered, worried, that he, too, should become so obvious, without disguises, become a place, a role, a stereotype. This complex soul of unexplored potentials, depths, boundaries subjugated to a simple definition.

"Don't worry," she said, demonstrating her ability to read his mind, penetrate his disguises, "you'll never fit in anywhere that well."

"ROBERT?"

"Hello, Mother."

"Robert."

"What's wrong?"

"Your father left."

"Left?"

"Walked out. He's gone."

"Gone where?"

"He left me, Robert. He's gone. He's someplace, an apartment."

"Are you all right?"

"He's just thrown it away. All those years."

"When?"

"Last week. I think he has someone else."

"What about you?"

"Don't worry about me. I'll be all right. You have enough to worry about."

"Are you sure?"

"I'll be all right."

And then she cried, whimpered, two thousand miles away, "I feel so awful, I can't sleep, I just walk around the house."

"I can't come out there."

"I know you can't."

"What are you going to do?"

"I don't know. I don't know."

And Robert, thinking, you drove him away, you've been trying to drive him away for years, asked, "What about Grandmother, can you...?"

"Don't be ridiculous. She'd be no help. I can't rely on her."

Not that Grandmother wouldn't be reliable, strictly speaking, Robert knew, but she would turn this to her own advantage, somehow, talk about it, talk around it, craft from it a message and a moral, a way of comparing it to her own suffering and find it unequal, a minor inconvenience. His father and mother had not agreed on Grandmother, their perceptions different, and thus seldom broached. And paradoxically his mother defended her mother, and then behaved like a reluctant slave in her presence, while his father thought her a tyrant, but behaved more like a gallant suitor when her eminence was on a visit.

His grandmother may have killed his grandfather, or so the story went. Grandfather, known to Robert only from photographs, black suit with vest, starched collar, pointed beard, high forehead, bald, cane and homburg in hand, a double for official portraits of King Edward. Robert had inherited his eyes and brow, but he feared his grandmother's genes were still searching for a room of their own in his body.

Grandmother had been thirty when she married, an independent businesswoman for ten years, Grandfather forty, an executive with Brackman Kerr, Canada Packers. As a child Robert sat at his grandmother's feet listening to her stories with more patience than any other member of the family. Afterward his mother would tell him, "It may not have happened quite like that." Her favorite dresses were of a deep royal purple shade, a bit of lace, a broach, square-heeled black shoes in her later years. A cane. But in her twenties, she said, she had been told that only a certain kind of woman wears purple, a lady of the night, and henceforth purple had become her color. "That story's probably true," said his mother. "It would be just like her. She loved to shock." Emily Carr walked the same streets with a monkey on her shoulder.

Two willful spirits, his grandfather and grandmother, Frank and Margaret. Frank lost all his money when the market crashed, and soon thereafter developed pernicious anemia. The remedy of the time had been a steady diet of raw liver. Whole, chopped, mixed. Thirty years later Robert had been asked on an oral exam, standing before three sitting lab-coated professors, to expound on the treatment of pernicious anemia. Injections of vitamin B_{12}, he told them. What dosage? they asked. By my calculations, he calculated, I might expect to run into a case once every five years or so. When I do I'll look it up. There had been more than a little of his grandmother in that answer. Insolence was the word the dean had used discussing the matter with Robert. Merely the truth, thought Robert.

Frank died of complications from pernicious anemia, his mother told him. He refused to eat the raw liver, said his father. Margaret nagged at him, pestered him, nattered at him day and night. It was the only thing he could do, said his father, refuse to eat. In that last year they were all summering on the beach at Cordova Bay, a hundred steps below McMorrans' dance hall. Blanket tents, picnic hampers, log windbreaks, salt cold Strait of Georgia, Gulf Islands in the distance, scavenging sea gulls, coiled seaweed, a raft, skirted bathing costumes. Frank, cold all the time, a blanket on his legs. Margaret had been at him all day. Criticizing, nagging, badgering, according to Robert's father, then Mother's fiancé. Frank was very weak. He begged Robert's father to take him back to town. Father carried him in his arms one hundred wooden steps up to the road, put him in the green Dodge and drove him to Victoria. He let himself die to get away from her, said Robert's father. He remembered how light he was, wasting away.

Now his own father had gotten away from another brand, a quieter brand of pestering, criticizing, nagging. The fear that picks at a wound.

"I'll see if there's a way of getting out for Christmas," said Robert.

"Don't worry about me, you have your own life to lead."

Ah, Christ, thought Robert, suddenly furious with his father for bequeathing this to him. "Have you heard from Michael?" he asked.

"About a month ago he sent a postcard from Samoa," she told him.

Robert, mouthing words of encouragement, then hanging up, now angry with his brother, as well.

IN THE EARLY morning he rode the subway along Bloor, crossed over to the trolley terminal and transferred for the ride down Bathurst. The trolley rattled along and he wished it would take something close to forever, stopping for the Italians, Portuguese,

Greeks, Hungarians to climb aboard, older women in black always with straw baskets or string bags on their arms, each, he imagined, part of a community, a family, linked together, doing the things they did every day. He, Robert Snow, the alien. I'm a doctor, he would say to himself. Big fucking deal.

THIRTY HOURS STRAIGHT on emergency. Now it was quiet, the last case sewn up, sent home or to a ward, the last drunk X-rayed, the big sloppy cut on his arm stitched together while he cursed and stank and then vomited. Two o'clock. Quiet. Pauline and another nurse at the desk. Long corridor, stretchers, bags of laundry, bloodstains. Snow sat and talked with them but his eyes drooped. He moved off to a small lounge where a soft chair waited, sat down and immediately drifted, his brain coming to a sputtering halt.

In his dream he heard a siren, and then another siren. His eyes opened and the sirens grew louder, two of them. He listened to them drawing closer, and then stopping right outside the double emergency doors, coming to a whimpering halt, one running down and then the other. Unsteadily he got to his feet and leaned against the door frame. Waited. The emergency doors flew open, propelled by two gurneys, attendants madly pushing from behind. On the gurneys, one big man on the first, one small older woman on the second, two at once, each of them mouth open, eyes closed, flat. The two nurses were scrambling, taking over, moving and steering the gurneys, one to the left, one to the right. The man was corpse-white, unconscious, blood down his chin, on his shirt. "IV, blood, cross match, normal saline, blood pressure," said Snow, awake now and moving across the hall to the older woman who was also unresponsive with an uneven, slow, weak pulse. "Oxygen. Cardiogram," said Snow. Back to the first, take blood, insert IV, examine quickly, oxygen mask, feet propped up, anything else wrong? Back to the woman, cardiogram quickly, in the middle of an infarct, morphine, procaine to prevent arrhythmias, get the medical resident, and back to the man, get a bag of O negative blood up, call the surgical resident, back and forth, keeping each one alive, taking some control of the situation, making decisions. Saying things, the nurses doing it, sometimes doing it before he said it, back and forth, up for it, pleasantly anxious, alert.

In the morning, though he hadn't slept but for a few fitful minutes in the last five hours of his thirty-six-hour duty, he walked several blocks up Bathurst before catching the trolley. The shops were opening, the people of the neighborhood already on the sidewalks, with the exhaust fumes, cinder air, telephone poles, proliferating wires, a heat haze announcing a hot humid day ahead. The shapes and forms of the street were startlingly clear to Robert, the colors vivid, and gravity diminished. He felt warmth toward the people, a connection, as he listened to them greet one another. The richness of their lives. Maybe he would fit in somewhere after all. Absolutely amazing, he said to himself, how good it feels to be competent, how good it feels to do something well. To be tested and succeed.

This time.

HE WORKED EXTRA weekends before and after to get a full week in late August to visit Montreal and Expo '67. Three his regular duty, two more, five in all. And then a week off. Ann had interviewed for a job and was waiting to hear. He came away from a phone call with his mother shaking his head and muttering profanities. He told Ann he wasn't sure he got it right but it seemed his mother had changed all the locks on the family home and then his father had hired a locksmith to change them back. On top of that, his mother had said, to add insult to injury, he paid a social call to your grandmother. Why, Robert had asked. No doubt to ease his conscience, to get her blessing, she told him. She seemed angrier about this than about the locks. I can't picture my father doing this stuff, Robert told Ann. His father, for whom appearances were important. Keep your voice down, he might say in the middle of one of Mother's tirades, the neighbors can hear. His mother then predictably raising her voice and declaring how little she cared what the neighbors heard or thought. At the kitchen table, his father sitting, his mother pacing the kitchen, Wearever pots on the Westinghouse stove, Tupperware containers, his father rolling his eyes, looking pained, hitting back with indignation, platitudes, this teacher being lectured, then walking out and working late and later. He did care what the neighbors thought. His mother's fury, triggered, it seemed to Robert, not then able to see the undercurrents, by trivial matters, both good and bad. His father's gifts: too expensive, wrong size, wrong model. His father's lateness. His father's mistakes. "Any fool would know…"

There was a small part of his father in Robert. He, too, was embarrassed thinking about the neighbors watching locksmiths come and go at the family home. Altercations in the driveway.

Ann said, "Let's leave it all behind for one week, Robert, please."

WITH SLEEPING BAG and small battered suitcases they took the bus to Montreal, down the 401 to *la belle province,* putting mileage between himself and the hospital, the immediacy of travel between themselves and his parents. A whole city celebrating, history left as history, English, French, *vive la différence.* They took a cab to an address in the east end. Robert had acquired, from a friend of a friend, a key to the door of an apartment, a crash pad in the jargon of the day, being passed around rent free. A thing done at the time, a flush of communal spirit, a strange and adolescent communism in the capitalist world. He didn't know who owned or rented this place. He didn't know the chain of covenance. He didn't even know if they would be sharing. He wore bell-bottoms and beads, peace symbol on a thong, and she, miniskirt, clogs, a bra sometimes, maybe, should I try it? Can I get away with it? The cabbie was skeptical hunting for the number, asking in French if they were sure, if they had it right. He dropped them off in a run-down section of town inhabited by blacks.

In that long hot summer it had taken paratroopers to quell the race riots in Detroit, and Robert had heard, through the medical grapevine, that the interns and residents of the Henry Ford Hospital had required armed escort, were being driven to and from the hospital in armored personnel vehicles, past the smoldering ruins, bottle-throwing rioters, snipers. It's okay, he said to Ann, these are Canadian blacks, mostly from the islands, and they walked by the curious stoop sitters, lamppost leaners to the building with the right number. Climbed two flights of wooden steps, banister pulling away from the wall, single light bulb. The key unlocked an anonymous door and they entered an abandoned, unfurnished room with sink, shower stall and small water closet. Old, fouled double mattress on the floor and the walls covered with graffiti. Well, at least the price is right, he said, examining some colorful, inspired flourishes around a grandly scripted Lucy in the Sky with Diamonds embellishing one wall. Ann inspected the mattress.

"I didn't think it'd be quite so bad," he told her.

"I guess it's too late to find something else."

"Hey," he said, his voice echoing in the shower stall. "There's water."

"Hot?"

"Not yet."

THEY SPENT EACH day at Expo, riding the rubber-tired Metro, returning only to sleep in the borrowed room, nights of ominous noises, reexamined locks, open sleeping bag on stained mattress, no sheets, no blankets, naked in the black heat, exhausted, awake, sweaty sex under Lucy in the Sky, sirens in the streets below, a small high window reflecting city light. Cold showers in the morning, croissants and café au lait, back to Expo, floating on the sea of life and color surrounding them, reveling in the unlikely promise of each exhibit, Habitat housing for everybody, Buckminster Fuller's geodesic dome, belief in a perfect geometry. A kind of adult connect-the-dots. Robert and Ann were prepared to suspend disbelief this week, to think truth, beauty, happiness were rewards for connecting the dots.

Or flying to the moon. America touted its Gemini program, podded capsules landing on a moonscape, postcards from space, photographs from orbit, the outline of North America, heavy cloud cover over what might be southeast Asia. The Czechs and Slovaks, fresh from their Prague Spring, liberated, photographs and glass, saying, hey, look at us, we can smell freedom, we can taste it—every country showing its Sunday-go-to-meeting best—it all caught them up. Everything was possible. Even Canada.

In the inverted open pyramid she climbed to the top and the open sky for a view of the city. He watched from the other side and saw her tiny skirt blow around her legs and her auburn hair sparkle in the sun. She turned and smiled at him and he fell in love again.

Robert, Robert, she said to him, I hate that apartment. I hate being alone all day and all night. I hate that city. But we're going to be fine, just fine.

Chapter Six

Pain waits for nightfall at the Salpêtrière. During the daytime there are drip solutions, injections, comings and goings of Green Pastures preceded by her laugh, other nurses who want to chat until the moment comes when I am able to answer them, tomorrow, the day after.... Although I am in little pain, I am far away, withdrawn into my fever. The mind surrenders itself to the groping fingers of death as it does to those of sleep.
— André Malraux, *Lazarus*

The leaves move in the garden, the sky is pale, and I catch myself weeping. It is hard—it is hard to make a good death....
— Katherine Mansfield

Just let me go nat'rally – Laura Nyro

ROBERT DID THE admission workup on George Martin on a slow Sunday afternoon. Mr. Martin had a very unhealthy appearance: recent weight loss, skin that looked like it smelled (though he didn't put his nose close enough to test this perception), eyes that telegraphed worry and pain. The older nurses always knew. Cancer, they'd whisper to one another, two, three months at the outside. George Martin had a large mass in his abdomen, which Robert took no pleasure finding, feeling through the otherwise soft and pliant skin, a foreign body, a baseball where it shouldn't be. It reminded him of the struggle he'd had as a medical student balancing the horror of finding terrible disease and the pleasure in making a correct diagnosis. Some of the other student doctors didn't seem to have that problem or recognize the paradox. A classic case of neurocystofibromoblastomo, they would beam, delighting in the discovery, the accuracy, the very pronunciation, the announcement of horror. The professor's congratulatory nod.

At bedside rounds the next morning, discreetly in the corridor, before entering the room, young Dr. Snow played out the script, telling the surgeon and his small entourage, of which Intern Snow was approximately number four, that Mr. Martin was fifty-two, that he had a wife and three children, that he had weight loss, energy loss, various bowel symptoms and a palpable hard orange- or grapefruit-size mass in his abdomen (for some reason unknown to Snow, size and texture of tumors was *de rigueur* compared to fruit), probably an adenocarcinoma of the large bowel.

Two mornings later they opened up George Martin, Robert second assisting the senior resident, Philip Trebilcock, who was first assisting the surgeon, David Armstrong. Snow had been awake since five-thirty, on the ward by six, going from bed to bed taking blood, filling the vials on a cart pushed along by a restive aide, had taken five minutes for breakfast, rushed back to the ward for rounds with Armstrong, students and nurses in his wake, Trebilcock joining them, not so much wearing as encumbered by a white jacket loaded with pens, pins, hammers, stethoscope and notepad. Armstrong, tall-and-tanned handsome, dressed tautly and expensively. Trebilcock, by contrast, tousled, bespectacled. His whites hung from his frail shoulders and bagged at the knees. He pushed his glasses up the bridge of his nose, thumbed through his notebook, asked the nurse for six charts in heavy metal folders, led the group from bed to bed and presented each case in turn.

Armstrong, not looking directly at his senior resident, said, "We have twenty minutes to cover six patients, Trebilcock, get to the point."

When they came to George Martin's empty bed Snow repeated his abbreviated history, announced that he was booked for an exploratory laparotomy at eight, given pre-ops and taken down already.

Armstrong turned to one of the two medical students and asked, "What do you think we'll find?"

"The differential would have carcinoma of the stomach or colon at the top of the list," said the student, beaming, knowing from Armstrong's expression that he got it right.

Trebilcock had to stay behind and write some of the orders into the charts. Armstrong, on top of his game, glanced at Mr. Martin on a gurney in the corridor outside the OR, visited the washroom, changed into greens, scrubbed and entered the operating room at precisely eight o'clock. Snow understood that if the anesthetist were to arrive a few minutes late Armstrong would be able to inaugurate the morning procedure, and establish caste, by admonishing him on the issue of punctuality.

Robert had his hands self-consciously aloft post-scrub when Trebilcock stumbled in, trying to walk and put on his surgical boots at the same time. He had yet to acquire style.

When they entered and were gloved they found Armstrong rearranging the drapes on Mr. Martin's abdomen, or *the* abdomen as it would hence be called. A nurse had done it not quite to his liking. *The* abdomen was a hairless quadrangle of human skin now coated and glistening with pink antiseptic framed in green cotton. The anesthetist had arrived on time and had gassed Mr. Martin to a level of unconsciousness satisfactory to the surgeon.

Armstrong asked for a scalpel and made an eight-inch vertical cut, the edges of the skin pulling up and apart. Trebilcock tied off bleeders. Snow kept the wound open with steel retractors, something like shoehorns with long handles, adjusting as each layer was ruptured.

Armstrong reached in and up with his gloved hand to feel the liver. Then he stepped back to give Trebilcock and Snow a look. There it was, a great mass, hard, lumpy, wet and oozing, attached to both the bowel and abdominal wall, nothing like a grapefruit at all, more like exactly what it was, mucosal cells multiplying recklessly, lumpishly, membranes, capillaries struggling to keep up. Its seedlings were spread all through the otherwise healthy abdominal cavity, a glistening pink sack of purple veins, mauve bowels and white connective tissues— hard bluish nodules growing, spreading, invading.

After a day in post-op recovery Mr. Martin was sent back up to the surgical ward. This time he was put in one of the three private rooms along the corridor, just outside the main ward. The dying was done in these three rooms.

"I GOT IT," she told him on the phone. Snow lying back on what he had come to think of as his pallet in a cell.

"Got what?"

"The job I was telling you about. The Toronto French School. They want me. I'll be teaching English to the hoi polloi, the filthy rich. The children of the filthy rich."

"They'll be paying you to do this?"

"Not as much as the regular school board, but not bad."

"You must be pleased."

"I'm delirious. I dreaded the thought of sitting in that apartment all year."

And Snow had dreaded it, as well, being in the hospital day and night, carrying that extra little burden of guilt in the back

of his mind, an unhappy Ann waiting for him, depending on
him.

"There's a real Russian who teaches Russian, and French
from France who teach the darlings Parisian French. *Pas de
patois* for the descendants of Timothy Eaton."

"Have you met them?"

"Some of them. The Russian's a real character with a mon-
strous beard, and the French teachers are thin young men
from the Sorbonne. *Très élégant.* They think my accent *Anglaise
est très jolie.*"

"They're probably queer."

"Robert, I do believe you're jealous."

"Ah, je suis fatigué."

They certainly were French when he met them, months
later, at a party, elegant, slim, charming, so socially at ease
with themselves. They wore tight-fitting slacks, small jackets,
longish hair, narrow leather ties, pointed shoes and knowing,
world-weary smiles. They were, without doubt, from Paris. The
embodiment of savoir faire, of *ensousciance.* Snow considered
donning a similar outfit but knew his heritage would betray
him. Rather than giving him a sophisticated Gallic appearance, it would place him in rural Alberta roping small four-
legged animals. Such were the vagaries of costume. Though he
was becoming moderately comfortable in whites, white barber's shirt, white parade monitor's slacks, white undertaker's
jacket, unpressed, usually a bit grubby, sloppy, spotted with the
fluids of his profession.

"Robaire, you're being very old-fashioned," Ann told him.
"But it might do you good to be jealous of something I'm
doing."

Jealousy was probably not the right word, envy perhaps.
Envious of a world of clever talk, lingering coffees, cultured
discussions, pursed lips exhaling smoke from colored Galloise.

Talking about the Free Speech movement, Free Love, student unrest at the Sorbonne, around the world, the naive Americans trying to do in Vietnam what the French couldn't. His unease, he understood, could also be explained by control, as in out of control, which his world seemed to be increasingly.

MR. MARTIN LAY on his back, alone in the room, thin and bony, rapidly losing weight and tone, his hair dank, stubble on his chin. An IV dripped into his arm and a catheter dripped out from under his bedsheets.

When they did rounds in the morning, Armstrong and his entourage floating into the room, spreading around the bed, asking the ritual questions about solids and fluids entering and leaving his body, George Martin rallied enough to ask when he'd be going home.

Armstrong answered, "Very soon, George, very soon. In time for a few more rounds of golf before winter."

Outside the room Snow said, "Shouldn't we tell him?"

"He doesn't want to know. Would you want to know?" asked Armstrong, not waiting for an answer. "Christ. I sure as hell wouldn't. We'll give him a course of methotrexate."

AND SO IT was that Snow found himself the next day sitting at Mr. Martin's bedside, injecting, very slowly, a thick amber fluid into the large vein in his patient's left arm. George Martin looked over at Snow with an odd expression on his thin face. The corners of his mouth offered a friendly smile, but his eyes showed an apprehension bordering on terror. He asked Snow how the drug worked.

"It kills the tumor cells," Snow said.

"That's it?"

"Well, it's not so specific. Some other fast-growing normal cells get damaged, too."

"But nothing vital?"

"Nothing vital."

And then he said it. The doctors hadn't said it. They hadn't said the C-word. Nobody used the word in the hospital, save whisperings between nurses. Nobody had cancer, nobody was dying, though undeniably some people died, had died; no case was hopeless. Where there's life, etcetera. They used instead technical jargon and euphemisms. Mitotic disease, neoplasms, metastatic condition, polyps, -omas with various prefixes, classes and stages, onco- with various suffixes. George Martin asked, "What happened to cancer patients before this drug was invented?"

Snow fumbled with the syringe and averted his eyes. His brain shouted out, they died you crazy bastard, just like you're going to die—no—I've got that wrong, first we'll give you false hope and make you sick as a dog and then you'll die, and I'm sorry I'm angry at you because it's not you, it's Armstrong swaggering around and your fucking cancer growing inside you and you being here asking me such a goddamn question. He had hoped, like all the rest, to slip by without answering that question.

He looked at George Martin and said, "It depends on the kind of cancer and how advanced it is." He waited for the next question, deciding, If he asks I will tell him. He gave it time, a good minute, before he busied himself cleaning up syringe, vial, tourniquet, alcohol swab, and mouthing platitudes. Mr. Martin looked the other way, turned his face to the wall. Snow gave his shoulder a squeeze and walked quietly from the room.

For five out of seven days that first week Robert sat at the bedside, used a tourniquet to find the vein of the cubital fossa and injected ten c.c.'s of yellow liquid into George Martin. George did become nauseous and restless, sick as a dog, and was given Gravol and more painkiller. They exchanged a few words each time about the weather or lunch. He told Robert a little about his family, visiting, waiting, passed occasionally in the corridor by Dr. Snow. But never again did he approach the big question. For this Robert felt grateful though guilty. For it hung in the air between them on each encounter, like a smudge on a mirror, blurring reflections.

By the end of the second week it became obvious even to Armstrong that the drug was not helping, and he ordered it stopped. Mr. Martin didn't comment on this. Snow wondered if he had come to understand the injections as some kind of hollow ritual in which they both colluded. Mr. Martin had eaten very little these few weeks, his appetite even further suppressed by his constant nausea, and his skin hung dry and yellowish over his bones.

"YOUR MOTHER'S COMING, Robert."

"She's what?" Snow was lying on his back on the small bed in his room on the second floor, the telephone at his right ear. He was in his whites, his sandals kicked off. He had tried rubber-soled white canvas shoes, but man, they stunk, the smell filling the box in which he slept. He had parked them on the outside window ledge, but the draft was incoming, then outside the door, in the corridor, but some self-appointed environmentalist had thrown them in the trash. Hence air-freshened sandals, socks beneath his white cottons.

Ann said, "She sounded bad. She's got a flight booked this Saturday."

"I'm on this weekend."

"I know. I told her I'd meet her at the airport."

"Jesus."

"I didn't know what else to say."

"Where the hell will she sleep?"

"She's been on the couch anyway. Hasn't gone near the bed

since your dad left."

"She's been sleeping on the couch?"

"That's what she says."

"What'll she do all day? I'm here. You're off to work.

"Robert."

"What?"

"Don't get mad at me, okay? She's your mother."

"Yeah, I'm sorry. What did you mean 'bad'? She sounded bad?"

"Angry, depressed, weepy."

"Shit."

"Robert, is that all you can say, 'shit'?"

"Christ."

"That's supposed to be an improvement?"

"How will you get there, the airport, I mean?"

"I have a job now, money coming in. I'll take a taxi."

"I'm sorry."

"It doesn't help to be sorry. Besides, I like your mother. It might work out okay."

She had had better days, moments, he remembered, but each touched with some cloud of misgivings. He had seen his mother and father flirt on a couch in a games room in their rented summer home. He had seen her laugh, pick Queen Anne cherries, play lawn badminton. Talk about the kneecap she broke playing field hockey for the girls' senior high. Her two small watercolors adorned the dining room, an unfulfilled promise. He had seen an eight-by-ten of his father and mother, taken by a street photographer, striding along Douglas Street, all decked out, his father in a summer suit with vest, spats, thin mustache, slick wavy black hair, a Clark Gable look-alike, his mother in cloche cap, flapper dress, good legs, one-inch heels, caught in midstride, father grinning, confident, mother smiling a little, anxiously.

He remembered Saturday family shopping on that same Douglas Street, coming out of Eaton's, where his grandmother, Margaret, had managed the millinery department, until, according to his mother, Frank, Francis, told her to quit, or until, according to his father, Frank was making enough money to afford the cooks and maids who would wait on Grandmother in the custom to which she was sure she was entitled. But then, in his mother's view of the world, events were determined by others, while his father had been brimful of the platitudes of self-determination: if at first you don't succeed, a stitch in time, do unto others, you have nobody to blame but yourself. Coming out of Eaton's, greeting people, the happy little family, the child Robert, bored, enduring the family outing, his father hearty, that was the word, putting a good face on everything, his mother polite, also enduring, saying something critical about the people they had just bumped into, provoking from his father a favorite father phrase, "If you can't say anything good about someone, don't say anything at all." Attributed to his mother, who had donated the organ to the Anglican church at Cedar Hill Cross Roads.

"Why the hell did they do that every Saturday?" Robert asked Ann.

"Do what?"

"Nothing. I was trying to remember something good and what went through my mind was the weekly Saturday family shopping trip."

"That doesn't sound so bad."

"It was a horror."

"Not all your mother's fault."

"What is it you like about my mother?"

"She's clever, she's warm, she's kind."

Yes, yes, but why is it those other memories dominate? He said, "I'll get home as early as I can Monday night. And I better try to get some sleep before the holocaust begins." It was nine o'clock. He'd been going steadily since six that morning. The admissions were done, all the extra work, routine and crisis, life-enhancing and scut, and now he was in a lull. It usually happened that way. Between nine and eleven everything quieted down. No emergency admissions, no one going into shock, no one infarcting, arresting, bleeding, dying. Then it would start up again, eleven, midnight. The smart interns got an hour or two of sleep during the lull. The trouble was giving up those couple of hours. Instead of sleeping Robert could read the newspaper, talk to somebody important about important things, shoot pool, watch television, lie around, maybe even look something up in the library, read a journal, in short, live. And then wonder why he wasn't worth shit come four in the morning.

"I love you," he said. And he did feel it, through all the other madness whirling through his head, anxiety, chaos, pulling him this way and then that way, he felt it, a small little beacon of possibilities.

GEORGE MARTIN'S BREATHING became labored, and he no longer said anything intelligible. His skin took on a dry parchment quality, loose in some areas, stretched grotesquely by edema in others. His chest began to fill with fluid every night, and he struggled for breath. He was given oxygen, and drugs to keep his heart pumping the fluid from his lungs. Then they weren't enough.

It began to happen every night, always at night. The fluid would rise in his chest cavity and he would begin to drown. At one or two o'clock a nurse would call Snow and tell him Mr. Martin was not breathing well, and he would get up from his bed, if he'd managed to get to his bed, and walk through the darkened quiet corridors to Mr. Martin's room. The nurse

would be there already with a tray of equipment for a thoracentesis. The room was always dimly lit with only a small table
lamp. Snow would sit in a chair by the bedside, paint the side
of George Martin's chest with alcohol and Cetavlon swabs and
then ease a long needle in between his ribs.

Each night Mr. Martin shifted and moved as if to get away
from the needle. He was too weak to escape and only managed
to make the procedure more awkward. And each night as the
needle slipped in he said the same words, "No, don't. No,
don't. No, don't."

The needle would go in through skin, muscle, fascia, hunting for the narrow space between the chest wall and the lung
and then, finding it, Snow would carefully pull on the syringe,
again and again, to suck out a jar of frothy pink liquid. And
Mr. Martin would breathe a little easier. Afterward, maybe
three in the morning, Snow would leave the room and thread
his way past the dormitory beds to the nurses' station. A couple of nurses on night duty would be there smoking forbidden
cigarettes, talking quietly, charting. They might offer him a
coffee. Doing what he was doing with Mr. Martin confused
him, and he gravitated to the light.

The nurse who had just helped do the thoracentesis fixed
herself a coffee and, before she sat down, said, "Why can't you
just let him go?"

Snow shrugged. It was the best he could do. He held his cup
in both hands, warming them.

"You know what kind of pain he's in. His family's here every
day asking the same questions."

"What questions?"

"It's all crap. They know he's dying. He knows he's dying.
They just want it over."

"You sure about that?"

"You oughta hear his wife. She keeps saying stuff like, 'when you get home,' but you can tell by her voice she knows he's not coming home. He just looks away from her."

"HELLO, ROBERT. I'M at your apartment now."
"I know. That's the number I dialed."
"I know you know. I'm not stupid, just because…"
"I'm sorry I said that. How are you?"
"How do you think I am after what your father's done?"
"How was the trip?"
"Well, I couldn't eat a thing, I haven't been able to keep anything down for weeks."
"I'm sorry I couldn't get off to come meet you."
"That's all right. Ann found me okay, but my God there are a lot of colored people in this city."
"A cultural mosaic."
"I'm sure it's fine. I'm just not used to it."
"How long are you staying?"
"I don't know. I've got nothing to go back to. Thirty years wasted, all a big lie. It was nothing but a big lie."
"Would you put Ann on for a second, please?"
He could hear his mother call to Ann and then Ann came on.
"How are you coping?" he asked.
"All right, I guess."
"What kind of shape's she in?"
"We can talk about that later, when you get home."
"Is she doing anything besides smoking and drinking coffee?"
"Watching TV."
"What about alcohol?"
"Robert, we can talk about that later."
"I'm sorry, you don't need this."
"Robert, for Christ's sake. It's all right. I know you can't be here."

"But what the hell will she do when you're at work?"

IT WAS THE fourth night or fifth night they called him, Snow had lost track. Mr. Martin was having difficulty breathing again. Snow dressed slowly, splashed cold water on his face, closed the door to his small room, walked down the two flights of stairs, out into the night, across the parking lot, into the back of the main building.

He sat in the same chair at the bedside, listened to the gurgling labored breathing and stared at Mr. Martin's profile. A nurse had set up the equipment for the thoracentesis and was standing in the shadows waiting to assist. Snow sat back in his chair. Without taking his eyes off George Martin he asked for a quarter grain of morphine. There was no movement behind him, so he turned around. It was the same nurse from a couple of nights ago, the one who asked why they couldn't just let him go. She left the room.

Mr. Martin lay on his back, eyes open, staring sightlessly. The horrible gurgling sound continued. The nurse returned with a syringe and vial and handed them to Snow. He drew the morphine from the vial into the syringe and George Martin began again his chant of, "No, don't, no don't, no, don't..."

He injected the drug into his patient's arm and sat back. The gurgling continued, the chant stopped. He left everything there, didn't look at the nurse, and walked quickly back to his room. On the way he thought about *no, don't*. No, don't what? Don't hurt me? Don't keep me alive? Don't make me suffer any longer? Don't kill me?

He stretched out on his bed. Various images assailed him, some undermining his action, some supporting it. The cancer, thick, bluish, oozing throughout his patient's abdomen, eating its way into his chest. Or maybe by a miracle receding, going into remission, and he had just killed the man, Christ, no, he had simply withheld a life-prolonging thoracentesis, no, he was dying, dead already, dying a most miserable death and he had helped it along, accelerated it with the morphine, and he no longer understood why. To help Mr. George Martin, to stop his pain, to help himself, to get some sleep, to have done with it, to end it, to get his miserable, gurgling, stinking body off the ward and into the morgue. Was it a kind, selfless act, or hateful, selfish? If it had been a decent thing to do why did he still feel so empty and anxious?

He finally fell asleep, but the ringing phone pulled him back. Five-thirty a.m. A nurse on the other end told him that Mr. Martin had ceased to breathe.

CHAPTER SEVEN

Yes to dance beneath the diamond sky
with one hand waving free,
Silhouetted by the sea,
Circled deep beneath the waves,
Let me forget about today until tomorrow
                           – BOB DYLAN

WHEN HE WALKED in the door Ann called from the kitchen, "I'm glad you could make it home, Bobby."

Snow said, "Bobby? Where the hell did that come from?"

Ann came around the corner, pressed herself against him and said, "Your mother's been telling me all sorts of interesting things."

She was there, sitting on the black vinyl couch, cigarette smoldering in an ashtray, coffee cup, a game show on TV. She got up and came over to him as Ann went into the kitchen. "My God. Have you grown or have I shrunk? And look at those sideburns, just like your grandfather's."

He hugged her and felt how much weight she'd lost and how tiny she felt in his arms.

She stepped back and said, "Let me look at you."

He looked at her face, her face looking more and more like his grandmother's face, white hair, wrinkled, watery blue eyes, though Grandmother was heavy and never lost her presence. "How are you making out?"

"As well as could be expected." Her eyes began to tear. "Damn it," she said, and turned away. She sat down, pulled a tissue from the box on the coffee table, wiped her eyes, picked up her cigarette and said, "Tell me about the hospital."

He sat in the other chair and said, "There's nothing much to tell."

"Well, what do you do there?"

"Everything. It's a hospital, I'm an intern."

"Today, for instance. What did you do today?"

"I was up at six, took everybody's blood, did rounds, assisted in the OR for about five hours, then worked up three new admissions, other stuff in between."

"What do you mean everybody's blood?"

"When blood tests are ordered I'm the one has to do the needlework."

"For the whole hospital?"

"No, no. Just the ward I'm on."

"Do you have a room there, an office? What?"

"I have a room. I'm on call every second night."

"It's like squeezing blood from a stone."

"I know. I'm just tired. Would you like something to drink?" He wasn't sure why he couldn't just sit and talk, babble on, entertain and enlighten her, why it was such an effort to get a few words out. He would have liked to blame his reluctance on his gift to George Martin but knew the constriction lay right there between them, in himself.

"I think Ann has cut me off."

"What would you like?"

"Gin and tonic. We picked some up today."

He felt better doing something, fixing drinks, seeing what Ann was doing in the kitchen, but when he brought the gin and tonic to his mother, she said, "Oh, Robert, I don't know what I'm going to do with myself. I'm no good for anyone anymore." Her hand trembled as she lit another cigarette.

During dinner she replenished her gin and tonic, smoked three cigarettes and ate very little. "I'm sure it's very good," she said. "I just don't have much of an appetite."

Ann talked about their day together and what they might do the next day, Tuesday, before she reported to the Toronto French School on Wednesday.

They stayed away from the obvious topic of conversation, though it seemed to claim most of his mother's attention, other topics approached briefly, distractedly. She would suddenly look away, or when lighting a cigarette mutter to the world, to herself, "That bastard, that rotten conniving bastard."

In bed that night, his mother still up smoking and watching television, he whispered to Ann, "Thanks for...taking care of her."

"She's not so bad, when you're not around."

"What do you mean? What's she like when I'm not around?"

"She looks better. She doesn't collapse so much."

"Maybe I should stay away."

"Don't you dare."

"What the hell's she going to do when you're at work?"

"I haven't the slightest idea."

He tried to make love with her but she whispered, "Your mother's in the next room." His unhappy mother. Had she been happy, he thought, they could exercise the springs with reckless abandon.

His brother miles away, address unknown until a postcard arrived. His uncle Tom, his mother told him, back in Victoria now, divorced, living with Grandmother in the old house on Yates, sleeping in his childhood bedroom, looking for work, playing piano some Saturday nights at the Douglas Hotel. His grandmother, no help, you know that, Robert, she's no help at all. She'll ruin Tom. She already has. She's finally got him right where she always wanted him.

He rolled over, his hand slipping away from Ann's breast, looked up at the ceiling. Mother love, motherhood, motherly, mothering, mothered, mother; he had discovered by accident one day a less common meaning: a mucilaginous substance produced by the fermentation of vinegar.

HARVEY RYAN WAS drunk, Trebilcock was drunk, Snow was drunk. Harvey, sprawled in a chair, focused on Trebilcock, moving nothing more than his lips, was saying, "Hey, man, Jesus, you shouldn't drink so much, you don't handle it so good."

Trebilcock replying, "So what're you now, some fuckin' basketball star?"

"What the fuck's basketball gotta do with it?" Harvey moving his head now.

"Ah, who the shit cares." Trebilcock stretched his legs out and slouched deeper in his chair, the bottle of beer clutched firmly in his right hand. The lounge party was dying out, a mess of bottles and scraps of food on the table, music still playing, interns, residents, nurses sitting around, some parts of the party gone private, retreated to the cubicles. Snow, Harvey Ryan, Trebilcock, Snow and Ryan in whites, Trebilcock in greens, gravity cementing them to soft chairs in the corner farthest from the music.

Harvey saying, "C'mon, aren't you on call tonight?"

Trebilcock looking up disdainfully, "Christ, what are you? My mother? You got four wards to cover yourself."

"Yeah, but I don't have to cut anybody."

"Looka this. Steady as a rock." Trebilcock putting the bottle in his left hand and holding out his right hand.

Snow noticed it didn't look too bad but it wasn't the hand, it was the brain they should be worried about. Harvey didn't say anything else. Exhaustion brooded on his face. Trebilcock put his hand down. "Radiology, fucking radiology, would you believe it?"

"What about fucking radiology?"

"They want me to switch to it."

"Who?" Harvey was coming back to life.

"Armstrong. Thinks I should switch to radiology."

"Wha' the fuck does he know?"

"Yeah, wha' the fuck does he know?"

Trebilcock tried to suck some liquid out of his empty bottle. "He's got feet."

"What?"

"Says the most important thing's to have good feet."

"Knew it wasn't brains."

"You see his feet? Thirteen triple E."

"Kicks a lotta butt."

"A radiologist, Christ."

"Ah, shit, there's worse things to do in life."

"Look at goddamn X rays all day long? You tell me."

"Dentistry."

"Whaddaya mean dentistry? You got cute little dental hygienists scrapin' your gums. What's a radiologist got?"

"A lotta money."

"Tha's a good point."

"But no patient contact."

"Fuck patient contact."

"Christ, am I horny."

"You got a wife and three kids, haven't you, Harv?"

"What the fuck's that got to do with it?"

"You ever see 'em?"

"Sure, four weeks ago."

"A radiologist'd probably get to see 'em every night."

"Maybe one does."

"Fuck you."

"I'm not that horny."

"So what are you gonna do?"

"I'm gonna get another brew."

TO REHYDRATE HIMSELF Snow drank some water from the tap in the bathroom shared by his duty room and the one next to it, occupied by Trebilcock when he was on call. He was thinking, all those years of medicine and the one piece of useful information he acquired was about hangovers. Dehydration was the main cause. Drinking a quart of water before going to bed made it a hell of a lot better, except for having to get up and piss in the middle of the night.

He stretched out on the bed and tried to sleep. He'd been exhausted but now he was past sleep, drunk and wound up, knowing he could get called and he'd have to sober fast, and wanting to sleep so badly, his guts churning, a horrible deep loneliness in the pit of his stomach, and a party next door. Four, five, six of them playing music, laughing, talking, clanking around, Christ, two in the morning.

Snow lay on his back on the bed feeling anger. Nausea, loneliness, exhaustion and anger. And nothing he could do about it. Bastards making all that fucking noise. It would be uncool to ask them to stop. They'd just hand him a beer and make room on the bed. Had to be up at six. Work another twelve hours, take shit from surgeons and nurses and then go home where his mother was camped in the living room. For Christ's sake, go to sleep. Main problem with joining them, if he was honest, was there'd be three guys, two women, one of the women attractive, fuck, if it's a fantasy, make it good, one of the women a bombshell with a major thing for Robert Snow, Vanessa Redgrave, and he'd sit back with his beer and not want to talk and drink and be friendly but wanting the one bombshell there, Vanessa, shit, probably flirting with or fondling one of the guys, and he'd sit there sipping the beer feeling worse and worse wanting to make a play for her and take her back to his own bed but not doing it for a lot of reasons, and being stuck there, not doing it and not letting it go, and finally getting back to his own room alone in worse shape than before.

He understood them partying next door. You go to bed, fall asleep, wham, next minute you're back on the wards. Stay up, drink, bullshit, laugh, get laid, anything to keep the next day away.

But it always came.

THEY'D BROUGHT THIS surgeon over from England with a newly designed stainless-steel hip joint nestled in tissue in a little wooden box. Head and neck, silver baseball at one end, jagged bayonet at the other, the greater and lesser trochanter in the middle, where those wonderful muscles, the psoas, the piriformis, the gluteous minimus, the vastus attach—burnished replacement parts. In the Toronto *Star* it would read: "Artificial hip. Exciting medical development. First hip replacement in Canada. Following a five-hour operation the patient is making an excellent recovery, according to a hospital spokesman. Within weeks he'll be back on the golf course."

If the damn thing worked it would be an exciting development for hip patients, old farmers, chars, hod carriers, hewers of wood and bearers of water, a new joint to replace the old one worn down to rat shit by heavy burdens and osteoarthritis, full movement restored, no pain. Well, less pain. It should be an honor to assist with such a historic operation.

Sure.

The surgeon was one of those slim, long-nosed, thin-lipped, nasal, upper-class English. With boyish haircut. A hyphenated name, something like Beresford-Smythe. No sense of humor, no kindness, no humility to be found in his features. His eyes registered the existence only of those he might consider of equal or higher class, of which by definition there would be none in the colonies. One thing, though, he didn't treat the other surgeons, residents, nurses any better than he treated the interns. And Christ, Snow noticed, those local surgeons, Armstrong among them, lording it over everybody most of the time, now disgustingly obsequious around their colleague from England.

The hangover and three hours sleep didn't help, left temple throbbing, hospital lights birching his retinas. He should have swallowed more water. That was one of the problems with the water cure. How could a drunk ever talk himself into drinking a quart of tap water? Snow scrubbed and gloved and tried to make himself inconspicuous in the OR. The other thing on his mind was the longer the operation took the later he'd get to the rest of the work on the ward. It never went away. Survival time, from seven a.m. until midnight.

Trebilcock was there to second assist, and not in good shape. The English surgeon lectured at the other surgeons and residents in the room. He wasn't happy with the arrangement. He had trouble getting the hip lying at the right angle. Irritated, it seemed, by the inflexibility of an unconscious human body. It had probably been easier on dogs and sheep.

It was a brutal operation. They had to cut long and deep enough so they could locate all the arteries and nerves, some of them rather important, femoral, pudendal, sciatic, then saw off the top of the femur, clean out the socket joint between the ilium and the ischium, insert the sharpened arm of the steel ball into the cut end of the bone, screw it down and fit it into the socket.

Snow couldn't find the right attitude within himself, standing, watching, waiting for a role, shifting his weight from tired leg to tired leg. He should have been enthralled, starry-eyed. He just wanted the goddamn thing over with and prayed he'd not fall asleep and pitch into the open wound.

"Damn it," said the surgeon. "I still can't get at it. Have you no wider stirrups?"

Trebilcock explained that they had nothing else that would fit on this table, maybe something from gynecology but...

The surgeon stepped back and rolled his eyes above his mask. "You," he said, looking directly at Robert Snow. "Hold his leg out."

Snow tried. There was no room around the table, with first assists and second assists and third assists and scrub nurses and observers, each, it seemed to Snow, having found the attitude he couldn't. Starry-eyed. And the anesthetist, and his resident.

"Higher. No. Not that high. Bloody hell. Wait a minute. I need the knee up and abducted, rotated about thirty degrees. Try it from under the table."

Eight years of university, eight fucking years, Snow was thinking, and no dignity, not a goddamn scrap. He was inches away from telling the English surgeon to stuff it up his ass. Inches and miles. He crawled under the table as directed. For the next five hours hunched under metal and vinyl, surrounded by green scrub boots, drapes falling in his face, shifting and squatting, his back aching, his own hips aching, he held onto an old man's dry, nail-curled foot and lifted it, pulled it down, twisted it left and twisted it right according to the imperious commands coming from above.

Under the table his mind wandered in mood, time and territory. Feet may be important for a surgeon, but also a good bladder. Squatting made it worse. He wanted nothing more than to let go and piss all over the green surgical boots inches

90

from his face. And while he was at it he should go back and have a talk with that counselor in university who looked at all his aptitude tests and his marks and especially at his performance in his own Philosophy 202 class and had told Snow, it looks like you could be a success at most things you try and teaching English seems a good bet but the one thing I'd advise you not go into is medicine. Clever bastard. The devil's own recruiter. Medicine, eh? Why not? He'd met a nice enough doc the previous week, gone to him because of a rash. Neurodermatitis, the doc had told him. When do you get it? Snow had said, well, the truth is I get it when drinking coffee and bullshitting all afternoon in the caf, and it goes away when I'm in the library. The doc had smiled and said, "The cure seems pretty obvious to me. That's one hell of a superego you got working on you there. Deny the superego at your own peril." Yeah, sure, sitting in the library, books spread open, distracted by every rhythmic click of heel, clack of clogs on marble floor.

Snow couldn't imagine Jack Kerouac having this kind of problem, or Norman Bethune, one of his other heroes, which was interesting in its own right, he was thinking, of all the doctors in the world the one who caught his imagination was Norman Bethune, late of Spain and China. To say nothing of Che Guevara.

So he had studied to keep the rash under control and gotten good enough marks, unfortunately, for medicine. Almost slipped away from it that other time when the faculty member interviewing him for the medical school had frowned at his transcript, brought his eyes up to Snow and said, It all looks fine except for this one mark, a fifty-nine in biology. Snow had looked at it and pointed out the fifty-nine was out of seventy-five, not one hundred, not gold-medal material perhaps, but... The interviewer had looked relieved, as if he wanted Snow to qualify, wanted him in his medical school, and being wanted was a fair aphrodisiac for what seemed now a prelude to a good screwing. Squatting under the table, his ears pained by that bloody English accent almost as much as his bladder and hips ached, Snow wished he hadn't pointed out the interviewer's mistake. He should have said, yeah, he hated biology, just couldn't get his mind around to it, or his hormones settled sufficiently, to memorize species, classes, genera and phyla, morphology, cytology, which wouldn't have been a lie, and let them turn him down. Reject him.

His mother had come to his graduation, and his father, and there was a picture, somewhere in a box, of him in his robes, one parent on either side, not curled in close, all three looking posed and uncomfortable, his two parents at that moment as close to one another as they had gotten all day, all year, for that matter, maybe all decade, come to think of it. Ann was in the picture, too, smiling gamely. Poor Ann. Didn't know what the hell she was getting into becoming the second, ignored half of Dr. and Mrs., now at their apartment with his depressed, betrayed, miserable mother. He didn't want to imagine what went on between them all day long.

"Dr. Armstrong, that intern of yours has a body-temperature IQ. I have just told him for the second time to rotate the foot medially."

He heard Trebilcock's voice then. "The other way, Snow, for God's sake, the other way."

Medially, shit, it depended, as far as Snow could see, from which vantage point you were coming. Although his was definitely a subordinate vantage point. Reminding him of thirteen-year-old Robert and his science teacher, Mr. Edmunston, telling the class the earth rotated around the sun clockwise, and Robert arguing with him that it depended where the observer happened to be sitting, which end of the universe, Mr.

Edmunston insisting on clockwise as the answer, Robert dis-
agreeing, then being sent down to see the vice-principal, to ask
the VP, also the head of science, the same question. The VP
agreed clockwise was the answer, and sent Robert back to
class. Nobody had told him about conventions, the governors of
imagination. Maybe Edmunston hadn't known the difference
between convention and reality. For instance, right here and
now, it was convention for the intern, arm aching above his
head, holding the heel of a foot, to eat shit. That the surgeon
with the accent from England should consider himself a superior human being. That Robert should be obedient, polite,
grateful. That he should exhibit superhuman stamina, that he
should be treated like a dog and yet care what happened to the
poor old bugger whose hip was being replaced. Whereas reality
had the intern conjuring a full range of sadistic operations he
might perform on the surgeon. First on the list: an external
laryngeal extirpation to remediate that abrasive accent.

"Pull down, pull down, man. That's better, ah, there it is,
we're ready for the hip now."

Ready for the hip now, Christ, it's been ten hours already.

"You had the right position a minute ago, and now you've
lost it. You, under the table, would you please exercise a little
consistency. I should think a review of your admission stan-
dards is in order, Dr. Armstrong. Ha, ha."

And now Snow found himself wishing the operation would
go bad. He didn't really wish any harm to the long-forgotten
patient unconscious above him, but a sudden hemorrhage,
a major drop in blood pressure, an arrest, would wipe
away what he imagined was a smug expression under the surgeon's mask. But then, he'd probably be blamed for it. The
first foot-holding-intern-provoked cardiac arrest in medical
history. Published in the *Lancet*.

This very moment, he pictured, his friend Tony would be

leaning against a lectern, eyes brooding over the edge, facing a room full of nineteen-year-old girls, explaining the dirtier passages in Shakespeare. Now there's an occupation with meaning. Sitting in the faculty lounge, arguing about the Vietnam war, the sexual revolution, long hair, new music, sit-ins. Other lives.

Then again, if the Russians dropped the bomb right now he'd be in a pretty good position, under a steel table. Remembering October '62, flipping coins or playing cards in the university caf, Kruschev and Kennedy eyeball to eyeball over Cuba, Robert telling Jim and Bryan he was going to do nothing until the bomb was dropped or the crisis resolved. Imagine spending the last days, hours of your life memorizing German poetry. What a waste. Jim thought they should sit on the beach drinking Logana, loganberry wine. Drive up the coast to a fishing cabin, watch the waves, wait for the fireball, the mushroom cloud.

"Snow."

Logana, the worst hangovers, reminding him of his current temple throb.

"Snow, you can come out now."

Robert Snow unwinding himself, crawling out from under the table, easing himself up, holding his legs together. The English surgeon gone, the acolytes with him, Trebilcock left behind, a couple of nurses.

Trebilcock: "They're letting me close."

Snow: "Lucky you. What the hell time is it?"

Trebilcock ignoring this, suturing the skin with black thread. Snow looking at the clock, two-thirty, six and a half hours. "Six and a half hours."

Trebilcock: "I'm done. Gimme his BP."

Snow and Trebilcock side by side at urinals, heads tilted back, masks down around the neck, boots and caps still on, mouths open, Trebilcock saying, "You know you can faint pissing this much at once. Knocks hell out of the blood pressure."

"I'll file that piece of information right next to the correct dose of B_{12}." Eyes meeting in the mirror, Snow seeing his own darkly colored, strained, hooded, but Trebilcock's alert, clear, scanning.

Trebilcock saying, "Fuck you." Throwing his cap, mask, boots, gown in a hamper, leaving, the front of his green cottons wet. Snow getting a Sweet Marie from the machine and heading off to the ward for six more hours.

SNOW GOT HOME at eight. Ann had been there since five. His mother there all day. Ashtray full, apartment stench of old tobacco, television on. Robert wolfing down leftovers, his mother telling Ann, "You should fix him something." Robert quickly saying no, no, this is fine. And asking, "What did you do all day?" of his mother. His eyes asking Ann what she was like at five, before, presumably, the three gin and tonics. His mother saying, "I walked to the corner store and back, down to Bloor. Your grandmother's family lived at Yonge and Bloor, did you know that?"

"There are sure no family homes there now. Does she know you're back here, by the way?"

"No, why would she know? I don't tell her everything."

Robert letting this slide, remembering the daily phone calls, a contentious issue between his mother and father, his father saying, for God's sake, you were on for an hour and a half, just tell her you're busy and hang up. His mother, unable to defend, going on the attack, just whose calls were more important.

Robert thought he shared a secret with his mother, mentioned it now. "You remember years ago when Grandmother phoned every single day?"

"Twice a day."

"And you'd be ironing or something and you'd rest the receiver on a table and Grandmother'd be telling one of her long stories and you'd just pick the phone up every few minutes or so and say, 'uh-huh,' and put it back down, and she'd never know the difference?"

"I did no such thing."

But he could picture it, even hear his grandmother's voice droning on. Even worrying for his mother that she might misjudge the pauses and blow her deception.

"I sure remember it," said Robert.

"Maybe once or twice."

The television news distracted them. Dean Rusk announced as truth, as given, as received wisdom—escalation is inevitable. Westmoreland asked for more troops. Then the body counts. An Army spokesman explaining the number of killed Americans was accurate whereas the number of dead Viet Cong a gross underestimate. They took the bodies away, carried them through tunnels to burial grounds. Norman Mailer had been arrested at a protest rally, joining Allen Ginsberg, Joan Baez. Hubert Humphrey saying they were winning the war.

"Jesus fucking Christ," said Robert.

"Where did you learn that kind of language?" asked his mother.

"I don't want to watch anymore," said Ann. "I can't stand it. It's so depressing."

"It's all coming apart. It's all unraveling, isn't it?" said his mother.

"Sure as hell seems that way," said Robert.

In bed that night, his mother again left sitting on the couch, television flickering, Robert tossed and turned, burned, muttered angrily, "I'm exhausted, I can't sleep, I've got eighteen hours on emergency tomorrow. Fucking asshole Americans."

96

"It's not going anywhere," said Ann.

"What?"

"Your mother. Where is this leading? I don't see where it's going."

"I don't know."

"We'll have to do something. Call your father. Something."

"I'm really sorry about it."

"It's not your fault."

"Of course it is. Everything's my fault."

"You're being melodramatic."

"All right. Let's give it a week then."

"Tell me about your day. Maybe that'll help."

"My day?"

"Yes. Think of it as counting sheep."

"Okay. Most of the day I spent squatting under the operating table. Praying for the materialization of a urinal."

"And they pay you for this?"

"I figured it out, actually. Twenty cents an hour."

"You will do something about it, won't you, Robert?"

"We'll have to." There was no escape this time, he could see that. Thinking about the many years before, an adolescent escape artist, home as little as possible, utilizing bed and refrigerator, his younger brother doing the same, any sport he could conceivably play without getting himself killed, jazz bands, Dixie bands, concert bands, chess clubs, school papers, jalopy restoration, long nights drinking, infatuations, beach parties. Escaping from his mother, herself trapped and resentful in the cage of his grandmother's making.

They talked briefly of Tom that evening, once a romantic figure in Robert's imagination, a musician, performer, escaping from the small town to the Royal York and then to the tropics. And now from alcohol nights in the tropics to a room upstairs in the old frame home on Yates. Returning to his

97

mother. There had been a period Robert's father and mother had worried Robert would follow his uncle's path, dropping out of university and running away with a band, during those years Robert played bass in jazz cellars on Saturday night, to make a buck or two, and drank too much. Margaret telling his mother and father there was nothing wrong with being a musician, an artist. Telling them Robert was a sensitive soul, like Tom, and Dinny, the one who died as a child. No one mentioning the alcohol.

There was Robert's grandmother, at the center again, the world revolving around her, held by her gravity, briefly escaping but always falling back. Michael trying for the moon, Tom crash-landing, Mother in low orbit. Robert's father achieving liftoff, maybe, Robert left on the ground as a member of the cleanup crew.

CHAPTER EIGHT

Will you still need me
Will you still feed me
When I'm sixty-four
  — LENNON/MCCARTNEY

The killer awoke before dawn,
He put his boots on,
He took a face from the ancient gallery,
And he walked on down the hall.
He went to the room where his sister lived,
And then he pays a visit to his brother,
And then he walked on down the hall.
And then he came to a door,
And he looked inside,
'Father?'
'Yes, son?'
'I want to kill you.'
'Mother, I want to…'
  — THE DOORS

DURING THE DAY Robert worked on emergency with Sandy, one of them finishing off an eighteen- or twenty-four-hour shift and the other starting one, overlapping for eight hours. Sandy was good, thorough, efficient, tireless. He had recovered from his Elsa experience, distanced himself and regained his confidence. Although he was noticeably less competitive. They moved separately from case to case, through minor problems, sprains, breaks, aches, pains, cuts, leather-skin working guys coming in affecting a nonchalant saunter, a smile-grimace on their faces and a heavy bloody towel wrapped around their arms, legs, hands, saying, "Little cut, doc."

Nurse Pauline saying: "Better look at the guy in seven. He's dripping all over the floor."

Then coronaries, infarcts, strokes, people passing out, suicides, bloody vomiting, multiple trauma, old ladies on stretchers from nursing homes. Casualties of life.

Robert felt clumsy, slow, lazy, incomplete, insecure next to Sandy. He was sure he was going to miss something. He knew it in his bones. Somebody was going to come in the emergency, see Dr. Snow, be examined by Dr. Snow, be given, as they say, a clean bill of health by Dr. Snow, step back out into the street and drop dead. He'd come close, and learned something about drunks: always X-ray their heads. Café patrons had escorted a drunk to the emergency, left him for Dr. Robert Snow, had told Snow that he was so drunk he fell off a stool. "Nothing fucking wrong with me," said the drunk. An uncooperative, ungrateful son of a bitch. Robert learned another thing. Always ask why. Why did you bring him to the emergency now? And if you don't get a clear answer, ask again. The part of the story they hadn't bothered telling Snow was, "When he fell off the stool he cracked his head on the floor and knocked himself unconscious." The next day, after Snow had sent him out, he returned with headache, double vision. Subdural hematoma.

They were always working on many cases at once, sending blood off to be analyzed, waiting for X rays, going on to the next while they waited, dropping everything when ambulances pulled up with the critically ill on board.

Pauline: "Blood work's back on Mrs. Jones."

"Who?"

"Your patient in eleven. She's been waiting since early this morning."

"Shit. Forgot all about her."

Old ladies from nursing homes. Sometimes old men. Mostly old ladies. Confused, dry, desiccated, frightened—toxic on pharmacological abundance, depressed, giving up, hanging on. Snow held their hands, touched their brows and brushed back their dry white hair with his fingers.

Throughout the afternoon Sandy had one he worried over, between all his other cases. Wire glasses pushed up on his nose, plastic case of pens in the breast of his white jacket, stethoscope draped around his shoulders, having graduated from the beginners' stuffed-in-the-pocket style, on through the novice necklace style, on to the journeyman draped around the shoulders as if just fallen there from the ceiling, his pockets still bulging with other instruments and notebooks. Intense and keen, he X-rayed all of her, this old lady who had arrived unaccompanied on a gurney in an ambulance. He systematically tested all her body fluids, her organs, her filtering organs, metabolizing organs, her pumping organs, her excretory organs. He wrote a three-page note. In the evening he declared her well and fit and sent her back to the nursing home.

At two in the morning she was brought back, dead. Sandy looked over his notes. "What the hell did I miss? I checked everything. There was nothing wrong with her."

Snow knew what he had missed. Pauline saw it, too. The woman was dying. "She was dying, Sandy."

"Whaddaya mean dying? You don't just die. You get sick and die. There was nothing wrong with her."

"She was dying, that's all there was to it."

"Whaddaya mean dying? What did I miss?"

"You didn't miss anything. She was dying. There was nothing you could do about it. It was time for her to die."

"Bullshit, bullshit."

Pauline: "You were supposed to be off at midnight. Go on home, sleep it off. It's okay, it was time for her to die."

Robert didn't mention he thought it a shame she had to spend the last few hours of her life being carted back and forth between institutions.

Perversely he felt a little better about himself after that. Not that he didn't still fret about making mistakes, and there was a voice in his head saying, "This is not a contest, for God's sake." But for all his self-perceived sloppiness, his aversion to detail, his lassitude, his distractions, the journals and books he never studied hard enough, he did seem to have something that usually didn't let him down, and which Sandy didn't seem to have. Instincts and intuition. He found he knew what people were telling him. He knew when they were dying. He knew when they were very sick. He knew when the pain was real and when it wasn't. He usually knew when he should take his time and when he should hurry. He also understood that he could never know enough to be certain.

HE WAS WAITING for the X rays for the man in two, the drunk in four was sleeping it off, the woman in seven was waiting for the neurology resident. In the late-evening lull he was sipping coffee and talking with Pauline. She didn't think much of him letting the drunk sleep it off. She said, "He should be out of here, if you're not gonna admit him."

"He said he was going to kill himself."

"So call psych."

"Sure. They're gonna say gimme a call when he's sober."

"Well, will you get him out before the supervisor comes?"

"A couple more hours he'll have changed his mind."

"You could send him to Queen Street."

"I'll think about it. It's not busy. We can spare the bed for a while."

An ambulance driver and an attendant walked in and sat down. There had been no sirens and they weren't in a hurry. "Coffee any good?"

Pauline said, "Help yourself." She was an attractive woman, dark eyes, black hair, olive skin, with an attitude all the emergency nurses assumed. Competent, efficient, flashes of empathy, but never showing fear, horror—a thinly layered veneer of indifference: who gives a shit, move it along, admit 'em or discharge 'em, get that wino out of my emergency department. Knowing who was faking, giving the regulars a coffee, a juice, ten minutes, out the door.

The two attendants got up and fixed coffees for themselves, dropping some change in the box beside the pot. The driver said, "Pretty steep for a small cuppa java."

Pauline said, "It's 'cause half you buggers don't pay anything."

They sat down not saying any more, sipping their coffees, smiling.

It was the smile that got Pauline. She said, "Okay, what's with you guys? You don't like the coffee, you don't wanna talk. You can always go up the street."

"We got a little present for you."

"Okay, I'll bite."

"Actually it's for the doc. Didn't think you'd appreciate us bringing it in."

"So?"

"It's in the wagon. Maybe the doc can take a look."

Snow got up and walked out through the emergency doors into the cool night air, not thinking clearly, not anticipating. The ambulance had been backed in, its back door only a few feet away from the entrance. He unlatched the door and pulled himself up and in.

Ah, the stench, thick, rotten, rancid, sweet, putrid. As solid as anything invisible can be. Reaching out to him, enveloping him, invading him. A vaguely human shape, black, on the stretcher. He staggered back, his stomach heaving, retching. He stepped away from the ambulance, settled himself and took several deep gulps of air. Then he held his breath and went back in. Even when he was not inhaling, the stink assaulted his nose, his mouth, his eyes. He looked quickly at the corpse and backed out.

"So, doc, is it dead?"

"It was dead before Confederation."

"You look a little green."

"Where the hell did you find it?"

"In a rooming house in Parkdale. Landlady thought there was a gas leak, called the gas company. They looked worse than you do. We coulda taken it to St. Joseph's but we figured your coffee was better. You wanna take a look, too, Pauli?"

She said, "Go fuck yourselves."

"Soon as the doc signs the papers testifying to the irrefutable fact that the John Doe in question is dead."

The stench seemed like a contagious thing to Snow, trying to take permanent root in his nose. He signed and went off to wash himself, briefly wondering about the life of the man and the manner of his death. And whether, on the last page, it mattered that he had died alone and rotted before burial.

ANN HAD TOLD him on the phone she had a meeting to go to, be back around eleven that night. He knew she had to get away. She'd said, "She doesn't sleep. If she's not sitting she's pacing. I try to keep her away from the bottle but she's your mother, it's sometimes easier to let her drink. It wouldn't be so bad if she helped out a bit, you know, offered to clean or cook or just wash the dishes, but nothing. She smokes and watches TV and complains about your dad."

He had said, "You wouldn't want her cooking."

"You know what I mean."

"She never could cook worth shit."

"She says your father wouldn't eat anything but overcooked meat and potatoes."

"Yeah, well, mealtime was a treat."

"I guess."

Ann wasn't there when he got to the apartment. His mother looked up and greeted him and then went back to watching TV. "You can learn an awful lot from these quiz shows," she said.

He asked her if she wanted anything to eat, and she said no, maybe later. He was thinking, this is not a frigging restaurant, but sat down beside her and touched her arm. He hated the smell of stale cigarette smoke wafting from her hair and sweater. Her glass was empty. Each time he saw her he was surprised how old she looked.

She said, "What'll I do, Robert? It's all over. There's nothing for me now. I raised you boys and now you don't need me anymore. Your father wouldn't let me work."

Robert said, "He didn't tie you down, chain you to the floor." And regretted saying it.

"You don't know how it was then. It's easy enough for you. Ann doesn't think twice about it. It wasn't so easy then."

"Yeah, I understand."

"You don't understand. The last ten years was a lie. I was living a lie. You work your fingers to the bone for thirty years and what do you get, what gratitude is there? None. Discarded like an old pair of shoes, that's what he's done, thrown me out like an old pair of shoes."

"You've got the house."

"I never liked it. It was your father's house. It was never finished. He was always big on ideas and small on finishing. I waited for ten years for the upstairs to be finished." Ah, yes. He'd grown up in a world where nothing was right, nothing pleased, not beyond the first few minutes. The car his father chose, the big DeSoto, the small Zephyr, the Christmas tree, shape, variety or size, the upstairs renovation, the kitchen addition, the cedar hedge, the summer lakeside motel, the camping trailer his father built, the washing machine, the tile sink, the freezer—the freezer, how could something like that become an issue for months, even years? He remembered the early days of home freezers when they were sold door-to-door with a year's supply of meat, maybe two years of meat and vegetables. The child Robert in the kitchen watching the salesman work his magic on his father, Mother coming in and out, father a sucker for sales talk, "A very wise decision, Mr. Snow." His father, of course, couldn't win. If he didn't buy Mother would call him a cheapskate, penny-pinching tight-wad. If he did, it would turn out to be the wrong size, wrong kind. This time, an even worse outcome. The company went out of business before the year's supply of meat was delivered to the empty freezer. Evidence for his mother. Evidence of his hapless, thoughtless ineptitude, to be added to the other piles of evidence and presented over and over again during the unending trial. Robert trying to make her happy, failing, escaping.

"Do you want me to get you another drink?"

"I don't mean to be a burden. If I just kill myself you'll all be better off."

"Gin and tonic again?"

HE WAS BUSHED from his last stint on emergency, the smell of the corpse still in his nose, in his hair, the image in his mind, so after he'd eaten some crackers and peanut butter while sitting with her on the black vinyl couch in front of the TV and then taken a bath he left her there and crawled into bed before Ann returned home.

She paced around the living room and then came into the bedroom, sat on the bed and said, "Help me, please, Robert. Help me."

He said, "It'll be okay, Mom. You can stay here awhile."

"Hold me, please."

He held her hand. She said, "That's not what I meant, you know what I mean." And began to get under the covers with him, lifting them, crawling in.

He got out of bed and led her to the living room, dusting this under the carpet as quickly as possible. Jesus shit, he was thinking. He knew exactly, didn't want to know, but knew, what she had in mind, and thought, Christ what a horrible loneliness she must have wanting that, wanting to be held and loved, held under the sheets, body to body, and more and more, and God help him, picturing it happening, and understanding and knowing the need, to be held by her son, to be loved by her son, to be fucked by her son. The old women in emergency, lying on gurneys waiting for verdicts, had wanted him to touch them and he had, holding their hands and stroking their brows, watching their eyes relax, mouths slacken, eliciting a smile. Endless need, endless demand. It was somehow harder to give his mother as much as he gave strangers brought to him by the ambulance service. He got himself back in bed and lay there, wide awake, listening to his mother sitting, getting up, wandering, sitting in the other room, on the other side of the thin wall. Waiting for Ann and thinking about Sigmund Freud and his father, not wanting to kill his father and fuck his mother, but rather have his father come and take his mother away, make her happy, fill her up, because he couldn't, not now, not before, not ever.

THE DOOR TO Trebilcock's room was ajar. Snow had knocked, heard water running and gone in. The door to the small bathroom was open.

"Jesus Christ. What the fuck are you doing?"

"I'm committing suicide. Wha' the hell you think I'm doing?"

"You're drunk."

"Of course I'm drunk. Sober I'd do a much better job."

"Put the razor down, for Christ's sake." The tap was on, the sink full but without a plug. Trebilcock had his left wrist in the basin, and the water was moderately pink. He put the razor on the ceramic lip. Snow pulled his hand out of the water and looked at the wrist. It was a superficial wound about an inch up from the hand.

"Here, wrap it in this and hold it up."

"I suppose you think I'm an asshole."

"You are an asshole."

"Lot you fucking know."

"Sit on the bed while I try to get Harv."

He dialed zero and asked the switchboard to page Dr. Ryan. Trebilcock was lying on the bed. His eyes were closed. When Harvey came on the line Snow asked him please would he kindly get his ass up here quickly. The blood was showing through on the towel but not enough to worry about. Trebilcock was snoring.

When Harvey came in the room in his rumpled whites, eyes sagging with exhaustion, skin a bad hospital pallor, he said, "What the fuck's going on?"

"Shut the door."

"Okay, the door's shut. Now what the fuck's going on?"

"Phil cut his left wrist."

"What, shaving his arm?"

"No. Deliberately."

"Deliberately?"

"Yes."

"What an asshole."

"Exactly what I told him."

"Now what is he? Coma, dead, what?"

"Sleeping it off."

"Is he on call?"

"I don't think so."

"Lemme take a look."

Harvey unwound the towel. "Piss ass job, just like everything else he does."

"I think that's why."

"Why what?"

"He thinks he's failing at everything. Surgery."

"No worse than the other assholes."

"Armstrong rides him."

"Armstrong's a prick. Stupid bugger's only got another year and a half to go."

"What now?"

"You sit with him. I'll get some thread from Emerge and we'll sew him up. Before he wakes up."

"Then what?"

"Put a bandage on it. He can tell everybody he had a mole removed, something."

"Yeah, and then what?"

"It's up to him."

IT WAS MIDNIGHT and quiet when she came in to Emergency. Snow had been on since eight that morning after four hours of sleep. Pauline told him the new patient was ready in room seven, call if he needed her. She smiled at him and

109

flicked her left eyebrow up over her coal-black eyelids.

He splashed cold water on his face and walked down to seven, her newly constructed chart in hand. She was sitting on the bed in a green hospital gown. She looked eighteen. He glanced at the chart. She was sixteen. She had straight blond hair. Her skin was perfect. The curving line from her ear to her shoulder had been what kept Renoir painting. The trapezius and sternocleidomastoideus, he told himself. He sat in the chair beside the bed. She told him she had some chest pains and stomach pains and didn't feel well. She'd been at a party and had asked her girlfriend to stop when they were driving past the hospital. Pauline had taken the girl's blood pressure, temperature and pulse. They were all normal. She was in the middle of her month. Could she be pregnant? No, she told him, without blinking. She spoke very little but her eyes were alive and watching him. He would have to examine her. With those, as they called them, chief complaints, he'd have to examine her all over.

He listened to her back. The gown was open at the back and she was wearing small white cotton panties. He checked her eyes, her mouth, her neck. He listened to the top of her chest in front, above the gown. He asked her to take it off and lie back and she obeyed without hesitating.

She had perfect breasts, small erect nipples, a lovely pink blush around them. He listened to her chest under and above her breasts. Her abdomen was flat, falling away under the ribs, slightly rounded at the navel, the cotton panties stretched across her pelvis so there was a half-inch gap between the elastic and the down that led to her... He quickly put the stethoscope on her abdomen and listened to normal bowel sounds. He felt with his hand for her liver, and then any tender spots, kidneys, spleen, bowel, and then pushed the elastic slightly down so he could feel, or try to feel, her uterus. His hand brushed the top of her pubic hair. It wasn't a complete examination. He couldn't bring himself to do a complete examination.

He sat back in the chair and she sat up in the bed. She didn't reach for the gown to cover herself. He was exhausted and exhilarated. Restless, fatigued, aroused, frazzled. Let's face it, he told himself, you're both dead and turned on. With her chart placed strategically across his lap he looked at her and she looked back. She sat there watching his eyes, looking at him as if waiting, expecting. She was gorgeous. She was sweet. She was pretty. She was perfect. She was also virginal and knowing at the same time. By appearance innocent and yet understanding her power. She didn't say a word. She just sat there watching him watching her, watching him watching her.

It seemed to go on for a long time. Snow couldn't make himself say anything or do anything. He couldn't bring himself to end the moment. His mind reeled with the profane and the sacred. Close the door, pull the curtains, do it now. Come up to my room, I'll meet you there. I won't touch, I don't have to touch. I'll just look. Let me lie beside you for eternity. Marry me and have my children. Magnificent angel please hold me and make me feel safe. Let me swim in your eyes and suckle your breasts. Wherever you go I'll go with you and keep you safe. I want you for myself. Already I can't stand the thought of other men touching you, of your defilement, of your growing old.

When he began to tell her he hadn't found anything wrong but maybe she could make an appointment with her family doctor for sometime this week, his voice was thick. He cleared it. Tried again. She watched him. He got himself up and down the corridor before she started to dress.

When he reached the reception area Pauline said, "You liked that, huh?"

He slumped in the chair. He watched the girl come down the hallway, jeans, sandals, small bomber jacket. She went out the door without looking his way.

Pauline said, "So, what's her trouble?"

"Just a confused kid," he said, and closed his eyes.

"Worried about pregnancy?"

He kept his eyes closed. "No."

"Then worried about fucking?"

"I didn't ask."

NOBODY NOTICED THE small bandage on Trebilcock's wrist. Snow figured the surgeons wouldn't notice if you cut off your hand, not until you were in the OR trying to hold the retractor with a stump. Armstrong would probably kick you out and say send me a whole intern next time. Dictate a memo to that effect. To the administrator, c.c. the board of governors, medical director: "I am alarmed by the recent decline in quality…"

Snow asked Harvey, "What do you think's going on with him?"

"I have no idea," said Harvey. "Maybe he's queer."

"Why queer?"

"He cut his wrist. It's kinda a female thing to do."

"He was drunk, didn't know what the hell he was doing."

"He's a troubled boy."

"Should we tell someone?"

"Are you kidding? He'd be outa here so fast."

"Reminds me. What happened to that Egyptian resident, the woman, what's her name? She just disappeared."

They were in the cafeteria, eleven in the evening, eating leftovers, drinking juice. Harvey pushed his plate away, said, "Stupid bitch. She got a call about two one morning. Nurses asked her to come see an old woman with a dropping BP. She asked how old the woman was. They told her the woman was eighty-six. Get this, she told them she doesn't get up in the middle of the night for anyone over eighty. She was gone the next day."

"Just like that."

"Shit, she was incompetent. Absolutely useless. They were just waiting to get her on something."

"This is not a particularly kind place," said Snow.

"Jesus, Snow, you're full of it. Answer me this: you want that incompetent bitch graduating and looking after your mother? You want Trebilcock hopped up on drugs, contemplating suicide, holding a scalpel in the middle of your gut? If they can't cut it they oughta drive taxi or something."

The word *mother* spun Robert's mind into his own preoccupations and he almost missed Harvey saying, as they gathered up their trays, "But I guess we better keep an eye on that stupid son of a bitch."

THEY WENT OUT to dinner. They'd asked his mother and she'd said she wasn't hungry. They didn't go far, just a few blocks away to the Café Europa, which meant Hungarian. Over cheap red wine and goulash, Ann, whose voice reclaimed its childhood north-of-London-but-cultured-by-elocution-lessons accent when upset, or as she might call it now, cross, said, "She's very depressed."

"I know."

"I either put up with her pacing and agitation or I buy her booze. I don't feel good about it when I buy her booze."

"I'm sorry about it."

"Don't say you're sorry. It doesn't help."

"Do you want coffee, dessert?"

"And don't change the subject."

"Okay."

"It isn't working, Robert. I'm beginning to worry all day at work. I don't know what I'm going to come home to."

"The mess, you mean?"

"No."

"What then?"

"Her dead body, Robert, her dead body. Or bleeding to death."

"You think she'd cut herself?"

"I don't know. Crawl out a window, overdose, use a plastic bag. I got rid of them the other day."

"Rid of what?"

"The plastic bags."

"Christ. You think she'd do that?"

"I don't know. You're the goddamned doctor."

He said, "They're listening at the other table." And as he said it he realized it was what his father would have said, his mother getting hysterical, screaming at him, calling him a weak pantywaisted two-timing fart in a bottle, and his father saying, a pained, affronted, condescending look on his face, saying, Would you please keep it down, the neighbors can hear, along with, If you can't say anything good about someone don't say anything at all. Robert suddenly experiencing, in himself, his father, his mother, his uncle, his grandmother. His father trying to maintain appearances, his mother given to rage, doubt, depression, his uncle escaping into romance, music, alcohol, his grandmother the rebellious puppet master.

Ann was leaning forward, saying, "I don't give a damn if they're listening or not listening. I can't handle it any more."

He put his fork down and drained the last drops from his wineglass. He said, "She did say something about killing herself, and the other night she was really over the edge."

"Tell me about it."

"We could send her back. I could call her doctor and then

114

send her back." He hated the thought of it, doing those things. He didn't want to deal with it. He used to escape from her house, but now she was in his house. He still had a partial escape, he realized, the all-consuming, all-embracing hospital, from which he would also like to escape.

"Is your father being as much of a bastard as she says he is? About the money?"

"I don't know."

"What does he say?"

"I haven't talked with him."

"You haven't called him?"

"No."

"I just assumed you had. From the hospital."

"No. I haven't called him."

"Not at all?"

"No."

"Why not?"

"Christ if I know."

"Robert."

"Okay. Okay. I don't want to get into it. I don't want to get into the middle of it. Him telling me one thing, her telling me another. I mean I want to ask him for Christ's sake take her back. She's not a piece of baggage. I can't fucking do it."

"You're going to have to deal with it, Robert, sooner or later."

"I know."

"I don't think I can handle it much longer."

"I'm sorry for this."

"Don't say you're sorry. Just do something."

"Like what?"

"I think she should be seeing someone."

"You mean a psychiatrist."

"Or be in hospital."

"You think she's getting that bad?"

"She just sits there all day, Robert, thinking about it, ruminating."

"It isn't good."

"So?"

"So?"

"Will you call?"

"My father?"

"No. Her friends, your relatives, the airline and her doctor in Victoria."

"To send her back?"

"You want to quit your job and look after her?"

"No."

"So?"

"I'll look into it tomorrow."

"Robert."

"I'll do it tomorrow."

But not tomorrow, not ever tomorrow.

THE TELEVISION NEWS that night told them that Woody Guthrie had died after years of suffering with Huntington's disease, and Robert immediately imagined, in this unfair, cruel world, that it had probably started with a clumsiness in his fingers. Ann in bed, Robert sitting on the couch with his mother, watching clips of Woody singing of tolerance and peace and boy soldiers being sent off to war. His mother asking about Huntington's and Robert answering perfunctorily but thinking of God, with more than his usual sense of irony, giving such a man Huntington's, the body going all to hell with involuntary movements described quite poetically in the medical texts as choreiform and choreiathetotic, with the mind following sometime thereafter. A genetic disease, he explained to his mother. Rare enough that he had never seen a case. And then remembering he had, but not telling her. Being taken as a student to see, to view, to observe, to inspect, to scrutinize an emaciated, hollow-cheeked, hollow-eyed, half-naked man tied down in a bed, thrashing in rhythmic bursts against his bonds. And howling, too, and howling.

The news then switched to the latest atrocities in Vietnam, where there were now four hundred and sixty-four thousand American boy soldiers serving in Vietnam and General "Westy" Westmoreland wanted more. Westy. Obviously not a fan of Woody Guthrie. Robert thinking about Westy and remembering he had been for a long time Bobby to his mother, and Bones, shortened from Lazybones, and then Rob on the football field, where a rough intimacy was called for, and Snow in the locker room, where a little distance was required. Monty, Westy, Ol' Ironsides. How could someone knicknamed Westy ever lead anyone astray? "Very comforting," he said to his mother.

"What's comforting?"

"Westy. Calling the man calling for more cannon fodder Westy."

But it was as if she could only attend to external concerns for seconds at a time, and not hearing his explanation, began to bemoan her lot in life, her abbreviated future, the wrongs done to her by his father. He held her hand, stroked her brow and brought her a glass of water and a sleeping pill.

CHAPTER NINE

I can see for miles and miles
and miles and miles and miles.
— PETE TOWNSHEND

ROBERT AND ANN took a Saturday afternoon and joined a peace march, an antiwar march, that wound its way down Yonge Street to City Hall. Ann had challenged Robert, who had gone on a rant watching the television news, about this American thing, this craziness, this stupidity, this corrupt, racist, self-destructive vortex, stubbornness, inertia, fragments of steel, flesh, a small child fleeing napalm, defoliation, drugged minds and poisoned souls, what could you do but stand at the border and shout, you're all fucking nuts.

"That certainly would be very effective," Ann had said.

"Do you have a better idea?"

"We could march."

"What?"

"There's a peace march on Saturday."

"It'll probably rain."

"Robert."

"You really mean it."

"Yes."

"Join all those hippies, radicals, potheads?"

Bunch of peaceniks, long-haired hippies, Hubert Humphrey

would call them, marching on a cold October afternoon down the main street of a Canadian city. Robert and Ann overcoming self-consciousness, reluctance, finding the gathering, falling in, walking with the crowd, chanting: "Hey, hey, LBJ, How many kids did you kill today?"

Robert remembering his discussion with his American pharmacology professor when it hadn't been too late, and now, when it probably was too late. Imagining him marching in a similar parade in Vancouver, forever determined to speak, no matter the futility. Belatedly developing an admiration for a man who could not change the world but could at least keep his own soul.

It also got them away from his mother for the afternoon.

It wasn't a big crowd. They were forced to use the sidewalk, not disrupt the daily commerce, the flow of traffic. Robert able to shake his self-consciousness for minutes at a time, his sense of being an uninvited extra on a public stage.

Arm in arm in the cold bleak afternoon, along Dundas to Bay to the new city hall, two oversize concrete spatulas facing off on a windswept square. The small crowd and its small voice overwhelmed by the size of the square and the buildings. Someone shouted, "Let's go to the American embassy." But nobody seemed to know where it was. "It's in Ottawa, you dickhead." "Yeah? What the hell. What about the trade center, they gotta have some kind of trade office here."

Robert recognized someone in the crowd, a psychiatry resident from the hospital, Joe something, with wire-rimmed granny glasses, masses of curly brown hair and a tattered duffel coat. He introduced Ann. Ann, Joe. Joe, Ann. Joe filled in the last name: Berkowitz. He added that a small group was headed over to a place he had on Dundas. It wasn't a direct invitation. It was said within the etiquette of the time. This is what I'm doing, suit yourself. They were stamping their feet against the cold and they followed along. Robert was wearing an overlong green scarf that Ann had knitted for him in a convulsion of domesticity. It was, Robert thought, a very confusing time. Women seemed to need new reasons, if not excuses, to do motherly things. To reinvent maternity. Girls wanting to be their grandmothers rather than their mothers.

Joe's pad was a small apartment over a Chinese restaurant. The odor of sesame oil and black bean sauce hung in the air. The two sparsely furnished rooms quickly filled. Robert and Ann found a corner and sat on the floor, shedding their coats and scarves and holding them in their laps. He listened to the conversation but it seemed the entire English vocabulary had been simplified to the word *man*. A gaunt young male with long dirty hair and sparse beard produced a guitar and began strumming the cords of "This Land." A plate of brownies was passed around.

Ann said something about not having lunch and took two. A hand reached in front of Snow with a fat smoldering joint in it. Snow took it, said, "Thanks, man," held it to his mouth and inhaled gingerly. Then he filled his lungs and passed the joint on to Ann. He held it in, stifling a cough, and watched Ann gamely follow suit. The guy on his left was saying, "Man, that's good shit, man."

There was a warmth in the room and the guitar player had been replaced by Bob Dylan telling them, "Once upon a time..." The whole thing felt to Snow as being on the verge of camaraderie, closeness, something profound being shared, some coming together in the wilderness, gathering around a fire and ignoring the screams of loneliness and terror out in the jungle. On the other hand he knew only Ann and Berkowitz, and Berkowitz had disappeared. All the others were strangers. He guessed someone in the room would say to him, if asked, "Names are not important, man." Neither were occupations. "They just get in the way, man." Snow could go with it, try to go with it, his shoulder leaning against Ann's. Someone said, "Shit, man, this is good shit."

But a faraway look was developing in Ann's eyes, her pupils wide with cannabis or fear or both. She held his arm tightly and her eyes said she wanted to talk with him but her mouth didn't move. "Are you okay?" he was asking. "Hang on, you're with me, it's okay." And then it hit him, too. The harmonica lengthened, intensified, lingered, and the song dragged on and on. "How does it feel to be on your own with no direction home?" The words repeated in his brain. He tuned in to a phrase and then drifted away for minutes, hours, came back and found Dylan repeating himself. How long had they been there? Ten minutes? Two hours? He was enveloped by a deep sense of lassitude with flickerings of anxiety. He had lost Ann. She was not with him. Some remnant clung to his arm, but her eyes were far away. Then her eyes focused and spoke but her lips didn't move. She was having a bad trip and he wanted to help her but the hell of it was he couldn't sustain that thought for more than a few seconds. And then it was gone and he was struggling to remember where they were and what the purpose was, the gathering, the game. Did they have something to do? Should they be someplace else? Did it matter? Could he help Ann? Did it matter?

He remembered reading that Rudolf Nureyev and Dame Margot Fonteyn had been arrested at a marijuana party in San Francisco, after escaping through a window and hiding on the rooftops. He figured the militia, the RCMP, the OPP, the city cops, they could all come crashing through the door and he wouldn't be able to summon the initiative to stand up, let alone flee over the rooftops. But then again, he was not a dancer.

"I am not a dancer," he said to Ann, who didn't respond.

They were still high when they got back to the apartment, shed coats and raided the refrigerator, bringing out bowls of day-old spaghetti, cold meats, potato salad, spreading them on the table, eating directly out of the bowls with tablespoons. His mother watched them, said, with something approaching a smile, "If you could just see yourselves, how foolish you look."

"What was in those brownies?" Ann asked.

"I have no idea," said Robert. "At least hashish, hash oil."

"You realize," said Ann, "we start off protesting the war and end up stoned."

"Stoned?" asked his mother.

"After the march there was some marijuana being passed around," Robert explained.

"Drugs. You took drugs?"

"Just marijuana."

"Oh, Robert, what if you were caught? What about your career, your job?"

Ann said, "We were protesting the war. Just what do you think is the more important issue around here? Killing children in Vietnam or toking up in Chinatown?"

"Well, I'm sure I wouldn't know," said his mother.

Robert, willing Ann to back off, not get into a thing with his mother, not say things someone would regret, was greatly relieved to see Ann begin to giggle. And he began to laugh, too. It was a pain in the ass having his mother being a mother but better than that other manifestation who had been living with them.

SHE WAS BROUGHT in by her mother, a Portuguese mourner dressed in black. They stood together in the examining room with Snow trying to make out what the problem was, through, it seemed, centuries and miles of cultural difference. The mother implored Dr. Snow and nattered at her daughter, a pallid sexless thin teenager. A few English words were drowned in Portuguese. The girl had her tongue out as if waiting for a throat examination. Snow acquired a tongue depressor and examined her tongue and throat. He found nothing unusual or pathological and shrugged. He listened again and felt for sure the mother was directing him to the area he had just examined. Her daughter's tongue was still protruding.

He said, "You can put your tongue back now."

The mother said, "Tha's a problem."

"What is?"

"She no put tongue away."

"What?"

"The tongue. It stick out."

"Yes."

"All day. It stick out all day."

It was still out, a little, dry, plump, pink, twitching thing.

He turned to the girl and said, "Put your tongue in now."

The tongue flickered a little, withdrew slightly and then popped back out.

He said loudly, sternly, "Put your tongue in now. Put it back in. Do it now. That's better. Now close your mouth. Close your mouth!"

The tongue went in, the lips closed, then they quivered and opened slightly. He shouted at her, "Keep your tongue in and your mouth closed!"

Mother beamed. "It's all right now. Thank you, doctor."

"ANN, YOU WON'T believe this one, this mother and daughter come in speaking Portuguese and the girl, maybe fourteen or so, her tongue is sticking out, and it turns out that's what the problem is, her tongue's been sticking out all day. I tell her to put it back in, that's all, and she does, and off they go... I don't have the slightest idea. I'd probably have to live with them for a month to figure that one out."

"HARV, TELL ME this one, why would a fourteen-year-old girl have her tongue sticking out?"

"Beats me, why would a fourteen-year-old girl have her tongue sticking out?"

"It's not a riddle, it's a case." A case that was a riddle, which would always catch Harvey Ryan's interest, and he put the newspaper aside.

"What are we talking about, straight out or crooked, off and on or all day?"

"Straight out all day long."

"Fibrillating? Anything else wrong with her?"

"Nothing."

"Hysterical."

"She put it back in when I told her to."

"Right, hysterical."

"Okay, but why?"

"Snow, you cured her, didn't you? Why would you want to know why?"

"Seems reasonable to ask why. Besides, I don't know I cured her."

"Well, Dr. Snow, you're asking me if I fathom the mind of a fourteen-year-old girl. I don't fathom the mind of my own wife."

"So what's your guess?"

"Jesus, Mary and Joseph. She probably had her tongue where it shouldn't be, or wanted her tongue to be where it shouldn't be, or stuck it out at her mother and then froze with guilt."

"I thank you, Dr. Freud."

"Reminds me, did you ask her if she enjoys cunnilingus?"

"Harv, her mother was there."

"Did you see this? Louis Washkansky died. Eighteen days he lasted."

Louis Washkansky, the world's first heart transplant patient, had survived for eighteen days with the heart of a twenty-five-year-old woman who had been killed in a car accident. Robert had assisted at a kidney transplant, as well as the hip replacement, an operation that took seven hours, which is what he would remember most about it, but the kidney had never been anything more than an organ. The heart, on the other hand, had always been much more than an organ, and now, quite suddenly, reduced to the lowly status of replaceable body part. In a fit of another kind of hysteria some magazine covers featured the long-fingered hands of Dr. Christiaan Barnard. Snow merely wondered about the poor interns and nurses who, undoubtedly, would have to endure the famous surgeon's vanity.

That evening Robert Snow performed his own medical miracle but was not featured on the covers of prominent magazines. The man lying on a stretcher in emergency was drunk, dead drunk, but not that drunk according to the blood alcohol levels. The internists had seen him, the neurologists had seen him. Nephrologists, endocrinologists, neurosurgeons. No one could figure out why the man was paralyzed from the head down. They poked, prodded, tested. They X-rayed, tapped, stuck pins. He wouldn't talk, presumably being paralyzed from the neck up, as well, which irritated the neurologists. Functional, they said, it's got to be functional, meaning hysterical, meaning in some bizarre way he brought it on himself.

Snow remembered a case he had seen as a medical student, a nice cooperative veteran of World War Two living in a room in a veterans' hospital. Snow had examined him, had completed a neurological and muscle examination and found the man to be in good health. Had found no reason for the man to be in the hospital. The man himself had complained of nothing. He explained this to his supervisor, who smiled slowly, with great satisfaction, having waited all afternoon for this moment. The supervisor asked, "Did you get him to walk?"

Snow admitted he hadn't.

"Well, had you," said the supervisor, "you would have found he can't walk. His legs are paralyzed. And have been paralyzed for the last twenty years."

"But his muscles are fine, his reflexes, his legs are strong."

"Yes. Interesting, isn't it."

The neurologists and internists threw up their hands and left the emergency case to Snow, the intern. He stood at the stretcher a long time and considered the situation. Then he went through the man's wallet looking for pertinent information. Among the credit cards, receipts, small bills, he found a torn piece of envelope with the name Brenda scribbled on it, and the name of a motel, an address and phone number. Another card requiring a next of kin, in case of, had Brenda printed neatly in the blank space.

Snow put these aside, leaned over his patient and took a flyer. He said, loudly, "So your wife, Brenda, is shacked up in a motel with another man. Right this very minute getting her brains fucked out." He repeated his message in several colorful ways, keeping an eye on the door to make sure no one was listening to him, and was beginning to feel he might have badly misjudged the situation when the man's mouth twitched, his eyes opened, focused on Snow, his fingers clenched, and he reared up screaming, "You fucking goddamn bastard." And swung a roundhouse right that barely missed. Robert took advantage of the momentum of the punch, grabbed him by the shoulders and lifted him up and off the stretcher. His patient staggered around cursing to himself, muttering, and finally plopped in a chair. Snow said he'd come back to talk with him after he'd checked on another case, but when he returned ten minutes later the man was gone.

"Walked right out of here," said Pauline. "What the hell did you do to him?"

"Well, now, let me tell you about it," said Robert, pleased with himself and his small miracle, but now wondering if the man, blocked from his chosen course of action, would act upon what must be his second, third and fourth options: kill Brenda, kill her lover, kill himself. Maybe he'd go the fifth route, back to the bar and alcohol oblivion.

While he was telling Pauline about this revival-tent experience (you can walk, praise God, you can walk once again, praise God almighty) they watched the chief radiologist hustle George Chuvalo through the door, a handful of reporters following.

"Did you see his face?" asked Pauline.

"Float like a butterfly, sting like a sledgehammer," said Snow. But the man had, without elegance, with limited skill, stayed on his feet for fifteen rounds. Something to admire there, thought Robert. Show up, stay on your feet, survive.

"ROBERT, YOU'RE GOING to have to do something. She's worse than ever."

"It didn't last, eh?"

"What didn't last?"

"The other day, she got a little better. She smiled. She got a little motherly."

"It lasted ten seconds, Robert."

"So, where do we go?"

"In Victoria she has a house, friends, some family, a car, a doctor who knows her."

"Send her back home?"

127

Ann had called the hospital from work, had him paged. Robert was standing at a phone outside the cafeteria. She said, "You're not abandoning her. We're not doing her any good here. My God, Robert, open your eyes, she's sick. And, besides, I'm the one…"

"I know. I know."

"Robert, ask someone. You're in a hospital, for God's sake, ask for some advice, some help, anything."

SNOW MADE AN appointment to see the head of the Department of Psychiatry, a Dr. James Tisdale, to talk about career options. He got there in his whites straight off emergency and entered with some trepidation. The office was decorated in earth tones, carpeted, chairs with wooden arms, full bookshelf, paintings on the wall, softly lit, a cocoon in the middle of the hospital desert. Dr. Tisdale beckoned him to sit in one of the armchairs. There was no couch in the office. Tisdale had shaggy graying hair over a high brow. His chin was long, his features Scottish. A pair of reading glasses sat on his nose. Above the glasses his eyes danced with inquiry and mischief. "So," he said, "tell me about yourself."

Snow was immensely uncomfortable. His grubby whites with small spatters of blood and God knows what other fluids blended anonymously in the rest of the hospital. Here they left him naked. Haltingly he told Dr. Tisdale a little about himself. Tisdale seemed interested in his adolescent athletics. "What positions did you play?"

Snow told him. Tisdale said, "I think you can tell a lot about someone from the positions he plays, especially rugby." He was still looking over his reading glasses, and either not really listening to Snow's answers or processing them and moving on very quickly to the next curiosity. He leaned forward and said, "Now, what did you really want to talk about?" Tisdale seemed somewhat pleased by his own cleverness, but his eyes were kind and so Snow told him all about his mother. Tisdale clasped his hands in front of his chin and encouraged Snow with small "Uh-huhs" and "Ands?" and Snow, in the telling, came to see how distraught he was. He came close to tears but fought them off with a voice in his head arguing for Christ's sake hold on and another telling him he's a shrink, you can let it all hang out. In the end Tisdale said, "Your mother needs to be in hospital. You're doing her no good, and your wife, and there's no sense sacrificing your internship year. The cost is much too high for all of you."

Not a word had been said about career options, which was fine with Robert. He had no real energy or taste for planning the next few years of his life. Get through this one. Just get through this one.

He left Tisdale's office somewhat unburdened, but questioning as always. It was nice to have some guilt lifted from his shoulders when he dumped her into a hospital, or was that just convenient and didn't Tisdale have a special interest keeping intern Robert Snow functioning at the expense of his poor mother and what the hell difference did it make if he played flying wing or scrum half? On the other hand, wings and wing halfs were the antelopes of that particular sport and scrum halfs were the coyotes and wouldn't it be nice to go back a few years and throw his gear in the trunk of his 1952 Plymouth, leave his intact family home and drive out to the playing field to spend a couple of hours being an antelope?

He called an aunt, his father's sister, and the family doctor back home and then he and Ann put his mother on the plane. Robert, you don't know what it's like. How can you do this to me? It's a terrible thing to be abandoned.

She was admitted to the psychiatric hospital, newly built on the grounds of the local general hospital, and now Snow was talking to the psychiatrist on the phone. Ship her back on the plane and into the loony bin. Terrific. The psychiatrist was saying to Robert, on the phone, "There are two kinds of depression, reactive and endogenous. Of course your mother's reacting to her situation, but we think there's an endogenous component as well."

Snow was thinking, reactive, endogenous? What about having your guts ripped out and nothing left but a hollow shell? Being a figment of your own mother's imagination. Being empty of life and reason. What about simply being lost? He said, "Drinking may have played a part here."

"Yes, of course. How much was she drinking, do you think?"

"I don't know how much when she's alone. With us it was only, say, four or five gin and tonics a day."

"Well, I don't think it's a problem of primary alcoholism."

"How's she doing?"

"She's quite agitated. We'll be giving her something to settle her, and then antidepressant medication, and then, if that doesn't help, we'll have to consider ECT."

Yeah, that ought to fill her up, give her a reason to live, put meaning in her life. "I understand." But he felt quite relieved she wasn't living with them or alone in the house but safe with the nurses and a doctor who didn't sound too bad if a little stuffy about this reactive-endogenous shit.

"Can I reach you at this number if anything changes?"

"Or at the hospital if it's urgent."

"I'm sure she'll be much better in a few weeks."

"I might be able to get a long weekend next month and fly out, maybe when she's ready for discharge."

ROBERT NOTICED A small column on the second page of that day's *Globe and Mail* telling of Isle Koch hanging herself in prison. She was the one, read the obituary, who had made lamp shades of the skin of her victims in Buchenwald. Snow wondered if the shrinks would label that one a reactive depression, but then, at least, it put his own guilt into perspective.

"SHE A NO make a me de sanwidge. What kind a wife is dat, *dottore*? She a no make a me de sanwidge. I say make a me de sanwidge. She say I a no a do it. She got a da knife, she make a hersel de sanwidge but she no make a me de sanwidge. I say make a me de sanwidge. She say, 'Show a me you hands, you gotta de hands.' I show her de fist. I say 'Here a de fist, now make a me de sanwidge.' But I no hit her. Before I smash a her in a de face. I no God. I use a de fist. But now I shy, I gotta de neighbors, I gotta de children, I a shy. She take a me to cot."

Snow had just entered the room when the man began telling his story. His wife was there, too, both over sixty, both heavy, short, broad peasant faces, rough-looking, laboring hands.

Snow said, "She takes you to what?"

"She take a me to cot."

"Oh, she took you to court. That's why you no use the fist, she took you to court?"

"I no a mind dat. I forgive. I gotta de good job, I gotta de five children. Thanks God. But she's a crazy woman, a *pazzo*, *dottore*. She no wash a my clothes, she no a wife to me. She's a need a de medicine. She's a sick woman, *dottore*."

"Why does she need medicine?"

"You a doctor, you can a tell. She's a sick, here, in *di testa*, de head. Vaaa! You no canna talk to her. Forty years I work. I gotta de five children. Thanks God. I gotta de house. I fix up, new rooms, *nuova cucina*. I make a de porch a new room."

His wife had been smoldering listening to him, making faces, rolling her eyes. She broke in, "You tell a *dottore* about dat, you tell a *dottore* about break my nose. Vaaa! No more. He's a no take a de fist to me again. *Finito*. I go back a to Italia."

"You can a live der. Her family can no stand her, *dottore*. You sister, she no want you. You a *pazzo*."

"Okay, okay, okay. So what's the trouble right now? She doesn't want you to hit her and you say you won't hit her anymore."

"*Dottore*. She's a no cook for me, she's a no clean for me. What kind a wife I got? What I gonna do? Who's a cook for me? My daughter have a to come a do my wash. I give her a good a machine. All she gotta do is putta de clothes in. Dey just a sit. She's a no touch. My daughter a teacher. She no should have a to come. All my children better dan me now. I no mind. I work forty years."

Snow said, for something to say, "You worked very hard for where you are."

"No, I no work hard. I just a do what I have a to do. I sixty-two now. Life a should be good but I no gotta de wife."

"All right. From your point of view, Mrs. Bardolini, what's the trouble, I mean besides your husband beating you in the past?"

"He wanna to kill me."

"She a *pazzo*. I no wanna to kill her. She crazy in de head."

"Mrs. Bardolini, why do you think he wants to kill you?"

"He's a bad man. He never good."

"I understand that. But why do you think he now actually wants to kill you?"

"You a man, *dottore*," interjected Mr. Bardolini. "I no perfect."

"Pig."

"Shutta you mout."

"Wait a minute. Hold on. I still don't understand why you think Mr. Bardolini wants to kill you."

"He's a gotta nudder woman."

"She's a crazy. I'm a sixty-two."

"But did he say he was going to kill you, Mrs. Bardolini?"

"He's a talk."

"Did he tell you he was going to kill you?"

"He's a send me messages."

"Messages?"

"Sure."

"What? Written notes? What are we talking about?"

"Through a de *televis*. He's a get de *televis* to tell me. But I a good woman, *dottore*. I no a do notting wrong. But I no more a wife for him. *Basta. I finito.*"

"You mean you get messages from the television and radio?"

"How you mean?"

"The radio and television. Do they talk to you?"

"Oh, sure, dey a talk to me alla de time. Dey say a Missus Bardolini, you marry to a pig, you buy a de Tide, you clean a de floors, you wash a de clothes. No more. I no buy a de Tide. I no wash a de floors."

"You mean you're sort of on strike?"

"Sure."

"See, she's a crazy, *dottore*. You canna talk a to her. She English no so good. She's gotta no friends. Alberto, our son, he's a just married, she no let him a visit."

"Alberto can come. But I don' wanna dat *puttana* he marry in a my house."

"Look, why don't you go home and fight. Maybe you can find a marriage counselor or something. Maybe talk to the priest."

"*Dottore?*"

"Yes, Mrs. Bardolini."

"I can no a go home. He's a gonna kill me tonight."

"How do you know he's going to kill you tonight?"

"De voices warn me. Dey tell me, *Seignora* Bardolini, tonight is de night. He's a kill you tonight."

"When did they tell you this?"

"Jus' now, *dottore.*"

"Maybe you had better come into the hospital after all, Mrs. Bardolini."

"Sure, *dottore.*"

"Mr. Bardolini..."

"Da's okay, *dottore*, you a call me when she a ready to come home."

HE TALKED TO his mother on the phone. They let her use the one at the nurses' station. "There are some really sad cases in here," she told him. "And so young." This sounded good to Robert, she was taking notice of the people around her, caring. But then she asked him when he was coming out and could she come back and live with them and what a terrible place it really was and you have no idea what it's like to feel the way she does and what a shame it is when they put you in a place like this.

They.

You won't be there long, he told her, and he'd try very hard to get a few days off to fly out. "Do you have any kind of recent address for Michael?"

"Maybe two months ago. On a postcard. I'm worried about him, Robert."

"That's good."

"Why is that good?"

"That you're worried about him, that's all."

"I don't understand why you think that's good."

"Never mind. Can you give me the address you've got?"

"I don't have it here."

LYING ON THE bed in his small room waiting for the phone to ring, listening to a restless Philip Trebilcock in the next room, getting up, banging into things, using the washroom, he forgave his younger brother, for now. "How does it feel to be on your own with no direction home?" But next time, Michael, it's your turn.

Chapter Ten

My weariness amazes me, I'm branded on my feet,
I have no one to meet,
And the ancient empty street's too dead for dreaming.
— Bob Dylan

ROBERT SPENT HIS days and nights doing things and not doing things that would affect the lives of others. The hospital was a large, hellish place, a world on its own. It had windows but everyone forgot to look out. It was as if they disappeared in imagination and then perception, leaving a surround of solid white walls and green curtains. The mind reluctantly focused on the business of the hospital alone. Always busy, always people moving about in ghostly whites, always on the verge of chaos. There was never enough time. A blur of body fluids, body parts, pain, suffering, carelessness, fear, anger, sometimes joy, triumph. But the interns, Robert Snow among them, were functionaries, foot soldiers. They experienced the losses, failures, cruelty. They weren't invited to the celebrations. They were left to deal with the patients no one wanted, the whiners, complainers, entitled demanders, neurotics, hypochondriacs—in their own language, the crocks. It was a world of euphemisms, of words not spoken, of missed opportunities. Lives passing through his life, seen as if in the periphery of his vision. A terrible collage, a conveyor belt of horrors. If it would only stop for a day or two, he thought, as he fell asleep at two in the morning wishing the phone to remain silent for at least an hour, if it would only stop he might grab a small part and wring from it some meaning and truth. Dying, from the verb to die…Cancer, the crab… Hope, from…

The laboratory technicians went on strike. Snow and the other interns filled in, adding routine lab tests to their other duties. Now the days ran from five in the morning to midnight without a lull, and then intermittently until five came around again. Patients clutched at him, literally and otherwise. He was learning to stall them, brush them off, mouth the platitudes of escape, be right back, see you later today, don't worry about a thing. He was seldom free of exhaustion. It walked with him, stood beside him, pounced upon him should he dare to sit down. It clouded his brain and made him short-tempered. He fell asleep if he sat for a moment, so he didn't sit. He fell asleep leaning against a door frame.

On the public urology ward they brought in old men who could no longer pee well enough and they shoved sharp instruments up their urethras and reamed out their prostates and then put them back on the ward with catheters and IV bottles. As they lay in post-op semicoma and confusion they passively pissed out bloodstained urine and clutched at their catheters and pulled out their IVs and complained to nurses. They all got infections. They all contracted very bad infections. The hospital housed an experiment in natural selection. With antibiotics all over the place, the bugs that endured were especially virulent, rare, resistant, little survivors with exotic names. They got in the old men's bladders and bloodstreams and shut down their kidneys. Snow had to watch the urine output and raise the alarm when it faded away, when the bottle stopped filling with thick amber bloody fluid. They often died, these old men. They all got infections and then powerful intravenous antibiotics and their urologists shook their heads and commented on these rare in-residence bacteria and moved on to the OR and the next case, blurrily on and over and through as the dormitory filled up and the delirious screamed in the night and the dead were wheeled away and Snow wrote histories and took blood and looked at urine and held OR retractors and walked from crisis to crisis and explained to relatives that a rare complication had arisen and wondered at night what the fuck this was all about and maybe it's important to piss a good strong stream and sure as hell not good to not piss at all but if all these poor bastards are dying from our very own hospital bugs with exotic names then why isn't somebody slowing down and asking questions like if the place is full of bacteria how about we at least do the ancient Greek thing and hang up raw meat here and there and move the operating theater and the fucking ward where the meat doesn't go putrid right away?

They were confused after their operations, losing their sense of time and place, some quietly, mumblingly, others loudly, disclaiming, accusing, asking, thrashing about, pulling out catheters, at first playing with them, turning the irritation to hurt, and then yanking hard, causing themselves excruciating pain, and then momentary relief, flooding the bed with blood and piss. The nurses tied their hands to the railings, admonished them, ignored them once the IVs and catheters were back in place, treated their delirium as naughtiness. Snow held their hands, talked with them, quieted them, undid their bonds, resisted drugging them, listened to the nurses tell him the unquestionable truth, that he did not have to live with them for a full shift, a full eight hours, and what about the other patients, the quiet ones, don't they have rights, too?

There was one old man, a Greek, hands that had worked a

lifetime with cement, who had just come back from the OR and Snow was checking his urine bottle every couple of hours to make sure it was still filling and it was doing fine, this dark bloody stuff dripping in steadily and so sometime in the late afternoon walking exhausted through his work after being up all night (and all those other excuses that would run through his head for days afterward) he didn't actually go and look himself, instead relying on an aide telling him the old Greek was fine and his urine was flowing only four hours ago, but he didn't actually go and pull up the bedsheets from the floor and look at the urine bottle himself this time and when he finally did, later that night, the level was the same as it had been some six hours earlier.

Kidneys shut down, packed in, renal failure. Blood pressure next to nothing. Heart erratic. Snow getting up a new IV. Pumping in all sorts of shit to get the blood pressure up, open the arteries, clean out the kidneys. Rewarded with a small trickle, a steady heart, a rising blood pressure. But then the man fading, the trickle stopping, blood pressure falling. Heart stopping, arrest team arriving, urologist arriving, Robert Snow hanging in the background, pushed to the periphery, but full of blame, sick to his stomach. How the hell did this happen? How long ago did he stop producing? Robert slinking away, telling himself to make no assumptions about the competence, care, motivation of others, lashing himself, but pulling the door shut so he might get on with the work of looking after forty other patients.

SEVERAL NIGHTS LATER, sometime around midnight, he was just finishing his routine work for the day when he was paged by the ward. He phoned over and talked with a nurse. She explained Dr. Brown had just been through seeing his patients. Why this late? I don't know, he'd been to a dinner or something, answered the nurse. Anyway, he ordered a urinalysis on Petrovich. What for? Just routine. Routine at midnight? It didn't get done this morning, he wants it for tomorrow morning, she told him. Jesus shit, said Snow, rubbing his face with his left hand, squeezing his eyes, getting paid a hundred and sixty bucks a month to work a hundred and twenty hours a week, which came down to something like twenty cents an hour, angry at the ward, at the hospital, at himself, still hurting about the old Greek, who had quickly been replaced in both bed and perception by an old Italian—you tell Dr. Brown, Dr. Snow said, you tell Dr. Brown to take his urinalysis and stuff it up his ass.

This nurse did what Snow had asked her. This nurse followed directions. This nurse carried out his telephone order verbatim.

When Snow got his call to visit the medical director in his carpeted office on the fifth floor he went there with no illusions. He was not about to be given a prize, a fatherly talk. Perhaps a little career counseling. The small portly man with the small white mustache did not rise from behind his desk. He did smile. He gestured for Snow to sit. Then he told him that if he, Dr. Robert Snow, wished to finish his internship he should endeavor to keep his mouth shut and his head low these next few months. Robert politely agreed to the terms presented to him, forgoing negotiations, and went back to work.

Smarting from these events, during a few minutes' respite in the lounge, Snow reads that George Lincoln Rockwell, leader of the American Nazi party, has been killed by a sniper's bullet. Snow understands the sniper and his need, his purpose, his wish, his anger, but if Dr. Brown wants his midnight urinalysis stat, Dr. Robert Snow will keep his mouth shut and do it, this year.

On the other hand, in a particularly gauche display of American conceit, Snow notes, Muhammad Ali, né Cassius Clay, is stripped of his world heavyweight boxing championship because he has refused to be inducted into military service. Cassius, baby, you can't tell the Dr. Browns of this world stick it up your ass and get away with it.

ON THE PHONE Ann said, "They called from the hospital."

"Why would they call? I'm here."

"About your mother. Her hospital."

"What's happening now?"

"She left the hospital. They don't know where she's gone."

"Christ."

"She had her car there for some reason. They say she just took off."

"No reason?"

"Well, the nurse said they'd been talking to her about having shock treatment."

"Yeah, well, that might do it."

"They'll call if they hear anything."

"Ah, Christ."

"There's nothing we can do from here."

Visions of his mother. What would she do, what would be her style? Plastic bag? Exhaust fumes? Pills? Drowning? "Maybe we shouldn't have sent her back."

"Nothing's happened yet, Robert. She'll turn up."

"Ann?"

"What?"

"Can you come down for the night?"

"Neither of us would sleep in that shitty little bed you have."

"Yeah, I know."

"You'll be up half the night anyway."

"You're right."

"Get some sleep so we can do something tomorrow night."

"I was a very beautiful woman once, you know," she said, taking a hesitant drag on the cigarette she held in her shaky, nicotine-stained fingers. "Bill Mulder loved me. He always said, 'Sheila, I don't know what I'd do without you.' I was always helping people. You know that, always helping people."

It was ten at night and he had been called to one of the private wards to see a woman a couple of weeks post-op who had told the nurses of a small pain, an ache, in her lower abdomen. When he got there she seemed to have forgotten the pain and he sat at the bedside where she had beckoned him.

"He was a drunk, too, you know, but not as bad as my husband." She looked sideways with a hint of pleasant memories on her face, and then a false note, tilting her head toward Snow, looking through her eyelashes, and then her head thrown back. "Oh, my God, how could I let it come to this, after all I've done for them—all of them, cleaned up after them every night, the bastards." Her flash of anger waned, she sniffled, teared and groped for some tissue. Only the wrinkles around her scarlet mouth changed, her eyes staying the same, suspicious agates buried deeply.

"I loved golf," she said, coming back to him with a wiggle of her head. "Bill was a golfer. We lived right off the course, it was beautiful. I used to stand by the window watching for him on Sundays. I knew when he'd get to the sixth hole. I could calculate how long it would take for each hole. And all the while George would be drinking in the other room. It was horrible.

"I could play. I learned from watching television. Were they ever surprised. So many things came easily to me." Her eyes sparkled with a little tilt and wiggle of her head. "That's when it all started. He wanted me to go away with him but I couldn't do it—not without marriage—I'm very old-fashioned that way—so I told him I still loved my husband. Silly. Why did I tell him that? It wasn't true. He left and I never saw him again. Now look at me. Oh, God, if I could only get out of this godforsaken city. I love the country. I love Elora. Do you know it? I must get back to Elora. The people love me there. This city is dull and dirty. Nobody cares about the finer things any more. I can't even find my flatware. Packed somewhere, some box. I had a full set of flatware from Birks and now I don't even know where it is. I knew about those things. It was important to have the table laid just right. I knew which kind of fork should be used for this course and which kind for that course."

In the middle of this she had reached for the glass of juice on her nightstand and taken a sip. Now she choked on it, a loud hacking cough, gurgling, sneezing, leaning forward, her face purple as she tried to breathe. Then it was suddenly over and she continued as if this breach of decorum had not occurred.

"My curtains were lovely. Everybody said so. I helped Maggie decorate her house, she had no taste herself. They all used me. Now where are they? The bloody hypocrites." She leaned forward in a clumsy way, fumbling with the ashtray on the bed beside her, and fished for a new cigarette. On her face, for a moment, was a vicious sneer.

She talked on, and he listened as he had often sat beside his grandmother listening to her stories, which had roughly the same self-deluding purpose as this woman's, though more coherent, more lyrical, more interesting. He looked at her thick makeup, her yellowing fingers, her negligee carelessly, carefully revealing her cleavage, the sheets revealing a bit of thigh and panties, and more when she shifted. She wanted him to love her, he decided. This repulsive, lumpy, bagged-up self-pitying old whore. As his mother had wanted him to love

143

her. He didn't want to equate the two, mix the images, but they refused to stay separate in his mind.

Her scuffed black boots sat under the bed and a dirty leather coat hung on a rack. A great fat cheap ring on her angry finger. Cigarette ash scattered down her front. Lips always moving, playing with her feelings, trying this one, then that one, wet, alluring with her tongue, surrounded by dry and cracked folds of flesh slipping down her jowls and neck. She wanted him to look at her body and admire her sagging tits. A coy smile, a little tilting come-on. He was included, he knew, in the bastards and hypocrites. If he looked closely he would see greasy nicotine hair and smell a faint whiff of old urine. A blond child with maggots, treated unkindly by the years. Perhaps the face and fate she deserved, perhaps not. The hidden parts of her attracted him as she intended, and they also horrified him, perhaps as she intended also. In his exhausted revery, his unconscious held insufficiently at bay, he was aware of her provoking in him the full mélange of human response. He wanted to run, to hide, to escape, to stay, to look, to feel, to fuck, to beat her to death. And to make her feel better about herself. That, too.

When he tried to regain himself, to pull himself away, her eyes glazed over and her body stiffened.

She said, "We haven't gotten very far, have we?"

She meant him and her, their relationship, help he might offer her, kindness, love, revelation, punishment. He thought of the question in a wider sense and agreed. We haven't come very far. And he thought of his mother, now lost, and this woman, lost, both little girls once, and then women in love with dreams, and then losing themselves somewhere in their dreams, and the rest, their bodies left behind, empty and corrupt. And he wondered why he can't give either of them what they want, they need.

On Saturday night he and Ann walked to the Brunswick, an old hotel beer parlor that had become inexplicably popular. They walked west on Bloor against the wind through ethnic enclaves revealed by languages on storefronts, Hungarian, then Chinese, then Greek, then Portuguese, mingling at the edges, pedestrians ebbing and flowing, chattering in several languages, migrating and recreating.

His mother had returned to the hospital. She had gone off to find a locksmith to change, once again, the locks on the doors of the family home, and when this was accomplished had taken herself back to the hospital. A nurse had called to tell them this. They'd be holding off on the shock treatment. She had cried all night when she got back, and this was probably very good for her, the nurse explained.

He was relaxed tonight, his mother was safely back in hospital, her nurse had sounded both capable and kind, the death of the old Greek had faded into his vaults of regret, there was no unfinished case left that morning, handed over but still itching at the back of his mind, no voices whispering you forgot something, you overlooked something, you weren't careful enough. He had also reached the apartment by one in the afternoon and slept for two hours. And he had decided to find a way and the money to fly out to Victoria for a long weekend, to visit, to see her, to ease his conscience.

Ann had asked, "Can you get off that long?"

"If I do double duty when I get back."

"What's double duty?"

"About four weekends in a row."

"Four?"

"Yeah. It's the only way."

Ann offered to go with him, but even one ticket would take them six months to pay off.

"What'll you do?" she asked.

"I dunno. I'll just be there. Help her settle back in the house if she's ready."

At the Brunswick they shared a table with a Portuguese family, a man, his wife, her brother, drank beer with them, talked, laughed, watched the crowd of regulars mingling with the hippies, the students, the young professionals, and Snow felt okay, warm, and thought about how the hospital was either hot or cold but never warm, never offering that comfortable inner warmth that he was feeling right now, right here among the people, living, breathing, drinking, talking, laughing, above all laughing, watching Ann so at ease with whomever she met, sharing stories with this family who were inviting them to visit, come for supper some day, which they'd try to do but would be pretty hard with his schedule and all, but maybe they'd really do it, sure, you come have supper, Mama she a good cook. Then they'd turn from this intimacy to laugh with the crowd because it was amateur night and people were getting up to sing their favorite songs off-key, and the beer kept coming to wash away the hospitals, the one here in the city and the one two thousand miles away.

THE VOICE ON the phone said, "Your Jesus friend is back."

"What?" It was two, three in the morning. He'd been sleeping fitfully on the hard mattress in his hard duty room, and then had jumped on the first ring as he would for the rest of his life and groped for the phone and got it to his ear before his brain cleared.

"It's Pauline. Your Jesus friend is back in Emergency, and this time he's carrying a cross."

"He's what?"

"The guy was here earlier. You let him go, remember. He's come back with a cross."

Snow stumbled off his bed, pulling his whites on, splashing

cold water on his face, retrieving jacket, stethoscope, getting the buttons wrong, doing it again, brushing back his hair. He imagined his bearded patient coming back in robes, adorned with crown of thorns, dragging some great wooden cross on his shoulders going from nursing station to nursing station.

They had him waiting in the observation room behind the green door. He was pacing, nervous, energized. He clutched a ten-inch metal cross in his right hand, holding it out between himself and Snow, as if warding off a vampire. Long brown hair, Jesus beard, jeans tied with rope, bare feet.

Snow left the door open and stood just inside the room. "What can I do for you?"

"You know, man. I have to reach them."

"It's Wayne, isn't it?"

"Yeah."

"You didn't go home?"

"Shit, no, man. Why do you want me to go home? They been talking to you?"

"No, no, it's the middle of the night. You should be somewhere."

"Nothing for me there, man. Evil. Bad vibes."

"Your mother's there."

"They got to her, man. She's contaminated."

"Why did you come back here?"

"I have to find them."

"Find who?"

"The disciples. They're here in this building. This is the place. This is where I'm needed."

"Have you been here before, in the hospital?"

"Yeah."

"How about we sit down and talk?"

"No. I have to find them."

"The disciples?"

"Peter and Paul. Peter and Paul. Peter and Paul and Simon. Also known as Saul."

"Maybe you should come in and stay a while, get a little help for yourself."

"I don't need help. I don't fucking need help."

"Yeah. Okay, man. Just stay cool."

"I'm cool. I'm cool."

"You've been on the psych ward before? Up on seven?"

"No sevens man, no sevens."

"There's a bed up there for you. People to talk to."

"I don't need help."

"Yeah, but you can help them."

"What the fuck you doing to me, man?"

"You need to be in hospital."

"No, man. I just need to find Peter and Paul, Peter and Paul, and Simon."

"Okay, but you're coming with me up to the seventh."

"No sevens, man."

"Up to the ward, talk to some people."

"Don't put me in a box, man."

"No boxes, no locked doors, just a bed for the rest of the night."

"No way."

"Wayne, we're going up there. You and me. Come on. We'll take the elevator."

"I don't need it, man." But he walked beside Snow, slowly, and stood at the elevator, cross in hand. That strange schizophrenic mix of godliness and fear, certainty and confusion, defiance and obedience.

The hospital was quiet except for small sounds, a wheeze-popping BIRD in one room, the slop and clank of a mop and pail at the end of the corridor. The elevator door opened. Solitary ding. Snow waited, watched, moved slowly. Wayne entered with him, and then startled when a buzzer sounded.

"It's okay, just an elevator noise, short trip."

"No needles, man. Don't give me any needles."

"Okay, no needles. Maybe some pills."

"No pills. Gotta talk to the people. Don't drug me up."

Snow looked at this kid before him. Early twenties, long unwashed hair, radiant, knowing eyes, searching eyes, scanning eyes, a sort of caftan robe over several sweaters, ragged jeans, very dirty feet. He said, "Must be hard sometimes. You pretty much knowing what you want and doctors coming along and saying you gotta come in hospital and you gotta take some pills."

Wayne had been staring at the door and the floor numbers changing above the door. Without turning he said, "The only trouble with you doctors is you never let yourselves be vulnerable."

Chapter Eleven

Waits at the window, wearing the face
that she keeps in a jar by the door
Who is it for?
All the lonely people, where do they all come from?
— Lennon/McCartney

S NOW FLEW OUT west on a Friday afternoon, flying with the sun, arriving in Victoria only two hours later after five hours in the air. He was restless on the plane, tried to read but couldn't concentrate. He took off his shoes and sipped Red Label Scotch, thumbing through magazines. At the airport he rented a small Chevrolet with his overwrought credit card and drove along the highway that had once been very familiar to him. Farmlands to his left, still green in contrast to Toronto's browns and grays, beyond them the rocky beaches of his childhood, the Strait of Georgia, Gulf Islands, the mainland. The sign to Butchart's Gardens, the small deserted beaches of Elk Lake, where he was sure he had been as a child on a family outing and later as a teenager. He came to the fork where he could choose to enter Victoria on Quadra or Douglas, chose Quadra, the least changed since his childhood. He drove directly to the institute, the local psychiatric hospital, recently built on the grounds of the hospital in which he had been born. In a homecoming to Victoria, he thought, one should drive directly to familiar landmarks: Dallas Road, the waterfront, Finlayson's Point, the Parliament buildings, the inner harbor, Beacon Hill Park, the Empress Hotel. Not a psychiatric institute, the existence of which, growing up, one kept in the periphery of one's vision.

This had been a simple task for generations of Victorians, because their psychiatric institute, their mental hospital, their asylum had been located on the mainland, up the Fraser Valley, to which people were taken, and then months later brought back. Without snapshots, albums or slides. Snow wondered which image was bleaker, more imposing, fearful, the Essondale imagined, fleetingly, in the periphery of vision, or the real Essondale up the Fraser Valley, the cluster of large buildings on the side of a hill.

He pulled into the parking lot of the new psychiatric institute. The premier's gift to Vancouver Island. This premier of the province that had once elected a man who called himself Amor de Cosmos, this premier had promised the electorate he'd do something for mental health, then personally acquired the plans for a building he had seen and liked somewhere in California and had it reproduced in Victoria, or so they said. They also said that once it was built he had flown in, from an old institution in Vancouver, a planeload of vegetables—Snow stopped his ruminations, corrected himself—a planeload of children and older children severely handicapped, needing around-the-clock care, microcephalics, Sturge Webbers like that one he'd seen in medical school with the tumor filling his brain cavity and growing out his mouth, which the surgeons wouldn't cut because he'd probably bleed to death, so he was just there, bedridden, two full-time aides looking after him, showing off the oldest Sturge Webbers in captivity, at nineteen—flown them in to occupy the fourth floor of this institution named

151

after the Cabinet minister who had broken the tie in the leadership vote that made the premier premier—in order to get fifty percent federal financing for the operation of this building with Snow's mother on the second floor.

He braced himself for the task at hand and was pleasantly surprised when he walked off the elevator on the second floor to find a large bright living, eating area, open nurses' station, corridors of semiprivate rooms. Ordinary people, mostly women, sitting around, playing cards, drinking coffee. She was waiting for him right there at the station, dressed, sweatered, made up, suitcase at her side.

Suitcase at her side.

She wasted no time telling him that the doctor, the psychiatrist attending her, had said she could go home with her son if she wanted to, a leave, or discharge, back to the house on a trial, that it would be a good time to do this with her son staying with her. He wondered what she had told him, what she had promised, how long she had said her son would be around.

He carried her suitcase to his car, walking beside this small woman, whose face and eyes looked bright and expectant. After the escapade the hospital had had someone pick up her car and drive it to the house. They took it away, she explained. "I haven't been able to go anywhere for weeks."

His mother used her newly minted key to open the door of the house, and he entered this familiar and very strange place carrying her suitcase and his, all the while glancing about seeing objects that evoked loss and sorrow in him, without specific memories. Familiar objects that seemed foreign at the same time, as if the objects and not Robert Snow were suddenly caught out of context, found in the wrong place. And this displacement heightened their reality while diminishing their innocence. Like the large red glass vase with thickly petaled aperture that had always sat on the mantel, front and center, which he had always seen and accepted but never looked at and considered. The house itself, he noticed, even with his mother living there, proclaimed its abandonment. And endorsed its abandonment like a poor and neglected beggar.

They drank gin and tonic and he was prepared to limit her but she didn't ask for a second. They watched an old movie on television, and she seemed okay, and talked about getting some things in order and looking for an apartment and selling the house and traveling, and she took her pills, the antidepressants, the anxiolytics. He slept in the bed that had been his parents' and which she had not slept in alone and the pillows were too thick and soft, the mattress too soft and old and the blond headboard too personal, too specific, and in this bed with him were the ghosts of his mother and father as intimate strangers. She stayed on the couch with the television on, turned low. She reassured him she'd be all right and fall asleep as soon as the pills began to work.

On the shelf of the headboard lay paperback mysteries, a Harlequin romance, *Reader's Digest*, a box of Kleenex. His mother had been, he remembered, an indiscriminate reader. A variety of perfumes, soaps, creams, pencils, sprays, polish lay randomly on the dresser, empty, full, half-full, the toiletries of a woman who no longer cared. It was on the edge of this bed his father sat years before with his mother kneeling before him when as a child he had entered without knocking and startled them and stopped them in whatever they were doing, which at the time he had not understood and not seen as a passionate act of fellatio between two assenting adults but rather as some terribly sad debasement. You only had to look at their faces. Were there tears in her eyes? Anguish on his face? Were they just surprised, embarrassed? Maybe his imagination had supplied the sexual connotation. Maybe she was fixing the cuffs on his pants and had dropped a pin. Maybe they were happy then.

It was five in the morning when he heard her moving about between the bathroom and the living room, muttering to herself in a low, plaintive voice. It wasn't long after she came into the bedroom, sat on the bed, got up, paced, sat down, her hands working together, rubbing, squeezing, wringing and rubbing the sides of her dressing gown, touching her face as if blind, and her voice coming out in breathless spurts, as if animated by horror, talking on and on, cadence ranging from low whimpering to high-pitched plea, with the same refrain over and over again that she didn't know what to do with herself, this self that Robert saw as her body and brain gone berserk, driven by explosions of dread.

He knew the textbooks called it agitated depression, which didn't come near the reality he was facing and she feeling as it drove her on and on so that she couldn't remember if she'd taken her pills that morning and couldn't think now which were which the white ones twice a day and two at bedtime or not or was that the blue ones and she'd be better off dead, what can I do, Robert, what can I do with myself?

He got up and made coffee and gave her another tranquilizer and sat with her and talked with her, feeling himself closing off and then relaxing and then closing off again. In small increments her agitation eased as the day wore on. He convinced her to have a bath and dress. The antidepressants had made her constipated and she sat on the toilet with the door slightly ajar moaning about that, not being able to do it, about her whole insides betraying her, about not being good for anything anymore. He was not comfortable with this intimacy and recoiled from it and was intrigued by it and saddened by it. He didn't want to see her half naked. He didn't want to know about the consistency of her shit. Revulsion mixed poorly with love. Revulsion the oil, love the water, the oil, no matter how hard he stirred, escaping to the surface.

He took her for a drive and for lunch and there were some moments when she calmed and they could talk about the things around her, the changes through the years, but most of the time she remained locked within her own agony. The long winding waterfront was clear and bright. The Strait of Juan de Fuca, separating the island from the brooding Olympics of Washington, moved restlessly, white-capped, deeply cold, dark, ominous. The gorse at the top of the cliffs bent with the constant eastward winds, coming large and fat off the Pacific. He had grown up with this, the rocks and beaches, the cliffs and perfect gardens, the ever-present ocean, the clean salty air, the moving skies, the quaintly decorated town, the cordial weather (even the rains were apologetic), and during that time this had encompassed reality for him, solid, immortal, friendly. Now it seemed to him illusion, misleading, an anxiety-ridden pastiche, a cover-up, a grand denial of the real nature of human existence.

In the evening he pan-fried some west coast oysters he had bought in a small tub in the local supermarket. She ate three of them and some dry toast and they watched television and he searched the newspaper for any reference familiar to his past. She sat on the sofa upon which she slept, leaning forward, smoking, rubbing her knees, watching intently, occasionally shuddering, pacing to the bathroom and back, but much calmer than in the morning. He hoped the worst was over when he went to bed but suspected the books were right when they told of something called diurnal variation, which meant, in less abstruse language: mornings are hell.

It began again at six on Sunday morning, this time with more references to if I had a gun I'd end it now and take all the pills and even begging that he was a doctor and would know how to put her out of her misery and if he cared at all he would do this but he didn't really care and nobody cared. And he would tell her he understood and she would tell him he didn't, nobody could, nobody could know what it's like, and he had to agree as he found his sympathy slipping to anger and back again.

He knew by now that if he spent the whole day with her he would end up seriously considering her request for assisted suicide and so he called a friend of hers, a widow, who agreed to stay with her for a few hours in the afternoon. He called his father and arranged to see him and perhaps play nine holes of golf if the weather kept up, which would help to limit the possibility of really talking, and when his father asked, as he inevitably would, "How's your mother?" he could answer, "Okay." And slice one into the woods.

"Are you staying at your mother's?"

"Yeah, it's why I'm here. She's been in the hospital."

"I heard about that. You know there's nothing I can do to help."

"I know."

The call was short even after his mother had said, "You can talk all you want. I'll stay in the other room." She also said, "I don't know why you have to see him."

HIS FATHER WAS renting a small house at which Robert did not want to look too closely, but it was clearly furnished in the fashion of a bachelor who was spending many nights sleeping somewhere else. The weather held and so they acquired clubs for Robert at a community course and duffed their way around eighteen holes, making Robert later than he said he would be getting back, but the crisp autumn air was fine, the breezes cold and the sun warm, the Olympic mountains snowcapped in the distance. All reference to his mother was avoided for

seventeen holes, and Robert, perhaps for the first time, actually observing his father: a handsome man who spent very little
on himself (too cheap, his mother would say), cautious (chick-
en, his mother would say), in some ways meticulous (when it
suits him, his mother would say), pleasant, gentle, doggedly
determined to dwell only on the sunny side of life (shallow, his
mother would say). It was a course Robert had known as a mix
of rocky outcroppings, dry stubble fairways, bogs and swamps.
He had come here as a child to catch tadpoles and small frogs,
later to collect and sell golf balls, still later sneaking on
halfway around to play. He would like to do this, get to know
his father, share something, anything. They were at their best
in parallel play, kibitzing about hooks, slices, duffs, choked
putts, water hazards, divots, his father playing a steady careful
game, Robert bolder, erratic. But his mother intruded on any
direct conversation, hanging between them, a specter of guilt
and accusation.

He told his father what he could about his hospital, routines, facts and figures, nothing of Elsa, George, the old Greek,
his interview with the medical director. He began to see his
mother as the evening news, bringing stories of fresh atrocities
in Vietnam, his father as "The Gardening Corner." Maybe
coexisting on the same network, but not living together. His
father did ask, "How is your mother doing?" while standing on
the last green after the last putt. No first names, disavowing
ownership.

Robert answered, "She's not doing very well. I may have to
put her back in the hospital." He watched his father's face and
thought how all his mother's demons were pouring forth, bub-
bling on her skin, in control of her tongue, and how by contrast
his father was utilizing immense reserves to sequester whatever pain and confusion he felt, staying with the gardening news.

They embraced when they parted, Robert explaining that

157

he'd left her with Freda, who they both knew had a good heart but a propensity for alcohol and he should get back to them, and next time he was out Ann would be with him and they'd get more time together. "I know it's difficult," his father said, "but you're welcome to stay at my place."

WHEN ROBERT GOT back to the house he saw them as two old broads deep in the sauce, which they were, exactly. A gin bottle sat dead empty on the kitchen counter. His mother was still agitated, but now drunkenly agitated, and Freda had gone the way she usually went when she drank—becoming maudlin, garrulous, generous, emotional, sloppy, talkative. She was upon him the moment he opened the door. "Yer mother and I are doin' jus' fine, jus' had a few little drinks, whoop, pardon my French, she loves you so much, you're her favorite, you know, like my own boy, Johnny'd do anything for me, he's such a darling, whatever he tells me to do, I'd do right away, he's wonderful y'know but he doesn't like me drinking so much, here, you should talk with him, I'll phone him up right now, here, you dial it, I can't see the numbers." And his mother still on the sofa, now rocking herself, and saying to Robert, "I don't know what I'm going to do with myself when you go back," and signaling to Robert with hand gestures that Freda had had a lot to drink, and Freda, very close to Snow, whispering, "Your mother's nuts, I been trying to tell her to get on with it, pull herself together, we could share a small house, she'd be jus' fine."

Freda had somehow gotten the right number and when John, Johnny answered and she had told him how much she loved him and when was he coming out so she could look after him, she handed the receiver to Robert and said, You talk to him, and whispered and mimed not to tell him she'd been drinking.

But John's first words were, "How much has she put away?"

Robert said, "I think they killed a bottle this afternoon."

"Jesus Christ."

"It's okay. It's under control. I'll look after things."

When he had hung up and sat down he thought about what he'd just said, "It's under control." He looked at his mother still rocking and moaning, slurring about what was she going to do with herself, and Freda rambling on about how she should look on the bright side of things and what a wonderful boy her Johnny was, but he'd be angry with her now, whoops, pardon my French, how naughty they'd been having a few drinks in the afternoon.

It's under control.

Robert thought about killing them both, allowed himself body disposal fantasies, and about just how far from being under control everything really was, and then he began to laugh. He laughed and he chuckled and he laughed again. They looked at him quizzically but were too drunk to be truly concerned that he'd lost it, gone over the edge, so he opened a beer, put his feet up and laughed some more.

When he called Ann long distance that evening she said, "You'll have to put her back in the hospital."

"I suppose."

"It sounds like she's worse when you're around. She regresses."

"Sure seems that way. She was pretty good when I picked her up."

"It's the best thing for her, Robert."

"I don't know when I can get back out, I mean to help her get settled when she leaves the hospital next time."

"Maybe you shouldn't be there."

"Maybe."

"Did you get any time with your father?"

"Some."

He convinced the psychiatrist to take her back in the next morning before he caught the plane in the afternoon, and she looked betrayed when he told her this, and pleaded with him, while he explained that there was nothing else he could do, and she'd be much better after a few more weeks (thinking at least two months) in hospital and he was sorry but he had to get back to Toronto and he couldn't leave her alone in the house. It just wasn't going to work.

To his surprise the next morning she packed her things and went with him quietly to the hospital. She was not as agitated. He told himself to remember this for future reference, these differences, these challenges to anything absolute. He said goodbye, left her there, feeling her eyes on his back as he walked away. He drove to the waterfront, parked, watched the fretful ocean from the cliff above, slow-moving freighters in the distance, sea gulls fighting over morsels, flying high, dropping clams onto rocks, swooping down to feed. Quite suddenly he decided he should visit his grandmother before flying back.

The old yellow frame house on Yates, small garage at the side with the 1937 Dodge up on blocks, full porch, leaded glass, the manual front doorbell that you twist. His grandmother, now eighty-seven. He parked on the street, opened the old iron gate between the square granite pillars, walked the path between patches of dry, dead grass and weeds and stepped onto the porch. There had been a time they had tried to talk her into a nursing home, and she had refused, and now her son was back, living upstairs, alone, working, Robert had heard, in the stockroom of an auto-parts distributor. A ghost-like figure in Robert's mind, slipping back home, stealing up to the room he had occupied as a child, quietly drinking the remainder of his life away, sleeping with his failures. Once a performer who banished the gray from his temples with old tea bags.

As a child Robert had visited the empty second floor and remembered unused beds, yellowing blinds, paintless sills, mysterious dormers, the tiny water closet with high wooden tank and pull chain. She came to the door in the manner he had expected: a voluminous dressing gown, slippers, thick, shoulder-length, unruly white hair. Zinc white. He was sure she had been brushing it at her dressing table, doing what he remembered her frequently preaching: one hundred strokes a day. And chewing fifty times before swallowing. Or was that fifty strokes and a hundred chews? It had always seemed, to Robert, a caution from the previous century.

"Robert. Is that you? As I live and breath. Dr. Robert Snow. I'm not dressed yet. You shouldn't call on a lady unannounced, not even an old woman."

"I'm sorry. It was a spur-of-the-moment thing. I'm flying back in a few hours."

"Come in. I'll make us some tea. Wait in the..." She hesitated here, with Robert knowing it was because the front room had not been used for years, heavily curtained, the dining room, parlor similarly archived, his grandmother's current geography being restricted to hallway, bedroom, kitchen. "Kitchen, while I get dressed."

He glimpsed his grandmother's bedroom as he passed on his way to the kitchen: large iron bed laden with satin comforters, piles of books on the old Oriental rug, newspapers scattered, tray of used dishes, clothing on chairs. Murky hallway, old wallpaper, large Victorian print in oak frame, single light bulb hanging from a black cord, oak hall tree, umbrella stand. The kitchen: linoleum floor, linoleum masquerading as carpet, pantry with porcelain sink filled with dirty dishes, old gas stove, wooden drop-leaf table and press-back chairs, all surfaces randomly covered with dishes, leftover food, newspapers, books, cloth, clothing, sewing equipment, letters, old envelopes. He took his jacket off and cleared a chair. The books, unlike his mother's, were mostly hardcover, biographies, nonfiction, classics, even poetry and a dictionary.

She hadn't changed from her dressing gown when she came in but had inserted her teeth, tied up her hair, fastened a brooch to hold her gown together. She found an empty pan, filled it with water from the iron tap in the pantry, lit the stove with a match, sniffed in her brown teapot, emptied it off the back porch and then dropped two tea bags in it. All the while talking. About the heart spell she had had yesterday, necessitating a visit by the doctor, a very handsome young man, who gave her new pills, which she wouldn't take, knowing the limits of apothecary in fixing old wounds.

"I had to take Mother back to the hospital," Robert interjected.

His grandmother paused only momentarily, hunting for two clean cups, before saying, "Emotional disorders have become very common, Robert. In my day we didn't speak of them. People were just sent away, or hidden. It's a curse to live long enough to see your children suffer. Did you see your father?"

"Yes. We played golf together."

"Don't be too angry with him, Robert. Your mother could be very difficult to live with."

Her disloyalty to her own daughter surprised Robert, but then Grandmother could always be counted on for the unexpected. And he almost felt relief to hear this viewpoint, contaminated as it was.

"You pour the tea, Robert. These damn dentures don't fit worth a hill of beans," she said, clacking them in her mouth. "Now, tell me about your hospital. There must be a biscuit here somewhere."

He began, but knew he wouldn't have to talk for long; any word might compel his grandmother to begin her own stories. This time it was the location of the hospital, and she told him, "There was nothing but farmland there when I was growing up, or stables and stockyards. I can't quite remember which, though the doctor thinks my memory is wonderful for my age." (Robert imagining the cycle of growth, maturity and decay that had occurred within his grandmother's lifetime.) "Here, these biscuits may be a bit stale but if you dip them they'll be fine."

"It's all Italian and Portuguese now."

"Your own family was poor Irish, Robert, on your mother's side. They came over after the potato famine. Your great-grandfather worked for the railway. Do you know you are looking more and more like your own grandfather, Francis, every day, except for the long hair and sideburns, but I suppose those are the style now. And don't worry about your hair thinning, women like bald men, Robert."

"They've got her on antidepressant medication," Robert interjected, for he realized he had come to talk about his mother.

"I've lived through Freud, the introduction of insulin, antibiotics, vaccinations and now organ transplants. These are miraculous times, Robert, though always a bit late for some. It was diphtheria that took Dinny away, before penicillin, and a woman who has ruined Tom, but perhaps there are treatments now for the heartbreak destroying your mother. Dinny was the smartest of them all, you know, a poet, a musician, eyes just like yours and your grandfather's, and a soul like my own. I always knew that, from the moment he was born." (Somehow Robert had always triggered memories of Dinny in his grandmother, and he had heard versions of the story before, but never really listened. This time he would listen,

163

and try to guess the truth among her embellishments.)

"He was the smartest of them all, by far. He would really have made something of his life. It was a terrible time, Robert, a terrible time. Just after the Great War. But there was no help for it then, and nothing more I could have done, nothing more. We had a nurse looking after him that weekend but the stupid woman didn't know enough to call the doctor. He was a beautiful boy, serene, not rebellious like Tom or so easily angered like your mother. Not a week goes by I don't think of him and what he would be like, and what we might have done together.

"He had a little cold all week, sniffles, and your grandfather was such a stubborn man, people often told me I was a saint to stay with him, a saint. He insisted I stay home that weekend while he went gallivanting in Vancouver. But I had my own business to attend to, which was every bit as important as his, though he would never admit to that. Twelve staff depended on me, Robert, twelve. And I couldn't ever bring myself to let them down. I drove Frank to the inner harbor early Saturday, to catch the Princess boat to Vancouver, and then went on to Eaton's. I supervised twelve dressmakers before they brought in ready-mades. They always said we made the best dresses north of San Francisco, by far. And some said my designs were even better than those from Toronto.

"That stupid, illiterate woman. I told her how to reach me. I wrote it down for her. We did have telephone then, but I don't think she knew how to use it.

"It was too late when I arrived home on Saturday. I carried Dinny to the car and then had to drive myself because she couldn't drive, but he was already blue and barely breathing. He died on the way to the hospital. A membrane closes the throat, Robert. It happens in minutes. There was nothing you could do about it in those days.

"Frank got back on Monday and I had to tell him. Nobody else would do it. You can't imagine the strength it took, Robert, to meet him at the dock and tell him his son had died, and my son, as well, although to Frank it was his son who had died, and died while in my care. But I had loved Dinny far more than he, far more. To Frank, business came first. He blamed me for not being there. Of course, he could have canceled his meetings and stayed home that weekend, but women had to fight for every inch, every inch, in those days. He only had a cold that Saturday morning, the sniffles. The doctors said it must have come on later. There had been no reason I should stay with him, no reason at all.

"Neither Tom nor your mother could ever fill Dinny's shoes, not in your grandfather's eyes. He never gave them a chance. He never got over it. Never. I stopped working then, to please him, and stayed home to look after Tom and your mother, but there was no pleasing Frank after that. God knows I tried. I was a wonderful mother, Robert. There was nothing I wouldn't do for your mother and Tom. You can't know how terrible it is to live long enough to watch your children suffer."

And Robert began to see the depth of the wound Dinny's death had caused, maybe extending into the next generation, neither Frank nor Margaret ever forgiving themselves, blaming each other. These two powerful forces from then on at war. And Margaret, the suffragette, the independent businesswoman, the Unitarian, the Freudian, turning her prodigious embrace upon Robert's mother and Tom. About whom, Robert realized afterward, there had been no mention: a thin man, perhaps still blackening his hair, slicking it back, saxophone propped in the corner of his bedroom upstairs, bottle in the drawer, under the mattress, returned to his mother's web, but hiding his substance, from her, from everybody. Maybe—and Robert hoped this was true—maybe he came alive emulating

Errol Garner, Coltrane, Jimmy Dorsey, Saturday nights at the Douglas Hotel.

FLYING BACK TO Toronto Robert Snow wonders if penicillin, vaccinations would have saved Dinny, and then Frank, Tom, his mother. He reads that the Red Guards have sacked the British Consulate in Peking and that paratroopers of the 173rd Airborne have suffered heavy casualties fighting for control of Hill 875. He has put his mother back in the psychiatric hospital. Penicillin has its limitations.

CHAPTER TWELVE

*What is meant by the touch?—an examination per vagi-
nam. What arrangements are necessary when this examination is to be made with the patient lying down?—
The proposition should be made to a third person; the
room should be darkened, and the female suitably clad
and situated.*

*If the patient is standing how should she and the
examiner be situated?—She should stand against something firm, and slightly recline upon the shoulders of the
examiner; the examiner should be seated upon a low seat,
or bend upon his knee in front of the patient, and pass
his index finger to the posterior commissure of the vulva.*
– *A MANUAL OF EXAMINATIONS*, J.L. LUDLOW, 1860

> *There'll be one child born*
> *And a world to carry on, to carry on*
> – LAURA NYRO

PICTURE THIS. EVERY boy's dream turned into nightmare.
Five naked women lying on their backs, legs up and
spread in stirrups. All in a row. Cunts like so many how-
itzers aimed directly at chest level, then eye level when Snow
sat on the stool before each one. Behind flimsy white curtains
in five hot and pungent cubicles. Entering and leaving from
the back like the exhibits of a carnival sideshow. The nurses,

assistants at this ceremony, undressing them and holstering them into the stirrups. Preparing them for the entry of Dr. Snow. (He felt apologetic for his fantasies, allusions, references, imagination.) And here we are, ladies and gentlemen, five, count 'em, five fresh vulvas, five vaginas. Brought to you courtesy of the poverty of the immigrant class. And what a selection we have for you today. Two from the Mediterranean, the hot steamy shores, redolent of olive oil and feta cheese with a touch of old urine, folds of flesh fiery red where the air hasn't reached it in years. The sweet pregnant smell of honey and old cheese. Wiry pubic hair that doesn't end, stretching in a wispy line up the belly, disappearing briefly and then reappearing around each nipple. Flaccid vulvar folds, labia majora, minora and Ibiza, too. And little Formentera. Swollen, engorged, abused by the passage of large heads.

The mystery solved. That hidden and forbidden land the subject of young boys' daydreams, bad jokes, misinformation, ignorance avoided, kept from the light, not talked about, except derisively over an illicit case of beer, often blanked out in the images of the mind in the manner of a police censor, a G-string, the topic of eternal male curiosity. Penis envy? Bullshit. Womb envy. Birth canal envy. Cunt envy. Not to have one attached, made part of, exchanged for the penis, but to own one...or two, or three. And retain a soft-focus image, a fade-in, fade-out, a glimpse, a glimmer, in soft lighting, maybe two-candle, partial view, to lightly touch, brush against, not this full-frontal in-your-face klieg-lighting all-flaws-all-realities-exposed approach. The touch in the prenatal clinic.

He remembered—age? must have been sixteen—four guys sitting in a car at the drive-in, hamburgers, fries, root beer, talking about girls, lying about women, and Kevin, in the backseat, skinny blond kid, played alto sax in their band, at that time dating the hottest number in the school, a Natalie Wood look-alike, Kevin talking about his last outing, being a little more explicit than usual, a little more personal, telling them that after the movie, parked at the waterfront, she let him put a finger in, he got a finger in. Three guys paying attention now, rapt, envious, knowing by the way he's telling it they're hearing a true story. And then, and then, and then?

"Boy, did it smell, I'm telling you. Wiped my finger on a good handkerchief and threw it away." And young Robert Snow, gallantly wishing he had not heard this, wanting to apologize to Natalie, wanting to retain his own inventions, wanting to get his own finger in.

Not one of the three asking, but what did it smell like? and thus reveal ignorance.

All right, all right, thought Snow. That piece of anatomy is a source of wonder and excitement and we have to find a way of neutralizing the encounter between a woman and her boy doctor, making it professional, but this way? Where the hell is there any dignity? For her, for him, for either of them.

As the context dictated, as the nurses indicated, Snow entered the cubicles from the business end, meeting and greeting each woman crotch first. Maybe it would be no easier the other way: "Hello. How are you? Let me just take a look down there."

What the hell do you say in such a meeting? I'll just be doing a routine prenatal, ma'am. Then he'd check the pelvis bones from inside, the cervix, the uterus, left hand on the belly, gloved two fingers inside, sitting between the legs, the swollen abdomen blocking his view of her averted eyes.

This one, next to the bulky Mediterranean women, was small, young and tough, or full of bravado, short blond hair and chewing gum, unwed, in her teens.

"Take it easy down there," she snarled. "What the fuck you

sticking in there?" Small quantity of brown pubic hair, straight, no curls, tight vagina, good thighs, well-shaped legs, a scowl on her face when he looked up. "I ain't had no bleeding," she answered his question. Her anger was palpable. Snow wanted to say, "Hey, sweetie, hey. Cool out. It wasn't me got you into this mess. But I'm sorry. I'm sorry."

Well, maybe she was scared and covering it with all this toughness. But Snow was far too intimidated to be fatherly and comforting. Two fingers in the kid's vagina, the kid snarling at him with her mouth while her eyes seduced, half his cortex deployed inhibiting his own emotions, which were pretty complicated if he had a moment to stop and think about them: a bit of lust, a touch of disgust, some censure, anxiety, profound embarrassment, maybe a little caring, a fair amount of caring, but reach out here and get your hand chopped off. All stirred gently with the Anglo rod stuck up his own ass. Just do the job, he told himself, be kind, get onto the next one.

And the one next to the chewing gum is an older woman, a maiden aunt, with nothing fecund about her except her positive pregnancy test. Skinny legs and knobbled feet, small varicose veins, clinging to a little dignity by clutching her white gown to cover her unused breasts, a little puff of pubic hair, everything powdered and clean, the smell of baby powder and tea bags. Her face has a startled look as if she hasn't yet figured out how she got here. She's over forty and almost virginal. Hard to imagine how she got pregnant. Maybe three martinis when she's used to dry sherry, a salesman taking advantage, fat salesman cock rasping down a dry vagina, or a gentle true love, a dream, the single adventure. It's dry and in spasm now, clamped shut so Snow can't get one finger in. She's uttering small cries and squeals when he simply spreads the lips apart with his left hand. Goop on the lubricant. Doesn't help. He has his right index finger in to the first joint when she arches her back and cries in pain. He imagines a moan of pleasure under the cry of pain, and squeals of protest. Forget it. Give her a few more weeks. He's not really sure why it's important to get his two fingers in, other than it's standard, it's done, it's in the book. What might he find that he would ever trust?

In the fifth cubicle there waits a woman who could be his sister, or his wife. She wants to know what's happening to her, all the details. She wants to eat the right foods and do the right exercises. She wants to know if the baby is growing with all its parts. She asks questions and lets him know that her body has a top end with a mind and some feelings. She's proud of her growing belly, and her worried smile awaits a few kind words. Her breasts are still fine, her hair is long and lingers on her bare shoulders. Snow talks to this one after the thing, the examination, the desecration. She wants the baby but she's afraid. She's embarrassed having her crotch waving in the breeze for this stranger to ogle. But she's here for good prenatal care, for the baby. Robert Snow likes this woman and likes her even though all the mystery has been taken from her vagina. A few minutes ago he had two fingers inside her and now they're having a pleasant talk about how she plans to go back to university when the baby's two or three. About her husband in graduate school and how they could afford a private obstetrician but they had talked about it and decided she should come to the same free clinic her neighbors use. Organic food, print dresses, incense, making love. No marijuana during the first trimester. He gives her his stethoscope and together they find the fetal heartbeat.

He prescribes iron for them all and gives them new appointments. The nurses help them unstirrup and dress and then guide them out and then they open the back curtains for five more to enter, undress and mount, their bellies small or swollen, large, taut, sometimes moving.

THAT NIGHT IN bed Ann said, "Will you stop that?"

"What? Stop what?"

"You're examining my breast."

"No, I'm not."

"Yes, you are. I can tell the difference between examining and fondling."

Well, he had been. His left hand across her body, gently stroking her right breast, had begun to knead and palpate and search for lumps. He had found a little ropiness as the textbooks described and was vaguely worried. He tried to shift his mind and look at her and feel her with the innocence and amazement he had once experienced. This gynecology rotation might ruin him, spoil something he didn't want spoiled. The pubic area, vulva, vagina, was not very attractive at all when examined with what was called, in a tradition of simpleminded optimism, clinical detachment. How could he ever want to touch it, feel it, lick it again? Ann's? Any woman's?

He took his hand away and lay on his back. She rolled toward him and kissed him on the cheek, then the neck, then pushing the sheet down she kissed his nipples. He pulled her face to his and the question that had sledged pessimistically through his mind seconds before was answered. Hormones and context. Context and hormones. Perception was soft clay in their embrace. And for too short a period of time magic took over, banished the hospital from his mind and made her and all her parts wondrous again.

The next morning Snow read that Jayne Mansfield had been decapitated in a car accident. The image haunted him, that body without a head, as opposed to the old photographs of Chinese executions he had once seen at his grandmother's, where the haunting image was that of a head newly separated from its body. He revised his formulation: context, hormones and object integrity.

THE PHONE CALLS with his mother took on a pattern. First few minutes she's doing fine, interesting people here, getting to know one or two, such sad cases and so young, then, "I'll be going home very soon, Robert." And just as Robert felt he could have a small comforting conversation, mutually reassuring, optimistic, then say goodbye, close off with peace of mind, she would add, "It's a terrible thing to be put in here, to be abandoned. It's just terrible."

WHY IN GOD'S name do we do it this way? Snow asked himself as he sat gowned and gloved between the legs of a woman he had met for the first time only minutes before. Her legs up, feet in stirrups, flat on her back, three, maybe four long feet above the hard tiled floor, a nurse holding her head, coaching her, now push, push, push, okay, relax, breathe, little breaths, wait for it, wait for it, now, again, push, push, that's it, one last push, almost there, push, push. The head crowning, coming out, this big sloppy mucous-covered head, slippery, twisting, pause, shoulders now, grab hold, Jesus Christ, almost slipped, great fat watermelon head slipping through his fingers and smashing on the floor, spewing its fruit at his feet. No, he's got it, thank God, arms, both hands, body, umbilical cord, legs, feet, he's got it in his right hand, in his lap, the little penis the first bit to work, pissing an impressive stream, and then baby's mouth sputtering, croaking, hoarsely crying. He's got it in his lap with the mother flopping back exhausted—squirmy, mucousy little puddle of life. All right. All right. He can buy the wonder of it, the miraculous nature of it. But mostly he feels relief: the thing had come out. It had come out whole. It had come out alive. And he hadn't dropped it. But why the hell do we do it this way?

SNOW WAS TOO tired to contemplate an answer to that question so he took himself back to his small room and dozed on his bed until they called him again, at midnight.

"Mrs. Didioto is in, Doctor. Will you be up to see her?"

"How close is she?"

"Three centimeters now, contractions every five minutes, strong."

"Okay. I'll be over."

Snow went through his usual ritual of shaking his white jacket out, filling the pockets with the tools of his trade and splashing cold water on his face before going down into the tunnel, crossing over to the main building and riding the elevator up to the obstetrics floor.

"Hello, Mrs. Didioto. It's almost time, is it?"

"Sure, *dottore*, it's almost time. You promise me she be a boy this time? Oh, oh, oh, mama!"

"That's a good contraction, Mrs. Didioto."

"Oh, it's a hurt. Don't a touch."

"Sorry. I'll wait till it's over."

"Oh, mother di Dio." She was sweating profusely and breathing hard.

A nurse came in and handed Snow a glove and some jelly for a rectal examination between contractions. Snow gloved and lubricated and put his finger in the poor woman's anus, trying to feel the cervix through both the rectum and vaginal wall. Which he knew was an impossible mission for all but a princess.

"I think it's three centimeters and soft," he muttered. The nurse grinned at him and left. He waited in the room timing the intervals between contractions. Mrs. Didioto moaned softly at first, but with each new contraction her moan increased in pitch and volume until it became a piercing wail with a cadence of appeals to the mother of God, Jesus, various saints, her own mother, sprinkled with a few choice words for her husband. There were a couple of hours to go. Not too long. This wasn't her first.

Snow waited at the nurses' station while the aides gave Mrs. D an enema. Her wails and shrieks penetrated the wall and reverberated in the station. The charge nurse looked up at Snow and said, "Can't you get her to quiet down? It can't be hurting that much."

He had no idea how much it hurt and guessed he never really would, but the charge nurse looked like she had no real idea, either, being an obviously dried-up, sour bitch who had never been screwed let alone pregnant. Pardon me. Loved, never been loved, thought Snow. They were a tough lot, the nurses up here. They seemed to gravitate to obstetrics, the unmarried bitter ones. They took a special delight making the male interns feel totally inadequate, and barely hid their contempt for the women in their care, women who not only allowed themselves to get pregnant but then moaned and groaned about it. He avoided the highly prejudicial act of contemplating their sexual orientation.

Mrs. Didioto's husband was probably out drinking with his cronies, boasting about the son who would soon emerge. Mrs. Didioto was carrying on as if she was the only woman on earth ever to go through this. The nurses were pissed she was making so much noise, and Snow was wondering if it was safe to give her another shot of Demerol.

He went to her room to examine her again. Maybe she was five centimeters and effacing, coming pretty fast, probably. At two in the morning. There seemed no point going back to his own room in the residence, trying to sleep and listening for the phone at the same time. Intermittently the nurses remarked on Mrs. Didioto's shouting, screaming, about how loud she was, keeping everybody awake, and looked at Snow. But he knew he shouldn't give her another injection, and even if he did the head nurse undoubtedly would turn to him and say, "Are you sure, doctor? It's very close to delivery." And he would say, "No, you're right. Better she screams all night than have a depressed baby." And the nurse would then intone, "Whatever you say, doctor." Whatever you say, doctor. There were patients who said it simply and trustingly and nurses who said it as if it were a sharp instrument.

Another nurse said, "I don't see why she can't behave like Mrs. Smythe." Mrs. Smythe was a private patient, two doors down the corridor, in her fourteenth hour of labor. She gritted her teeth, sweated and panted, never complained, didn't even moan, thanked the nurses for their many favors. Afterward she would leave them a box of chocolates, flowers.

"Oh oh oh mama mia mama mia mama mia!"

Snow left the station to visit his patient again. "*Dottore*, give me somet'ing. Please a give me somet'ing."

"I'm sorry, I can't give you anything more. It would hurt the baby. But it won't be long now." He took a cloth and mopped her brow. She looked heavy and old, with oily sweat and a mustache. He took her hand in his and held it. Not a small, delicate, female hand. A worker's hand. Laundry, garden, a thousand dishes. With the next contraction she was a little quieter but almost crushed his hand in her thick, callused fingers. With stethoscope he listened to the fetal heart and heard it optimistically pinging away.

"I'm a gonna die this time. I gotta three girls. Who look after my three girls?"

"You're fine. You're doing just fine. You're not going to die. It won't be long now."

There was a smell of sweat and garlic mingling with the honey-sweet perfumes of pregnancy. He withdrew his hand, and the volume and pitch of her moaning increased. He took her hand in his again and she quieted. It looked like the thing to do, and after a moment of embarrassment when the head nurse looked in, saw them holding hands and curled her lip, he pretty much knew it was the thing to do and he felt okay about it. Trouble was he was about to lapse into a coma, having worked the last thirty-six hours straight. There was an empty bed behind him, beckoning. He took his hand away, reassuring her that he wasn't going anywhere, he was right there, just hold on for a minute. He moved the bedside cabinet out of the way and rolled the empty bed up against Mrs. Didioto's bed.

He fluffed the pillow, slipped off his sandals, lay back on the bed and took her hand in his once more. She gripped it tightly. He dozed. Her soft moanings and mutterings invaded his dreams. He opened his eyes to see a new nurse standing at the foot of the two beds. She smiled at him and said, "How very sweet."

He ignored her, closed his eyes and listened to her retreating footsteps. He dozed again, drifting through a landscape of hospital monitors, white curtains, thought for a moment the woman beside him was his mother, then his grandmother, felt himself recoil from her strong grip, but didn't let go, couldn't let go. The next thing he knew his ankle was being shaken and Pauline was standing at the foot of the bed saying, "She sounds very close. How's the cervix?"

"What are you doing here?"

"They're short tonight. I'm covering."

"What time is it?"

"Almost four."

"Do you have a glove?"

Snow pulled himself off the bed, gloved and tried his finger in Mrs. D's rectum once again. "I can't tell," he said. "Cervix feels hard. Harder than before. But it must be close by now."

"Oh mama mia mama mia."

"Here. Let me try." She said it nicely, kindly.

"Go ahead."

Gloved efficiently, professionally. "I think it's nine centimeters and fully effaced. That's the head you were feeling. Better call the anesthetist, and Saunders."

Snow left the room to put in the calls. When he came back it was obviously too late for anesthetics and chief residents. Pauline was saying, "Don't push, Mrs. Didioto, don't push, don't push. It's not time yet."

And Mrs. Didioto, between gasping and moaning, was saying, "I gotta push, I gotta push, baby coming, oh."

The crown of the head was showing between Mrs. D's legs, spread wide on the bed, not in the delivery room, not up in stirrups.

"I don't think we have a choice," said Pauline.

They pushed away the extra bed, pulled on new gloves, moved to opposite sides of Mrs. D, held her knees up and delivered her right there. Snow recognized that as being something of an overstatement. They talked her through it, tried to slow her down, but Mrs. D gave one last ear-shattering scream, pushed with all her might and the head popped out into their hands. They guided the rest of the nine-pounder out, awash with fluids and already screaming at a pitch and volume comparable to mama's.

An anesthetist looking half anesthetized poked his head in the door, muttered some profanities and wandered away. Saunders, the chief res., arrived in a flurry of green, just behind the head nurse. "Well, are we having fun?" he asked, pulling on a glove. "Any bleeding? Did she tear the cervix?"

"No. I don't think so."

"Let's take a look at that placenta." Pauline had been scooping it off the bed into a basin. "Looks all there," he announced. "You seem to have everything under control." The scowl on the face of the head nurse seemed to be too much for him. He made a show of adjusting his unused glove hand, then twisted and goosed her with his thumb.

It was four-thirty in the morning. An unhappy anesthetist was trying to get back to sleep, Mrs. Didioto was quietly moaning a different refrain, "Thanks be to God. Dis my last one, you hear, *dottore*, dis my last one." Snow and Pauline were cleaning up the baby boy, showing him to Mrs. D and bundling him for the bassinet. The kid was kicking and screaming. And the scowling head nurse was shrieking like a schoolgirl, chasing the obstetrics and gynecology chief resident, Kevin Saunders, down the hall, shouting, "Come back here, you bastard."

Pauline said, "I'm impressed, Snow."

"What? That delivery?"

"No, you asshole. Before that."

"What?"

"Staying with her, holding her hand."

"It was merely the most practical and expedient thing to do."

"Bullshit." Said with a nice flirtatious smile that helped him negotiate the elevator, tunnels and stairs back to his bed for, looking at his watch, three hours sleep if he was lucky.

A pediatric resident would soon be called to check over Mrs. Didioto's new son. It wouldn't be Dr. Benjamin Spock, Snow mused on his journey. That was for sure. Dr. Spock had just been indicted for counseling young men, boys really, to resist the draft. It seemed a reasonable thing to do, thought Snow. Undoubtedly Spock, like Snow, had stayed up half the night delivering some of them, maybe held their mothers' hands,

179

reassured their mothers. He would want to see a few get past their twentieth birthdays.

PHONE CALLS WITH his mother, a little longer, more hopeful. She was taking her medication, looking forward to getting on with her life. Tom had visited, but he didn't look well, she said. He needs to move out of there. He needs to move a long way away. He did try that once, said Robert, he did try that.

A FEW NIGHTS LATER, responding to the insistent pounding, puzzled it was that and not the phone that had awakened him, Snow opened the door of his small room to find Saunders standing there saying, "C'mon, it's time."

"Time for what?"

"Harvey's birthday party."

"It must be after midnight, for Christ's sake."

"The witching hour," said Saunders as he moved on to rap on the next door.

Snow followed in bare feet, tucking his intern's shirt into his white pants. "What the hell are you talking about?"

Saunders was giving the same pitch to Sandy, somnolent, surly, leaning against his door frame. Sandy wasn't so forgiving. "You fucking asshole, what are you up to now?"

When he had three of them he stopped to explain. "It's for your old buddy Harvey, poor bastard hasn't had a night off in two months and he turned thirty today. He needs a blow job in the worst way."

"Yeah?"

"So do it yourself. I'm going back to bed."

"No. It's all arranged. We just need a small crowd to make it more effective."

He was leading them down the hall and up one flight of stairs, explaining over his shoulder as they followed. "We got the Great Dane in on this. Birthday cake, champagne, the works."

Snow followed Saunders through the door on the next level and found himself part of a small gathering of men and a couple of women in dirty whites and sloppy greens, smiling, giggling quietly, bottles of beer in hand, talking in whispers, one of them holding a birthday cake with candles, another a bottle of domestic champagne. Pauline was there, just one of the crowd. Harvey Ryan wasn't there.

Saunders took over, issuing instructions. "Okay. Keep it quiet. We're right on time. I've got the key. Light the candles and follow me. Oh, yeah. Who can sing? Probably none of you shits. Anyhow, we need a loud chorus of 'Happy Birthday.' "

Saunders led the assembly down the hall to the fourth door, signaled everybody to gather around behind him and keep quiet, the resident carrying the cake beside him, candles now aflame, slipped the key in the knob, twisted it quickly, pushed the door wide open and shouted, "Happy birthday, Harv."

They didn't manage to get a chorus of "Happy Birthday" started for maybe five or ten seconds, just long enough to hear this big blond woman saying, "C'mon Harv, let's get it up. You can do better than that." She was on top, straddling him, her uniform three quarters off, large breasts set free, Harvey under her, on his back, eyes glazed, head twisting toward the door and this crazy mob of grinning whites and greens, now breaking into an off-key chorus of "Happy Birthday." Happy birthday, dear Harvey. Happy birthday to you.

The Great Dane, who Snow now recognized as the tall, powerful and Scandinavian head nurse for the OR, began pulling herself together, skirt falling over her legs as she got off, saying, "Saunders, give me a beer, you prick."

Harvey, rendered speechless, pulled the sheet and blanket over himself. Everybody crowded into the room, sat on the desk, the edge of the bed, the single chair, the floor. A couple of cases of beer were dropped in the middle.

"Shit, man. You should've seen your face."

"How'd you like our little present, Harv?"

Harvey took a beer offered him and began to guzzle from his prone position, looking up at the ceiling. "Fuck off," he said.

"Hey, I'm worried about you, man."

"Fuck off."

"A toast to Harv on his thirtieth birthday, and to the prodigious talents of our favorite nurse."

"To Harv."

"Fuck off."

A small room, crowded and close, one-thirty in the morning, a good supply of beer, bedside rounds at seven, the OR by eight, Snow wondered for a moment if Harvey had been truly affronted but he looked in no great pain. Snow could go back to his own room and try to get enough sleep to survive the next day, or he could sit here on the floor, drinking beer, pondering such important questions as: was the Great Dane wearing panties? Was Harv really having trouble getting it up? How many nurses was Saunders laying? Pauline looking his way, now coming over, sitting beside him, shoulder to shoulder, back to back.

The Great Dane was a handsome woman, her body just part of her, an extension of her big laugh and warm smile. She had half buttoned her blouse, leaving a lot of cleavage and the possibility that if she leaned forward just enough... It wasn't exactly Nirvana sitting there on the floor in the small hours, feeling the warmth of Pauline's back against his, smelling her perfume, watching the Great Dane, watching Harvey smile, watching Saunders be irrepressible, but it wasn't bad.

The Beatles, according to the newspapers, bored with

Western fame and fortune, were seeking "absolute bliss consciousness" somewhere on the Ganges with the Maharishi Mahesh Yogi, having changed their tune, so to speak, and having decided love, after all, is not all you need. It would be kind of nice, thought Snow, bliss consciousness. He mentioned it to Sandy drinking beer on his right.

"Define bliss," said Sandy, cracking another Labatts.

"Define absolute," said the white jacket next to him.

"Define consciousness," said Saunders.

"Fuck off," said Harvey.

"Where's Trebilcock? asked someone else.

"Appendectomy," said Saunders.

"Oh, yeah, forgot."

Snow figured forgetting probably had a lot to do with bliss consciousness. He opened another beer, hoisted it in a mock toast and said, "Here's to ya, John, Paul, George and Ringo."

"And here's to the maharishi."

"To the maharishi."

"Who the hell's the maharishi?"

"Some silly old fuck with three Mercedes."

"Yeah? To the maharishi."

"Who's got more beer in his room? We're running low."

"Hey, we forgot the champagne. Somebody open the champagne."

"Where's Trebilcock?"

"Harvey, old bud, what was it like? Was it good?"

"Fuck off."

There may be many paths to absolute bliss consciousness, thought Snow. He had trouble taking his eyes off the Great Dane's ample cleavage, her nipples pushing on thin cotton. He was aware of each and every one of Pauline's movements, struggled to decipher their code, struggled to not respond to their code. He couldn't imagine bliss consciousness being more than a temporary state of mind. Bliss unconsciousness, that could last a little longer. He was surprised to feel a touch of relief when Trebilcock joined the party, still gowned and slightly blood-spattered.

Chapter Thirteen

Surry down to a stoned soul picnic
There'll be lots of time and wine
Red, yellow honey, sassafras and moonshine
— Laura Nyro

THERE WAS A party in the residence lounge every Friday night with different ethnic groups taking responsibility for the food. The Ukrainians put on the best spread, a table laden with cabbage rolls, breads, sausages, cheese, smoked meats. Beer was the beverage of choice, but on special occasions someone would mix a basin of hospital alcohol with Welch's grape juice in unlikely proportions. It didn't take much to find a special occasion. Hey, we gotta celebrate the first microwave oven. What the hell's a microwave oven? Well, man, you know about X rays. Of course I know about X rays.

Some sliced orange or lemon might be floated on top, or might not. Esthetics was not a priority. This deadly potion was known as Purple Jesus. Snow thought it notable that one did not ask for or drink *a* Purple Jesus, as in, I'll have a Bloody Mary please. One simply drank Purple Jesus. Neither singular, nor plural, nor a portion thereof. Which gave the proceedings some affinity with Communion. Or so he liked to imagine, though the relationship was tenuous. It was a quick way to get drunk, a quick way to forget, a quick way to regain some lost optimism, the latter perhaps being the connection with Communion.

On call or off call they drank, though those on call stayed away from the Purple Jesus and limited themselves to beer. The music would get louder as the night progressed, with interns, residents, nurses, aides joining as they finished shift or, in the case of interns and residents, when they could steal away between emergency and routine duties. And some of the senior residents would become more outrageous as the night progressed. The word *resident* was fairly accurate. For four years they lived in this and other hospitals, breathed its air, smelled its smells, ate its food, slept when they could, escaped when they could, watched patients die, suffered humiliation, failure, some triumphs, conquests. People with volumes to tell passed through their lives like stray dogs. In front of them one moment, yapping in pain and need, clutching small offerings in gratitude, servility, suspicion, entitlement, gone the next. They witnessed pain and suffering and they were there to learn to become healers, good healers, respected physicians, some of them imagined. But they experienced frustration, impotence, anxiety, fear, helplessness.

It all hung out on Friday nights. In greens and whites, surgical hats and boots, they danced wildly, shouted and sang above the music. They collapsed in drunken corners of remorse and self-pity, then revived and blasphemed themselves back into the center of the undertaking. They grabbed at willing nurses and slyly slipped away to find momentary bliss consciousness, and then came back and danced some more. The interns participated as initiates, novices, in confusion and admiration.

It was not surprising, thought Snow, that it took so long for someone to notice that a window was wide open to the January night and Trebilcock was outside sitting on the ledge.

ROBERT'S MOTHER HAD been released from hospital for Christmas, suffered through Christmas. Phone calls got her through it. She was taking her antidepressants and her sleeping pills. But it would never be the same, she said. From now on it would be a season to endure. Robert explained to Ann that he didn't really see how that would be a major change. He told her how the Christmas season had always been a gathering storm, his father determined that it should be happy and celebratory, spending too much, his mother waiting for her moment of disappointment, momentarily softening with the music, lights, rum punch, but always finding her moment.

Grandmother may be coming this year. Well, is she coming or not? She says her heart's been troubling her, she's not sure yet. The turkey well-cooked to his father's approval, mashed potatoes, Brussels sprouts, sweet potatoes, onions, gravy, cranberry sauce, bread stuffing, sausage stuffing, pudding with two kinds of sauce, crackers and silly hats. Waiting for Grandmother Margaret. Then the old Dodge appearing, trundling up the center of the road, into the driveway, Father gallantly trotting out to open the door for her, offer her his arm on the pathway, through the front door. (Later Mother might point out the futility of this gesture; Margaret would never part with any of her money—and Father would look pained, insulted at this challenge to his motivation.) Grandmother arriving, large and ominous, cane in hand, feathered hat pinned to her speckled bun, black fur coat, under this a flowing purple dress, pearls, Victorian brooch, a wrinkled décolletege. No presents. And no embarrassment about not bringing presents, either. Her own presence sufficient, her gift to them. Occasionally mentioned later, but not often, for this would lead to an argument over which parent contributed the most at the time of the wedding or house purchase.

And now that Grandmother was in the house, she filled it. She would find a chair, sit regally and be catered to, served. And she would talk, tell stories, dominate the dinner table.

About her dentures, about the latest young doctor, young entrepreneur, accountant, agent, stockbroker in her life, what she said to this person or that person, what they said to her, how she put them in their place, how they thought her wonderful, courageous, generous. Lecture them about eating too fast, not chewing enough. Then have dyspepsia herself, Robert's father having to fetch a glass of water, his mother asking if her heart pills were in her coat pocket. But then, after being helped to a better chair in the room with the Christmas tree and taking a moment to recover, indefatigably reviving and, like a magnet, pulling them all to her, to gather around her once again. At some point telling again, one version or another, the story of Dinny.

Ann asked Robert if that was why he got stuck with Christmas duty at the hospital. Had he volunteered? He vehemently denied volunteering, which was true, but he knew Christmas among strangers and acquaintances might contain less tension. He promised her they would have Christmas on the day after.

And Christmas in the hospital had been peaceful. Generally people avoided dying on Christmas day, or having major accidents, eruptions. They were pleasant, friendly, rooms were decorated, a few colored lights here and there, carols played on the overhead, family members visiting with gifts, on every ward, at every nursing station, Christmas cookies, cake, chocolates, gingerbread. Ann talked with him on the phone, went off to spend the day with Tony and Beth.

Mrs. Didioto gave him a big sloppy kiss and thanked him for the boy child, the *niño*. It was the least I could do, thought Snow, but he did feel good inside. Mr. Didioto came in bearing not chocolates but a forty-ounce bottle of homemade wine. He insisted the *dottore* drink with him and pulled glasses from his pockets. He insisted the nurses join, as well, but they made themselves busy. Snow sipped the raw red wine, received a kiss on each cheek, noticed Mr. D's eyes looked worse than his wife's, full of sleeplessness, worry, gratitude. He was a spent but still simmering Roman candle of paternal emotions. *Grazie, grazie, grazie.* Or a Calabrian candelabra, thought Snow, pleased with himself, as he sauntered off to visit his other patients. *Prego, prego.*

BETWEEN CHRISTMAS AND New Year's Day he talked Ann into trying another night at the hospital.

"You probably won't be finished before midnight," she protested.

"You could bring a book, or watch TV in the lounge."

"I feel out of place in that lounge. Besides, I hate what's on television. I can't stand to see one more bombing report, one more dying kid." He knew she could feel immediate hurt and anger about something happening twelve thousand miles away, while he remained detached or better insulated. She had joined protest groups, antiwar sit-ins and discussions, rap sessions, some nights he was on duty. He told himself that the immediate deaths and tragedies surrounding him were all that he should be expected to bear. To shoulder those other burdens, as well, would be futile. "What then is a man to do?" he misquoted Tolstoy to himself.

"Or some knitting," he suggested to her. "You could bring some knitting."

"Knitting?"

"Do me another scarf."

"A shorter one this time?" He knew the reference to the scarf had broken down her resistance.

"We can have supper in the cafeteria."

"You sure know how to show a girl a good time."

"I'm sorry. This is it, that's all."

189

"It?"

"You know what I mean. I'm working. I'm on call. There's nothing I can do about it."

"I know, I know, I understand. How about I come down around eleven. Will you be in your room?"

"If I'm not there I'm tied up in the OR, something like that. Wait for me in the lounge."

"Sitting there with my overnight bag I'll feel like a whore."

"They're calling me again. I'm sorry. I gotta go."

"Robert?"

"Yeah?"

"I'll be there."

HE WASN'T THERE to meet her at eleven. He was in the OR assisting with a ruptured ectopic pregnancy, an overanxious or possibly quite lazy embryo that hadn't bothered making the complete journey from ovary to uterus, taking root instead in the nearest Fallopian tube. What a mess when something goes wrong with God's intricate design—unnecessarily intricate, thought Snow, whenever he contemplated the long and dreary hours he had spent studying anatomy and physiology. There was little elegance to it, he decided in those tired hours. An evolved patchwork. A Rube Goldberg contraption. Nothing straight or straightforward. Everything winding around or through everything else. The true wonder was that the damned thing worked at all. Why should an egg, newly erupted, newly penetrated, leap the gap to the entrance and wind its way down the Fallopian tube before nesting? Why not homestead en route, as it had in this case.

Afterward they took the woman to post-op with IV drips in and catheters out and Snow walked over to the lounge in the residence. Ann was waiting for him curled in a big chair, book in her lap.

His small, dreary room had a single bed. "It's a single bed," she had said the first time they tried this.

"Yeah, it's not too bad."

"No. I mean really single. I didn't think they made them this small anymore."

They had spent the night together in a bed this small in the past. But that had been a time when they might lie awake in each other's arms, astonished at their circumstance, commenting on the cool when they were cool, the heat when they were hot, and when either slept the other asked, "Did you sleep?"

"Uh-huh."

"Me, too." As if talking about a small gift they shared, unnecessary but sweet.

Now he was exhausted and she was aware the morning would be coming quickly when she would lose him to the hospital, six a.m., seven a.m., dressed in his whites, no longer listening to her, anxious and full of dread, and she would quickly, furtively use the shared bathroom, which could not be locked from the inside, pack her case and sneak down the back stairs, passing a few residents or interns who might look knowingly at her.

"Did you call your mother today?"

"Yeah, I talked with her."

"And?"

"She's holding her own."

There was a private party in a room down the corridor from which filtered waves of laughter and Jim Morrison's voice promising to light their fire, take them higher. The single radiator made the room hot and dry. It could not be controlled individually so they had to leave the window open a couple of inches, and because of this they were sometimes hot and sometimes cold, but they didn't whisper about it as they once had. With the window open they could hear the late trucks and cars

191

on Bathurst Street, and sometimes a siren growing louder as it raced for the building next to theirs. The small bed was hard and they slept very little. Twice he was called from the ward and once he had to dress, leave her, walk through the tunnel to the main building, reestablish the drip on the woman in post-op, worry about her, check her blood pressure, her urine output, her temperature, and then come back to their shared bedroom, undressing, lying on the edge of the bed on his back, trying not to disturb her, watching the shadows play on the ceiling until the hospital called again.

"God, that was awful," she said in the morning.

"I'll get to the apartment Monday night six or seven."

"Robert, I can't get any sleep here. I won't be worth a damn at school."

"Yeah, I guess we shouldn't try it again."

They had made love, sometime in the night, when the room was cool, but half his mind was waiting for the phone to ring, the bed was too short and very noisy, Trebilcock snoring in the room next door, and she had told him how awkward she felt there, like a whore brought to the front for a soldier to fuck between battles, a comfort woman. It's not like that, he told her, but he knew that without the sex, two people of any persuasion, any relationship, would feel crowded sharing this room and this bed.

Something was unsaid, unfinished between them in the morning, but the hospital was beckoning impatiently and she was steeling herself for the lonely trip from the room to the sidewalk, and then to the trolley and subway to their equally lonely apartment, before she could escape to her interesting and happy friends at the school.

"Trebilcock, what the fuck are you doing out there?"

"Shit, man, get your ass back in here. We gotta close the

192

window."

"So close it."

"C'mon, man. It can't be that bad."

"How much Purple Jesus did you drink? How much did he have, anybody know?"

"C'mon back in. We'll go have a talk or something."

"It's only the second floor, Philip, you'll just break a few bones."

"Not if I go headfirst."

"That's true, but they say it's awful hard to do."

"Who's on call for psych?"

"He doesn't need psych. Silly bastard just needs his ass kicked."

"C'mon, you're spoiling the party."

Snow got close enough to see Trebilcock just out of reach on the ledge, sitting there in his whites above the parking lot, hands held under his arms, face as pale as his jacket.

"It's too cold to be doing this, man."

"Ah, leave him out there. He'll come in eventually."

"Hey, Trebilcock, we're gonna close the window partway. Any time you wanna come in just knock on the glass, okay?"

Trebilcock eventually came off the ledge. The Purple Jesus made the whole thing pretty hazy in Snow's mind. He remembered the Great Dane having something to do with getting him back in. And he remembered dancing with Pauline, who had come off emergency shift at eleven. Pauline was taut, firm, in control, sober. Snow was sloppy and drunk. He wanted to tell her about his mother and take her to his room. There was, he recognized belatedly, something very erotic within this woman, behind her glasses, in her soul. He learned she had a small apartment not far from the hospital and then took himself to bed with some new fantasies to sustain himself through those lonely few minutes in his barren room, the clock ticking, the shadow of the hospital pressing against his window, before he fell into a few hours of bliss unconsciousness.

ROBERT SNOW WAS reading the newspaper in the lounge when he was paged and told to come to the medical director's office. General Westmoreland was quoted as saying, when asked about the Tet offensive, that the Communists' "well-laid plans went afoul." Bullshit, thought Snow, it's coming apart, can't you see it? The Viet Cong blasting a hole in the American Embassy in Saigon, armies in disarray, the sacking of the ancient city of Hue. A photographer catching the moment of impact when the Saigon chief of police shoots a man about Snow's age in the side of the head. Summary execution. That's when he was called to the medical director's office, while reading about summary execution.

The U.S. had shifted its bombing targets from North Vietnam to Laos, a soft four-letter word, difficult for a Western tongue to pronounce without making it sound like a small parasite, but conjuring images of an ancient kingdom, little kings, tiled castles, bamboo huts, rice paddies nestled in warm and humid jungles. Boom. The dropping of bombs.

Snow had no idea why he was being called up this time. The first time had not been a surprise. You don't tell the chief of urology to shove his urinalysis up his ass, even through a third party, and expect the universe to proceed on course. But he had no idea this time what it might be about, except the frightening possibility some news had been received from home about his mother, or father, or Ann for that matter, that someone had deemed, in an unusual convulsion of sensitivity, that someone had thought should be broken to him in privacy by the kind and caring medical director, father figure to them all.

The office was the same as before, and the gray-haired man behind the desk was the same, and again Robert was not asked to sit and so he stood, waiting, while the director signed his name to a few more papers.

When the director finally looked up at Snow he said, "I understand you had a woman in your room a few nights ago."

Snow was about to deny the accusation, thinking about the many times he thought about getting a nurse to his room, most recently Pauline, his halfhearted, ambivalent attempts on a couple of Friday nights, his complete failure in the seduction department, and how he knew he must be confused with one of the other guys who got laid quite regularly. And then he realized the director was talking about Ann.

"Do you mean Ann?"

"I don't know her name."

"Ann. My wife. She spent a night with me last week, and a month ago."

"Those rooms are for single occupancy, Dr. Snow."

"Well, yeah. You couldn't fit two midgets in them. We've got an apartment downtown."

"But she did spend the night with you?"

"She's my wife, for God's sake. We're married."

"That's the very point, Dr. Snow. Those are not married quarters."

"You're worried about my wife spending one night a month with me?"

"It's very bad for morale."

"It's not bad for my morale."

"For the others who spend so many nights here alone, who live here."

"You're worried about my wife sleeping over a couple of nights, and what you've got there is the biggest brothel in Toronto?" His voice, he noticed, was growing shrill, uncontrolled, whiny, in comparison to the medical director, in complete and utter control of his game.

"I don't know what you're talking about."

"There's a lot of fucking going on over there. Nurses in and out all night long. And Ann and I are married, for God's sake."

"Dr. Snow, I don't countenance that kind of language!"

"Okay, but I still don't understand."

"You've been in my office once before, Dr. Snow."

"Yeah."

"The warning still holds. I don't want to see you here a third time."

"Yeah."

"No more conjugal visits, Dr. Snow. You can close the door on your way out."

"It didn't work out very well, anyway."

"What was that?"

"Nothing."

Snow was on his way out when he felt a sudden need to defend Ann's honor. With one hand on the doorknob he turned and blurted: "There's war going on, the world's fucking falling apart, kids are dying, and you're upset with one good woman spending a night with her husband in your precious residence."

"Dr. Snow!"

The director's secretary didn't look up as Snow quickly walked out of the office, before he said any more, before he found himself driving taxi.

He steamed about it on his way to the lounge. They were making love in Haight-Ashbury at the time, lots of it according to the newspapers, maybe fucking right there in the Avalon ballroom, strung out on acid, flying with the Jefferson Airplane, the Grateful Dead, Janis Joplin. He wished upon the medical director that his children might drop out and migrate to Haight-Ashbury, or at least Yorkville, or Fourth Avenue in Vancouver, smoke dope and engage in fucking. Christ. The peace talks in Paris had broken down again and Lyndon Johnson had said American offers had gone "as far as honorable men could go." He had given Westy a few more troops to push the total to just over half a million. Half a million boy soldiers lost in the jungles. And the medical director had time to worry about conjugal coupling in the interns' residence. He didn't want Snow curled in his wife's arms, at least not on his time, in his hospital. It's a wonder he hadn't given him a pack of condoms and told him to find a bar girl down the street.

There was a time, Snow knew, that the all-male interns and residents were not allowed to be married until they finished their apprenticeship, their servitude. Was it a belief that the dissipation of their sperm would be accompanied by an equal dissipation of their energy and intelligence? Where goeth the sperm goeth the brain? No. These were medical people. They understood that the sperm would be squandered one way or another, usually another, paying little heed to the admonitions of schoolmasters, scout leaders and medical directors. It probably had to do with babies—working a hundred and twenty hours a week, getting paid less than minimum wage and having babies. He wondered if he should go back and tell the medical director about the pill—which had recently been invented and was changing life as we know it. For one thing, very few parents would be producing such a surplus of boys that they would willingly donate a few of them to the General Westmorelands of the world. For another, the medical director would soon have to contend with more and more female interns. Silly fucking bastard. Worst part of it was, thought Snow, he'd still be angry when his chance came to get three hours sleep. Vengeful insomnia.

"Harvey, would you believe it? I was just given shit for having Ann stay over one night in my room."

"By whom?"

"Grant."

"Ah."

"What's ah?"

"We're slaves here, Snow, slaves. Time you accepted it."

"I can't believe this shit. It doesn't make sense."

"Did you ever read that contract you signed, Dr. Snow?"

"No."

"The fine print says they can do what they want with you, work you around the clock, say who you fuck and don't fuck and summarily dismiss you at their pleasure. I believe the exact wording is 'without cause'."

"I guess I should have read it."

"You'd have still signed it, Snow, you'd have still signed it."

"HAVE YOU BEEN drinking?"

"Just one or two. I'm entitled to one or two at my age."

"Sure."

"Tom was here. He has to go for liver tests."

"Is he sick?"

"He doesn't look good, Robert. I think it's caught up with him."

"I'm sure it'll be all right."

"He's lost a lot of weight, Robert. But he hasn't been drinking. He says he has no taste for it anymore. Alcohol makes him nauseous. At least that's good."

That's probably bad, thought Robert, as he hung up. A very bad sign.

CHAPTER FOURTEEN

There must be some kind of way out of here
Said the joker to the thief
There's too much confusion—
I can't get no relief

— BOB DYLAN

S NOW LEARNED A few Italian words. *Parole italiane. Dove* was one. His favorite phrase hitchhiking through Europe in his late teens had been, *"Dove la strada per Roma?"* Now he had to add the word *dolore*. It was far more expressive than *pain*. You could roll it on your tongue, stretch it out, make it sound agonizing, sharp, or dull, deep, intense, even sympathetic. *Dove dolore?* Which translates as, "Where pain?" *Dove il dolore? Teste? Stomico? Petto? Qui?* The rest could be accomplished with signing, about which the world knows Italians are not shy. Except for morto, as in I'm a *morto*, to which Snow always replied, No, *non*, no.

And blood: *sangue, mucho sangue, sangue pressione,* and crazy: *matto, pazzo.* Someone once observed that a wonderful uncomplicated friendship could develop between two people who spoke only a few phrases of the other's language. It's true. It's true, thought Snow. No nuances, no subtext, no irony. *Dove dolore? Qui. Qui? Si, dottore, mucho dolore.* Okay, I make better, *migliore. Migliore?* Better, *bene, bene. Grazie, dottore. Grazie, grazie.* This accompanied by much two-hand shaking and shoulder grasping.

199

The entire family brought Papa in one Sunday night. Eight or ten of them. They had been eating dinner, *il padre* at the head, Mama up and running about, serving, making sure everybody had more than enough, three generations at the table, heaping plates of pasta, roasted veal and pork, oil, breads and homemade wine. Talking incessantly, telling Mama to sit and eat, discussing the nuances of the veal, the pasta, the pork, Papa insisting the son-in-law have some grappa, another helping, the dinner table a magnet, a celebration, an offering. Robert always pictured these scenes with great envy, contrasting them to his own family Sunday dinners, the tension rising with each clank of fork on plate, the overcooked roast, or shepherd's pie, bowl of boiled onions, glasses of milk, no alcohol, his mother angry at something already, his father at the head of the table, sharpening the carving knife, finding the roast too pink, or tough, commenting on this, his mother slamming the next dish down with unnecessary force.

Snow could easily, perhaps fancifully, picture the lushness of this Italian family dinner, and he had to ask for every detail because the whole family, all talking at the same time, hovering around *loro padre, loro nono*, in the hospital corridor, were telling Snow that in the middle of the first course— "No, he'd finished his pasta," "He hardly touched a thing," "That's not true, he was filling his wine glass," "No, *dottore, uno, due, soltanto due*," "He was eating well, *mangiare bene*," "No, no, he no eat well, he work too hard"—somewhere in the middle of a perfectly normal Sunday dinner, Papa had gone crazy, *pazzo*.

Snow got the family settled in a waiting area and took Papa to an examining room. He was a healthy sixty-year-old, short, stocky, gray hair and a broad face. He had spent his Canadian life building, bricklaying, pouring concrete. He had come to Toronto after the war and had built foundations, for buildings

and for *famiglia*. He talked to Snow, and muttered to himself—
mangiarsi le parole, his wife said. His eyes were confused and
fearful. He was speaking in half sentences, none of it made
sense, something about the fireplace and the chimney, his
daughter told Snow. Snow examined *il padre* and found nothing
physically wrong. He questioned the family about his work,
alcohol, toxicities, family history of insanity. His neurological
examination was, as the jargon goes, unremarkable. He called
the neurology resident. The neurology resident, an Anglo, a
tall, elegant, clean man of thirty or so, went over Papa with his
ophthalmoscope, his little hammer, pins and tuning fork, and
pronounced the problem psychiatric.

"But it doesn't happen that way," said Snow.

"What doesn't?"

"A psychiatric disorder. It doesn't just happen suddenly in
the middle of dinner."

"There is nothing neurologically wrong with this man," said
the resident as he stalked out. "Call psychiatry."

Snow called in the psychiatry resident. It took a while. Joe
Berkowitz had to come in from his pad on Dundas. Bushy
beard, hair a little longer each time Snow saw him, granny
glasses, as they were being called, on his nose, moderate bell-
bottoms, sandals, leather jerkin. He must have appeared to
il padre as someone who wandered in off the street, but then
il padre was already quite confused. If he was put out coming
in he didn't show it, having already acquired the mask of
aloofness most of the shrinks wore. Snow told him the story
and together they stood and watched Papa, who was still sitting in a chair in the examining room, now in the gown and
slippers the nurses had provided, and still talking, sometimes
to them or at them, and sometimes to himself, or an imagined
friend, or to God. Berkowitz pulled on his beard. It was no use
bringing family members in to translate, Snow explained,

they just got very upset and cried, *pazzo, pazzo, papa, nono, nono.*

Snow added, "There is one thing."

"What's that?"

"When he talks, he only talks with one hand."

They examined his arms and hands again, finger squeezing, muscle strength, pins for sensitivity, little hammer for reflexes. There was no difference. They could convince themselves there was a difference between his right and his left but there really wasn't any.

"See, he only talks with his left hand."

"Is he left-handed?" Berkowitz asked.

"No. He's right-handed. I checked. Besides, Italians talk with both hands."

"There are hard signs and soft signs. This is very soft." He cleaned his granny glasses on his shirt.

"But you agree it's not psychiatric?"

"Neurology doesn't want him?"

"The resident said to call psychiatry."

"I could ask the chief of service to take a look."

So later that night the head of the neurology department arrived. He was obviously put out, called in on a Sunday night, and disdainful of the whole procedure. He, too, applied his little hammer and pins to Papa and then, before straightening up, made his pronouncement: psychiatric. That which we do not understand is psychiatric. It seemed to Snow to be a rather simple pattern of reasoning.

Reluctantly they admitted Papa to the psychiatry ward.

THREE WEEKS LATER Snow attended a Grand Rounds presented by the Department of Neurology in the amphitheater of the hospital. The subject was Papa: Seignor Brazziani, a sixty-year-old Italian male—diagnostic problem.

Ann had called to tell him Robert Kennedy had declared his

candidacy for the presidency. He told her he saw it on the TV in the lounge. Maybe it'll all stop, Robert. Maybe this craziness will end. Maybe we've all got another chance. Robert wasn't so sure you should pin so much hope on one person, so many expectations. Pierre Elliott Trudeau photographed in swimming trunks executing a nice dive, the new messenger for Canada. Longish hair, arrogant, in-your-face. The times they are a-changing. Oddly, Canada seemed to be embracing these changes, whatever they really were, while the Americans were fighting among themselves, divided, destroying themselves. And the North Vietnamese, after trying and trying again, managed to shoot down an F-111. Robert pictured it: fifteen hundred miles per hour over rice paddies and bamboo villages. What a shock it must have been.

In their weekly phone call his mother told Robert that Tom had gone back to drinking. He'd lost his job at the car-parts place. He was skin and bones. But he'd teamed up with an old buddy, another musician-alcoholic, alcoholic musician, Bunk McEwen, and they were playing together at the Douglas Hotel. And Grandmother? What could you say about Grandmother? She's got Tom to run now, she's leaving me alone. Have you heard from your father? No, why do you ask? asked Robert. No reason, said his mother.

The neurology rounds were delivered in English to an English-speaking audience. "A sixty-year-old Italian male was admitted to the psychiatry ward on such-and-such a date after presenting in the emergency department in an acute confusional state." Snow, in the audience, thought that the word "presented" was not an adequate parole for the large family milling about in the corridor, all talking at once. But even with the simplicity of the language there were nuances and subtexts in the presentation, to the effect that, as usual, at least as Snow heard it, interns, residents and psychiatrists had all screwed up. They had missed an obvious neurological problem and admitted this poor man to the psychiatry ward, where he languished in bed for two weeks surrounded by crazy people, until his symptoms were so blatant, so severe even the cleaning staff might notice them. Belatedly, the Department of Neurology had been called in. He was now on their ward being properly diagnosed and cared for. Their diagnosis: an infarct or a blood clot or a small hemorrhage in the midbrain, perhaps the caudate or lentiform nucleus, the real centers of movement, coordination, communication, over which the cortex, some centuries ago, had laid language skills with all possible nuances and subtexts. Most of the discussion that followed centered on the question of which specific parts of the midbrain might be affected and which might not.

Snow went up to see Papa and wished afterward he hadn't. Papa was twenty pounds lighter now, lying in a bed with the railings up. He was writhing, like Woody Guthrie must have, in choreoathetotic gestures of despair and bewilderment, neither beseeching nor lashing out, simply flailing in his bonds. His eyes held even more confusion and fear than before. And somehow it wasn't just the disease that was so terrible, the vascular accident in the middle of his brain, it was also the room, the railinged bed, the gown, the whiteness of it all, the isolation within the hospital machinery. Images of this, Papa struggling in his white gown, laced to the bed railings, white on white, and of the last lush, colorful, noisy family dinner collided in Snow's head. Fifteen hundred miles per hour. Tons of steel landing on a bamboo hut, the family sitting around the fire, rice bowls in hand. Boom. Snow never learned whether Papa died, recovered, stayed the same. He never saw the family again. Fifteen hundred miles per hour.

So they danced and drank on Friday night. Beer for Communion. Purple Jesus for amnesia.

PAPA MAY HAVE recovered. It's possible. The fat woman had. Dorothy, Dot for short. Snow was on emergency the night they brought her in, unconscious, in a party dress, her hair colored and coifed, lips and nails brightly painted, laid out on a gurney. Rings, necklaces, dancing shoes. They had to intubate her and breathe for her. Put her on the BIRD. Intravenous, life support. All this while she was still lying on the emergency room gurney. Still in her party dress, all two hundred fifty to three hundred pounds of her. And when one of her arteries had decided to either leak or clot in the middle of her brain, while she was pounding out a polka on the old Heintzman upright, her sphincters had relaxed. She and her party dress were lying in a pool of feces and urine. Shit and piss. Surprising amounts of excretory matter. Her heart quit, too, after the insult to her brain, so Snow and Pauline took turns up on top, pumping. Thud, push, down, harder, one, two, squoosh, splash, breathe. One, two. She didn't have a chance. Not a chance. Arrest team arriving.

"Oh, shit."

"You said it."

"Can't we move her?"

"No way."

"Get her dress off, at least."

"You gotta be kidding."

"Jesus Christ. This is hopeless."

"Remember your mother telling you about wearing clean underwear in case."

"Shut up, Harvey."

"All right. Everybody stand back. On the count of one." Thud. "Again, everybody back." Thud.

"Oh, Christ. It's on everything."

Dorothy had been a piano player and the life of every party she attended. When she woke up on one of the medical wards a few days later she couldn't speak, she couldn't talk. But she could smile and wink, which she did. And as she gradually regained her speech and her hand movements, she laughed and joked and flirted as if her midbrain infarct had been but a minor inconvenience to her, like breaking the heel of her shoe. She insisted her hair and nails be done so that she might look her best for gentlemen callers. And there were a few, in relationships Robert could not decipher. Friends? Lovers? Agents? She continued to have trouble with some words, but she worked at them, and sat up on her own, and then moved to a chair with help, and then to an aluminum walker, which she named Sam. She could lean on Sam. She could depend on Sam, she told Robert. And one day when Sam bored her she could divorce him. She had every intention of regaining her old life, and she probably did, against all odds. Dorothy, Dot. A whole different species than his mother. Perhaps the same genus as his grandmother.

So they danced and drank on Friday night. And told one another stories of failures, mistakes, disasters and miracles.

EVERYTHING THAT HAD not been eaten during the day, for breakfast, lunch and dinner, was available to the interns and residents free of charge from eleven until midnight. The leftovers. They ate mounds of food and still lost weight. The roast beef left over from dinner, the corned beef from lunch, a drink called Honeydew from breakfast, untitled casseroles dreamed up by nutritionists: noodles, process cheese, tuna flakes, parsley, canned peas, a sprinkling of peanuts, even a scoop of peanut butter for extra protein. Residual corned beef was the favorite; it kept well, could be drowned in mustard. Tuna noodle casserole the least favorite. It aged badly, dried at the edges and held little promise to begin with. They often missed breakfast, lunch or supper and thus were perpetually hungry, and dehydrated, by the evening. The kitchen staff filled their plates as they escaped from their duties and filed through the line, eleven till midnight. It was, Robert reflected, a cheap way to keep them, if not happy, at least tame. Throw food at them. He usually put three or four glasses of Honeydew on his tray, with bread, gravy and whatever meat might be left. They ate quickly and talked, shoveling the food in, one ear always tuned to the overhead speakers. Dr. Snow, 4785. Dr. Robinson, 3976. Code ten, Seven East.

They talked of how tired they were, how long they'd been up, how long standing in the operating room, about their interesting cases, and comic moments, too.

"Would you believe, this guy comes into the Emerge, he's got lacerations all over his penis. So I ask him, 'How did you get those?' And you know what he tells me?"

And, "You wouldn't believe what she had stuck in her vagina." For this the others at the table offered predictable suggestions: "Saunders's left index finger." "The Queen Mary." "The left tie rod from a 1927 Model A roadster." "A string of Mexican pleasure balls." "Those are for an entirely different orifice, you asshole." "Yeah? Tell me about it."

Snow had his own you-wouldn't-believe story. "You wouldn't believe, I'm on Emerge since eight in the morning and it's now three the next morning."

"Christ, I was on forty-eight hours once."

"Maybe it was since eight the previous morning. Anyhow it's three in the morning and I'm getting a couple minutes snooze in the big chair down there when this guy walks in, registers and asks to see the doctor. So Pauline wakes me up, tells me I've got a patient in room seven."

"Hm, Pauline."

"She can wake me up anytime."

"So I go down to seven and you know what this guy wants? He wants his ears cleaned. He usually gets his family doctor to do it but he just happened to be driving past the hospital at three in the morning and thought he'd drop in and have it done, not bother the family doctor this time."

"So, whadya do?"

"I cleaned his ears."

"Ah, man."

Snow didn't tell them about the sleep-deprived fantasies he had while holding a basin in one hand and a large syringe of warm water in the other. Acting upon them would have brought about a third trip to the director's office, and perhaps a coroner's inquest.

And they talked seriously about diagnostic puzzles, the latest technology, finding rare diseases, known as canaries, being a kind of linguistic slippage from *rare* and *rare bird*. Common things are commonest, they were told in medical school, as indeed they are, but their commonness left them less interesting than canaries. Which may have been one of the reasons they didn't talk about death and suffering and fear. But not, of course, the only reason.

Snow had his own canary to talk about. "This black guy comes in with a pain in the left side of his abdomen, a long way away from appendix, or stomach, or where the bowel usually hurts. And we didn't find anything, not a thing."

"Renal cyst."

"He said in the side, not the back."

"So?"

"Let him finish."

"Ryan wants to send him home, says it's hysterical, you know these island people, somatize all over the place. But I tell him I don't think so, the guy's a graduate student, and there's something about the way he talks about the pain. Different from the way hysterics talk about pain." Halfway through the telling Snow realized the point of this anecdote was to make himself look good, so he quickly altered his story here and there. "Well, I haven't the slightest idea what's going on so Ryan admits him and tries a few more X rays and finds a swollen spleen. The guy's too healthy for a major blood disorder, and he's not a football player, so we're no further ahead. What they eventually find is parasites. The guy's spleen is full of parasites, some kind of little worms from the Caribbean."

There was a woman intern at the table. She blithely named the parasite. The others raised their eyebrows and ignored her.

"I knew there was a reason I wasn't taking a three-week holiday in Bermuda this year, had to be something, couldn't simply be the fact I'm in debt up to my eyeballs."

"Since when does anybody get three weeks?"

AND NEAR MISSES. They were fond of near misses. He could imagine air traffic controllers on their coffee break doing the same: so there I am, watching four screens, one big sucker coming in for a routine landing, me dozing off, slipping into dreamland, when out of the corner of my eye I catch this blip, blip, blip coming in fast at ten o'clock, I swear to God, the guy thinks he's landing at Da Nang.

Snow told this story: Maybe I got two hours sleep in the last thirty-six, and I'm finally back in bed and out cold at five in the morning. Six o'clock and I'm somewhere between level four and coma. The phone rings. The hand reaches out and gets it to my ear but I'm still only responding to pain. A voice says, Dr. Snow, do you want Mrs. Sarcovich to have her insulin this morning? You didn't cancel the order. It makes no sense to me, this question, but then dreams don't have to make sense, so I

209

say sure and hang up. A half hour later the same nurse calls back. She says, Are you sure you want Mrs. Sarcovich to have her insulin? So I figure it must be a trick question and I say wait a minute and get up and splash cold water on my face and think about it for a minute. Then I pick up the phone and ask if by any chance Mrs. Sarcovich is having an operation today. Nurse says, bland as zucchini, she's booked for a total hysterectomy at eight. Well, then, I think we better hold the insulin, hadn't we. Yes, doctor. And he wondered had he said, Yeah, I'm sure, for whatever reason one might say, Yeah, I'm sure, some of them having nothing to do with certainty, had he said this, would she have injected Mrs. Sarcovich with insulin, Mrs. Sarcovich who would get no nourishment until very late in the day, Mrs. Sarcovich who would go into hypoglycemic shock on the table?

Sandy said, "The anesthetist would have picked it up."

Trebilcock, coming in late, said, "Like shit. They never read the chart."

"Sure they do, the night before, they have to."

Trebilcock, his mouth full: "You're all fucking naive. You're all babes in the woods."

And then a cardiac arrest call on the overhead, and Trebilcock saying shit, spilling his Honeydew, knocking his chair over, rushing off.

"What the hell's got into him?"

"He just needs some sleep."

"Sleep? What the fuck is sleep?"

WHEN HE CALLED Ann before midnight she told him Lyndon Johnson had announced he would not run again. He'd thrown in the towel.

"Must have been that peace march we were on. The final straw. Pushed him over the top."

"Robert, be serious. This is important. It means there's a chance McCarthy or Kennedy might get in."

Dorothy had been a miracle, given and taken a second chance. His mother was still out of hospital, Tom playing his horn in the Douglas Hotel.

"I should get home by noon on Saturday," he said. "Maybe this would be a good weekend to see Niagara."

CHAPTER FIFTEEN

I heard the roar of a thunder—it roared out a warning
Heard the roar of a wave that could drown the whole world
Heard one hundred drummers whose hands were a-blazing
Heard ten thousand whispering, and nobody listening
Heard the song of a poet who died in a gutter
Heard the sound of a clown that cried in the alley
Heard the sound of one person who cried he was human
And it's a hard, it's a hard, it's a hard, it's a hard,
    it's a hard rain gonna fall.

                    — BOB DYLAN

KIDS WERE ALWAYS cutting themselves. Infants, crawlers, toddlers, children, latency-age children, as they had been called in his child-development classes, as if they were going through a dormant phase. Who dreams up these titles? When they cut themselves they were brought to the emergency ward. For infants, crawlers, toddlers and young children this was the standard technique: they were adequately undressed to expose the cut, held on a surgical table, examined by the doctor who would ask for the appropriate cleansing equipment, needles and thread. They were told this won't hurt at all, or almost not at all, and be over in a minute, and then they were bundled. Bundled meant quickly wrapped in a cotton sheet, all unaffected appendages pinned to the body, nurse's body over the kid holding the kid down, nurse saying make it quick, willya. Parents in the waiting room, the kid screaming its head off, fighting every inch of the way, Dr. Snow would sew. And the prevailing wisdom was that cuts on little girls' faces should be sutured with tiny thread and great care, while it mattered not at all with boys.

Robert tried it another way. He told the kid this is going to hurt. He showed the needle and thread to the kid. He had the kid watch him. He talked the kid through it. He told the nurse to forget the bundling and just hold the kid's hand. "Are you sure?"

"No. But let's try it this way, huh?"

It worked a few times, and Robert liked it much better: the child not screaming, instead asking questions, curious, trusting, being brave. But the nurses waited him out, standing there with big white sheets in hand. He failed with one wounded little boy who screamed for his mama. "I told you so," said the nurses. "I told you so." And, "You've really got him worked up now."

Like most great medical advances: inconclusive results. All right, bundle the kid, let's get it over with. His overwrought sensitivity, idealism, was no match for the way, as in, this is the way it's done, the way we've always done it.

ONE MID-MORNING, AFTER rounds, after a coffee, during a lull, the ambulance brought in an eight-year-old girl, quickly, quietly, and the nurses and doctors, including Robert, quickly gathered around her. They breathed for her. They pounded her chest. They put needles in her. They pounded her chest again. The arrest team came and did it all over again. They paced and rubbed their eyes and looked at tracings over and over again, wishing them to change, as if they might have missed something the first time and the second time, until Harvey Ryan finally called it. Snow had been the one trying to find a vein in the girl's foot. When the equipment was packed away and they had left the room, and somebody, not Snow this time, went to talk with the parents, he stayed to take a final look at the child.

A dead child does not look the same as a dead adult. You would think it would, only smaller, but it doesn't. Snow had a need to look carefully in order to believe what he was seeing.

This child appeared to be sleeping. She looked like she was sleeping, on her back, partially covered with a sheet. A dead adult looks dead. A child appears to be sleeping, or at least that was the only way Snow's eyes would let him see her.

HE AND ANN took the promised weekend to visit the winter Niagara Falls. He rented a car and they drove to the cold bleak town. They walked through the tunnels to the lower levels where they could watch the ice chunks growing and dissolving, torrents of emerald froth, crystals in the air, an inhospitable roar. The cold cut through his coat and reminded him of other nights, other winters. A wet cold that paid little heed to any clothing.

They drove to the American side in search of a steak, known by rumor to be better, always better than a Canadian steak. The flags were out, on the porches, in front of buildings, the flags of a nation at war. The Canadian side had been carnival, pure American glitz and glitter, or at least winter remnants of it. The American side was a timeless Norman Rockwell illustration. They have the power and the money, thought Snow, thinking of what he'd read of Saigon, to make whores of us all, and pretend innocence for themselves. But he wasn't above eating one of their T-bones.

They found a restaurant entrenched in 1949, after World War Two and before Korea, the new fascination with shiny plastic, Naugahyde, Formica, chrome, cavelike curves where the chandeliered ceiling met the wall. The steaks were good, and the baked potatoes, which someone had recently decided always needed sour cream and bacon bits as well as butter.

"You know," he said, "it was asthma. That's all it was, asthma."

"What was?"

"What killed this kid yesterday."

"A child?"

"Uh-huh. Eight years old."

"Don't tell me about it, Robert, please."

The waitress, the timeless waitress—mid-forties, thin, curling bottle-blond hair, too much rouge and lipstick—served the red wine chilled. He tried warming it over the candle and only succeeded in blackening the carafe.

Well, he hadn't started that conversation very well. It had become increasingly hard to talk about his work, the hospital, a possessive bitch, that hospital. When he entered it the shutters closed, absorbing him, using him, filling his heart and every conceivable space in his brain. But what else could he talk about when his entire perceptual apparatus was focused on the hospital? The wine was poured, the candle lit. All right now, let's talk about disease, death, that kind of thing.

"Robert, I'm sorry. I don't like to hear about children, that's all."

"So how about this guy we got on the ward who lost his larynx to cancer and breathes through a little hole in his throat—right here—and you know what?"

"I hate to ask."

"He sticks cigarettes in the hole and smokes."

"Do I need to hear this stuff, Robert?"

"He won't give it up. Would you believe that?"

"Doesn't anything good happen?"

"That one's good."

"Just how is that good?"

"Demonstrates an indomitable spirit."

"And stupidity."

"Yeah, that too. And another man walks very slowly into the emergency department, white as a bedsheet, and says he can't climb three steps anymore. So I do the usual and get a hemoglobin of four point three. He should be dead or comatose, but he's sitting there talking to me. Turns out he has pernicious anemia, and I get my chance to look up the correct dose of vitamin B_{12}."

"Okay. I'll bite. How is that a good story?"

"Two ways. First it shows the body can adjust to anything given enough time. And second, it's completely treatable nowadays. Did I tell you my grandfather died of pernicious anemia?"

"Once or twice. How was your steak?"

"I guess I wolfed that down, didn't I?"

"D'ya know a couple of the kids at school get picked up by chauffeurs at lunch time?"

"Like real chauffeurs with limousines?'

"Uh-huh."

"They don't get to brown-bag it?"

"And I feel sorry for them."

"You feel sorry for them?"

"They're deprived, Robert."

"Deprived of what? Mickey Mouse lunch pails? Dry peanut butter sandwiches? Wet tomato sandwiches? Brown bananas?"

"I don't know. The whole lunch hour experience. I think it was the best part of school."

"You'll never be a revolutionary, Lara."

"And why is that, Yuri?"

"You have much too much sympathy for the ruling class."

"The children of the ruling class, Robert. The children. And wasn't Lara a bit of a whore?"

Avoiding that question and thinking of Julie Christie, Robert said, "Would you like some more wine before we find our own ice palace?" He felt better now. Warm. A little more wine might lick comfort into all his wounds.

THEY DROVE BACK to the Canadian side and found a cheap motel with king-size beds, avoiding the heart-shaped beds and heart-shaped whirlpool baths, and Snow refrained from over-explaining to the desk clerk. The carpet was worn, the floor of the bathroom cold, the air cigarette-fouled.

In the middle of the night he woke to find his face wet with tears. She sensed his restlessness and asked, "Are you all right?"

"Yeah, I'm all right."

PIERRE ELLIOTT TRUDEAU won the election and became Canada's prime minister. Wow. Style, wit, Gallic charm, brilliance, decisiveness, to lead a country of indecisive plodders. Ann loved the idea. A man comfortable in the world's capitals, who could thumb his nose at the Americans, a rake, a bon vivant, an intellectual representing Ann and Robert and all the other Canadian Anglos who felt cowed by American confidence, threatened by Asian deftness, alarmed by French sophistication, irritated by English superiority. Robert Kennedy had won a primary, Dubcek was hanging in, Robert's mother was better, his uncle was playing on Saturday nights, his father, it seemed, building a new life for himself, his brother still sending postcards, there weren't many months left in his internship. Ignore the Soviet troops massing on the border.

THEN TREBILCOCK LOST it during a cardiac arrest.

For a month they were on the team together, carrying beepers, Snow and Trebilcock, Snow a minor player attaching elec-

217

trodes, getting IVs started, Phil Trebilcock in charge, the team leader. There hadn't been many, Snow thanked God, for every time the phone rang or his pager went off, he jumped a good three inches. They hadn't done badly with the few in the middle of the night. For these they were alone, working, doing their best, just the team, the white room, small machines, the windows black, the city quiet, the arrested patient. Not that their record was very good. But when called they ran from all parts of the hospital, their adrenaline surging, the nursing group arriving with equipment, and did what they had been taught to do. There were only two possible outcomes: "All right. We've got sinus rhythm. Let's get her up to coronary care."

"Okay, people, let's call it. We've given it a good shot."

On the surface this arrest seemed the same as all the others, although the man was younger than most. What was different, Snow thought afterward, was the daylight, and the family. He was a Ukrainian man in his forties, a heavy, muscular man, and he was just being admitted that day, for investigation of a lump on his elbow. His wife was there with him, his children and his mother.

It was midafternoon when they got the call, dropped what they were doing and ran to the designated ward. The family had been herded out into the corridor while the ward staff thrashed around, someone up on top of the bed shouting get a board, someone get a board, someone else saying let's put him on the floor, an IV, get an IV in him for Christ's sake, what the hell happened, he was fine just a minute ago. The cardiac arrest team took over but the ward staff didn't leave. They milled about in the manner of witnesses to a road accident.

He had no veins. Everybody's got veins, but this man had no veins. Thick skin, fat and muscle. Unlike many of the dying, cancer-ridden patients they had jumped earlier that month.

Snow tried arms, hands, feet. The man was intubated, electrodes placed, sternum pumped. Snow found a vein in his right foot. They were tripping over one another. Clear out, said Trebilcock, but nobody did. He did not have a commanding presence. Bicarb. Cardioverter. Everybody off. Let's do it. Whap. What have we got? What have we got? Nothing. Still flat. Shit. Clear out. Everybody clear out. Let's go again. On the count of one. Whap. There are too many people in here. I can't see the goddamn monitor.

Snow considered afterward why nobody left. It was a small, single room to begin with, now filled with machines, poles, bottles, white jackets, green scrub suits, nurses, aides, interns. They were in shock, having just admitted this healthy man, talked with him, learned about him, met his family. And that was probably the other reason: the family in the corridor, hovering at the door, one of them wailing, the wife clutching at anyone leaving the room.

So they were all there when Trebilcock shocked him a third time and his body arched up and fell back. And they were all there when Trebilcock couldn't pump any longer and Snow took over up on the bed, precariously straddling the large naked man, and they were all there when Trebilcock tried an injection of adrenaline directly into the heart. Nothing.

How are his pupils? Fixed. One dilated. Let's keep going. Blood gases. Get his blood gases. The collapsed rubbery femoral artery evaded Snow's needle.

"How much time now?"

"Twelve minutes."

"Shit. More bicarb. Give him ten more. We gotta have blood gases. Lemme try."

"We're not seeing any pulse."

"Harder on the sternum. Don't worry about ribs."

"Anything yet?"

"Nothing."

"Pupils?"

"Fixed and dilated."

Fifteen minutes. Twenty minutes. Twenty-five minutes. They took turns squeezing the air bag and pumping on his sternum.

"His pupils are dilated and fixed, Phil."

"Let's hit him one more time. Everybody off. On one." Whap. "Anything?"

"Nothing."

"Check the electrodes."

"Electrodes okay."

"Let's hit him again."

"Phil."

"On one." Whap.

"His pupils are fixed and dilated, Phil."

"Call it, Phil."

"It's my responsibility."

"You gotta call it, Phil. He's gone."

"I'll decide."

"We can't keep doing this. There's no point."

"Trebilcock. For God's sake."

Snow was bagging, squeezing air into the dead man's resisting lungs. Trebilcock was dithering, looking at the machines, checking the wires, the intravenous lines, the bottles, the tracings. He was sweating profusely. His face was red. The dead man's mother was keening, the regular staff still standing there in shock, someone repeating, he was fine just minutes ago, just minutes ago.

So Trebilcock couldn't call it. He couldn't bring himself to make the decision. Snow understood what was going through his mind. It was always possible. It was always possible one more minute would do it. It was always possible the pupils are sluggish, not fixed. It was always possible the readings are wrong, something not plugged in right. It was always possible they were getting enough oxygen into the man's brain that he would survive twenty minutes with a dead or fibrillating heart, and if twenty minutes, why not twenty-five, thirty, thirty-five.

When Harvey Ryan arrived he quickly cleared the room of all but the arrest team. He asked for the time, checked the man's pupils and called it. These were the words he used: "All right. Let's pack it in."

He asked the arrest team to clear out, as well, and leave him alone with Trebilcock, which they did. But when Snow was almost at the door, the last out, Ryan said, "Robert."

"Yeah."

"Talk to the family. Take them somewhere and talk with them."

ROBERT SPOKE WITH the family of the Ukrainian man. He herded them into a waiting room and asked someone else to leave. He told them their son/husband/father was gone. The children didn't understand. One asked to see him. The youngest asked when he was coming back. And Snow stood there shaking his head, the mother weeping and keening, the wife beseeching him, hearing himself muttering those empty words, Did all we could, he didn't suffer, it was his heart, I don't know, I don't know, I don't know. He watched their disbelief. He watched them recoil. He watched them fight with him, plead with him, beseech him. He watched them weep. And he stood in the center of it all, helpless.

"I will see him. I will see him," said the wife.

"I will show him to you," said Snow.

ALWAYS, THE MEDICAL director had told them during their orientation eight months before, always ask permission for a postmortem examination. And always the chief of service's first question would be, "Did you get permission for an autopsy?" The hospital wanted first cut.

Snow didn't ask this family. He couldn't bring himself to do it. It felt like shit on his tongue.

The coroner might order one anyhow. He could tell them that. It still felt like shit on his tongue.

HE LEAD THE wife across the hall to see her husband. Harvey was coming out with Trebilcock. Harvey asked, "Where you going?"

"Taking her to see her husband."

He motioned Snow aside for a moment while the woman stood frozen before the door. He said, "It's not a good idea." But Snow went ahead anyway.

In the room she threw herself across his body and cried and asked over and over again, Why he did this, eh? Why? Why?

In the bathroom of his room Robert washed his hands. He noticed her husband's blood on his sleeve. Then he went looking for Pauline, to share a coffee with her, to hold the warm cup in his hands, to watch her eyes and receive her smile.

ANDREW JACKSON, SNOW remembered from a *Life* magazine, or *National Geographic*, named Memphis after an ancient Egyptian city. Cotton mills on the ponderous Mississippi, birthplace of the blues and home to Elvis Presley.

Martin Luther King was leaning over the balcony of the Lorraine Motel in Memphis talking to Jesse Jackson when the bullet killed him.

ROBERT SNOW WAS looking after infants, thousand-gram ones, fifteen hundred, two thousand, keeping them alive, little butterfly needles under their skin, blue babies, pink babies, yellow babies, brown babies, black babies. And older ones not growing fast enough, failing to thrive, thriving being the task and right of all. Kids with shaven heads, with cysts where they should have kidneys, with holes where they shouldn't have holes and no holes where they should have holes. Kids with livers that didn't work, arms, speech, bladders. Kids who couldn't breathe except in a mist-filled tent. Holding back the flood of nature's mistakes.

He still had the eight-year-old girl on his mind when he learned what happened in Memphis. They've done it again, he said to Ann. They've fucking done it again. And it seemed to him that nature didn't need any help in these matters. In the tide of mistakes, disasters, accidents. Ann cried, said she needed him home. Tomorrow night, he said, tomorrow night.

And now everyone felt the rage that James Earl Ray must have been nursing in his flophouse down the street.

Robert didn't know why King's death hit him so hard. He was white, privileged, Canadian, for God's sake. It had nothing to do with him. Nothing. Still, his eyes filled whenever he thought about it.

ON FRIDAY NIGHT they danced and drank.

Two Fridays later, breaking away from the hospital, he found a meeting in the lounge before the beer, the food, the music. The residents and interns were forming a union, an association. They had tried before and it had been scuttled in two ways. The senior residents had taken the lead, drafted documents, sent around applications, filed papers and then, come the end of June, left the hospitals to go to practices or staff positions. And those who were prepared to carry on were told such activities were incompatible with post-residency fellowships, or with surgical privileges at leading hospitals. In short, they were told to stop.

They had a new plan this time. Junior residents were to carry on the work, and a lawyer would be hired. They wanted the same lawyer who had organized the National Hockey League Players' Association. They said they had taken their employment contracts to this lawyer and he had laughed. The contract stated, as the medical director had twice reminded Snow, that the above-named intern or resident could be terminated at any time at the discretion of the hospital. Terminated. Wasted. No appeal. The bitch goddess could withdraw its meager love at any time.

All right. They couldn't live on the wages paid them. They couldn't support the families they seldom saw. They worked in feverish exhaustion. Snow had told the medical director, during one of his interviews, that things would change, "Someday things will change," he said, feeling, at the time, more like a whining child than a prophet. The medical director had looked mildly amused. He had said, "Rites of passage are very important."

Maybe so, maybe so. While the world unraveled, he signed petitions, applications, joined a subcommittee. Their careers might be threatened but, all in all, it was probably much safer than organizing sanitation workers in Memphis. They passed resolutions, elected chairs and vice-chairs and secretaries, and then they danced and drank.

SNOW HAD SEEN this alcoholic man earlier in the year. He was back, heavy mournful body slumped on a stool. He had been sober a few months and then fallen off the wagon. Just coming off a long binge. He was saying to Snow, "I'm really scared, doc. I can't remember things. I don't remember what I've just done. I start something and forget what I'm doing."

Snow, a very tired Snow, heard himself thoughtlessly ask question number two, the question always asked: "How long have you had this problem?"

And the drunk said, "What problem, doc?"

A wave of hopelessness hit Snow but then he slumped back in his chair and began to laugh. "I'm sorry," he said. And laughed some more.

His patient didn't seem to mind, even began to chuckle with Snow, as if a joke had been told that he hadn't quite understood.

"The trick," said Snow, "is forgetting what should be forgotten and remembering what should be remembered."

The drunk said, "Huh?"

"Never mind. Let's do this properly. I'm going to tell you five numbers. You memorize them and then in a few minutes I'll ask you what they are."

He was actually thinking about the damage alcohol had done to this man when his mother phoned to tell him Tom had died quite suddenly. Admitted to the hospital for investigation, possible cancer of the bone, of the spinal column. Four days later he had gone into seizures and died. The doctors said the cancer had spread to his brain. And Robert, two thousand miles away, knew clearly what had happened. Four days. An alcoholic, abruptly denied alcohol, four days later going into DTs, trace elements, electrolytes thrown off balance, agitation, hallucinations, delirium, then seizures. Some stupid goddamn intern missing it, not asking, not taking a full history, maybe not knowing how dangerous DTs is. He didn't tell his mother this. Said instead, If he had cancer that bad it's the best way to go. I mean quickly. She said, I know, I know. And talked of arrangements, her nephews and niece, his grandmother. How's Grandmother taking it, Robert asked. You know your grandmother, she said. She's playing the role to the hilt. She's in her element. The grieving mother.

In Emergency, during a lull, he talked to Pauline about it.

She concurred with his diagnosis. It wasn't metastasis to the brain, she said. It just doesn't happen that fast. Then she asked, "What did he mean to you?"

He said, "I don't know. I didn't really know him. But for a long time he was the artist in the family, the one who escaped, who got free, I guess. A romantic figure. But I guess he never really made it."

"No one makes it forever," she said. "No one."

THE FEMUR BREAKS and then they fall down. This bone juts in at a precarious angle before forming the ball that fits into the socket of the hip. They tell the doctors that they slipped and fell and must have landed on the hip and broken it. The doctors know the bone breaks and then they fall. A weak link in God's design. Older women, osteoporosis thinning their bones. They came in on stretchers, one set of toes pointing the wrong way, and then lay in beds on the ward awaiting decisions about surgery. Is there enough bone left to cobble it together with steel rods and screws?

After surgery many of them got in trouble, and that's when Snow's partner on this rotation invented the Davis Drip. Heart and kidneys giving out. Adrenals overloaded. They had very little to combat this. A drug called Isuprel to dilate the vessels when there wasn't enough blood getting to the kidneys, a drug called Aramine to tighten up the arteries when the blood pressure dropped, cortisone when the adrenals had decided enough was enough. Trouble was, when you think about it, the heart, artery, kidney system is more subtle than that. But Davis had been a pharmacologist before he entered medical school. He knew his drugs, as they say.

So when these poor old post-surgery ladies went into shock he hooked up one bottle with Aramine in it, another with Isuprel, a third with cortisone and ran them into one line and the fattest vein he could find. Blood pressure's down: a little faster with the Aramine. Kidneys aren't producing: a little more Isuprel. Temperature spiking: get some antibiotics in the cortisone bottle. Add potassium. And a touch of morphine. All coming together in a fine broth. And, for a while, it seemed to work. But then everything, for a while, seems to work.

They were alchemists madly mixing their chemicals, adding this, subtracting that, making notes in little black books, their concoctions dripping down transparent plastic tubes and mingling with the fluids and chemicals being equally and madly adjusted by little factories in the blood, kidneys, heart, adrenals, liver, every organ in the body of this—this...body.

"What the hell are you doing?" Ryan wanted to know. But Davis could outtalk him when it came to pharmacological matters, and so Ryan shrugged his shoulders and left him alone.

The Davis Drip dropped into history the day Snow said, "Hey, look at this."

"Look at what?"

"This. The stuff's turning yellow."

"What do you mean turning yellow?"

"Where it all comes together. It's turning milky yellow like Pernod."

"Lemme see that. It shouldn't be doing that."

"Well, it is."

"Shouldn't be happening. Their substrates are all compatible. Did you put anything else in?"

"No. Nothing."

"Here. Let me see that thing."

"Now it's becoming sludgelike."

"There's no reason to be doing that."

"Look. The stuff's solidifying. It's like egg yolk, or that Dutch liqueur, what's it called, Advocaat."

Davis was muttering something about water base, pH,

227

alkaloids, salts. "It shouldn't be happening."

"Well, it is."

"You got a Goodman and Gilman? Lemme check Goodman and Gilman."

"At least it's too thick to be getting in her vein."

"You sure you didn't put oil base in there by mistake?"

Ryan came in about that time. He looked at this bottle of yellow stuff very slowly oozing down the plastic tube. He said, "Turn the goddamn thing off." He checked their comatose patient, pulled her eyelids up. He said, "For God's sake, let the woman die in peace." And then he walked out.

The yellow stuff continued its journey to solid state. They pried some out of a tube. It was rubbery and tenacious.

"Hey, Art, look. You've invented a new plastic."

"Screw off."

"I think we better call NASA. They might have a use for this stuff."

"Give it a rest."

"Or maybe you've got a new embalming technique here."

Later that evening Snow walked back to look at their patient. She was still alive, but comatose, and her breathing kept stopping, starting again, stopping. The dismantled intravenous tubing was draped sadly, obscenely, over a pole in the corner. Hadn't he learned this lesson once or twice before? Beware the detail men. Beware the befuddlement of technology. Keep your eye on the real issues. If you could only figure out what they are at the time.

FATHER PHILIP BERRIGAN was sentenced to six years in a federal penitentiary for pouring duck's blood over draft files at the Selective Service headquarters in Baltimore.

"The real question is," said Harvey Ryan to Snow, in Ryan's room, sandals off, feet up, working on a six-pack, "The real question is, did the duck give its blood voluntarily or was it drafted?"

"I'm worried about our own Philip," said Robert.

"Trebilcock?"

"How'd you make out with him after that arrest?"

"All right. I got him calmed down and covered for him for twelve hours."

"He couldn't call it."

"He hasn't been sleeping."

"None of us has."

"I mean when he's actually off. He says he still doesn't sleep."

Snow reached over to get another beer. He looked at Ryan. Always rumpled and tired. Just doing the work, surviving. Not brilliant. Not quick. But stubborn and sometimes kind. "You can't do this without sleep."

"I told him to take some time off."

"What'd he say?"

"Says he'd lose his year. Armstrong told him sure, you can have a month, but no guarantee there'd be a slot open when he came back."

"You mean lose the whole residency."

"Something like that."

"That's shit."

"That's not the worst of it."

"What else is there?"

"You didn't ask why he's not sleeping."

"Why's he not sleeping, Harv?"

"I think he's taking uppers, bennies, amphetamines."

"You know this?"

"You share a bathroom with him. I thought you might take a look in his things."

"Lot of guys take something to stay awake."

"I'm trying to tell you I think he's hooked, man. And he's on the edge."

"Would he see one of the shrinks?"

"Are you kidding?"

"I was serious."

"He tells the shrink he's hooked on amphetamines, the shrink has to get him off the wards, he's lost his year and maybe more."

"You said he was on the edge."

"It was pathetic. The guy was weeping. Pathetic."

"I thought you wanted to help him?"

"I do, doesn't mean he's not pathetic."

"Say I find something, what then?"

"We confront him. Beat the crap out of him. Straighten him out."

"Sort of the American approach, eh?"

"What?"

"I'll take a look, first chance I get."

"There's only one left. D'ya want it?" He was speaking of the beer.

THAT NIGHT SNOW went through Trebilcock's bathroom kit and found aspirin, cold remedies, after-shave, cotton swabs, stamps in a little plastic envelope, nothing else. Because the doors of the bathroom didn't lock he could have gone through Trebilcock's room. He could have tossed it. But he didn't. He lay down on his own bed and waited for Trebilcock to return from whatever call he was on.

He heard the door next to his open and close a little after midnight. He went into the shared bathroom and knocked on Trebilcock's door.

"Phil."

"What?"

"Can I come in for a minute?"

"What for?"

"To talk."

"Suit yourself."

When Snow entered the room and looked around he said, "What a fucking mess."

Trebilcock was on his bed, head propped on a pillow. Books, papers, wrinkled clothing, empty beer bottles were scattered everywhere. "You came in here to tell me that? That this hole's a mess? You think I don't know it's a fucking mess?"

He wasn't wearing his glasses and his eyes were sharply suspicious in their tired, darkened sockets. He went on his subdued tirade. "This isn't a fucking mess. It's a fucking disaster, man. A fucking disaster."

"You don't look so hot, Phil."

"You standing there telling me I don't look so hot? You look like shit yourself."

"You got a beer?"

"You find a full one, you let me know."

Snow rummaged through Trebilcock's things until he came up with a bottle of beer. Then he hunted for an opener.

"Careful with those papers. They're in order."

The beer was warm, but it helped. "Phil, we're worried about you, man."

"Cause I couldn't call that goddamn arrest? Well, you tell me this, Dr. Know-Everything Snow, when is dead dead? When do you give up? When do you throw in the towel? You build it up and some asshole tears it down. They're just waiting for me to fuck up, that's all they're doing, waiting for me."

"Who's waiting?"

"It doesn't matter. I'm gonna pass my exam and come back and piss on the lot of 'em."

"Look, Phil…"

"Go to bed, Robert."

"You need some time off."

"You think I can't handle this?"

"No. That's not it."

"You been talking to Ryan?"

"No."

"Well, I can handle it."

"You look worn out, Phil."

"Gimme the rest of my beer and fuck off, Robert."

"I finished it."

"Then fuck off. I've got studying to do."

"It's after one."

"I can't stand you sitting there with that look on your face."

"Are you on anything, Phil?"

"Good night, Robert."

"Phil?"

"I said good night."

He went back to his own room and lay on his bed alone, and imagined Trebilcock lying on his, and Ryan on his, and Sandy on his, and all the others in this squat brick building, in their small rooms, waiting for the phones to ring and the dawn to come.

CHAPTER SIXTEEN

I pulled into Nazareth
Was feeling 'bout half past dead
I just need some place
Where I can lay my head
Hey, mister, can you tell me
Where a man might find a bed?
He just grinned and shook my hand
No, was all he said

— THE BAND

HE HAD BEEN neglecting to call his mother, telling himself the worst was over, she was on the mend, she had managed her brother's death really well, arm in arm with Grandmother at the funeral. Believing her when she had told him she was shopping, playing bridge with the girls on Tuesdays, planning a bus trip to Reno, maybe a trip through Europe next year. Yes, she was sleeping. Yes, she was eating.

But this time all his optimism, all his wishful thinking could not disguise her agitation. On the phone almost as bad as in person, the torrent of words, the breathless agonies: "There's nothing left, Robert. I don't know what to do with myself. You don't understand, nobody can understand what it's like. If I had a gun I'd shoot myself. I'm no good anymore, it's terrible, just terrible. What's wrong with me, Robert? In God's name what's wrong with me? My whole insides are shaking. I can't sit still. Can I take another pill? I don't know. I don't know. I've got them all mixed up, I can't keep them straight."

He was beginning to have trouble remembering her in other ways, and yet she must have been. "Would you go back to the hospital?"

"I'd rather be dead than go back to that place."

"I thought it was okay. You told me it was all right, it wasn't so bad."

"I don't deserve to be put away like that."

"It's not being put away. It's going for treatment when you need it."

"He wants me to sell the house."

"Who? Dad?"

"Of course, your father. I can't face it, all this furniture, all this stuff, what'll I do with all these things?"

"It'll work out, somehow."

"I can't live with myself, Robert, I can't."

He told her he was going to make an appointment for her, extracted a promise that she would attend. Hanging up, he said to Ann, "Shit, you know how hard it is to get through to doctors, especially shrinks?"

She said, "Use the doctor stuff, Robert, use it this time."

So he did, Dr. Snow calling Dr. Walters on an urgent matter. The switchboard patched him through to an answering service. He pushed the long distance, doctor to doctor, urgent matter. They found Dr. Walters for him. Robert explained in detail, found Walters hadn't seen her in a month. He'd make time at noon tomorrow if Robert could get her in.

He called his mother back. No difference in her pressure, her agitation, this time found she'd lost ten or twenty pounds, had not been playing bridge with the girls, had canceled each week, had not been shopping for ten days, except to the corner store for smokes. He made her promise to visit Dr. Walters at twelve noon tomorrow.

The next day he found they'd readmitted her, and the nurse suggested he call back in a couple of days, after they'd had a chance to assess her. He did this, and was told: "She's seriously depressed, lost maybe fifteen pounds in a month, and not responding to the medication. We'll be starting electroconvulsant therapy tomorrow."

"That's ECT."

"Yes, that's ECT."

"You think that's necessary?"

"Yes, definitely. It's perfectly safe and very effective."

He told Ann, "They're going to give her ECT, for God's sake."

"Maybe it's what she needs."

"Jesus, shit. Have you ever seen it done? They put electrodes on your head, and then provoke a full grand mal seizure." He could picture his small mother arching up in the manner of Elsa under the defibrillator paddles and then convulsing. "Shit, shit, shit."

"Robert, she needs to be back in hospital and she needs treatment."

"There's nothing I can do. There's nothing I can do about it."

"Robert, come to bed. You have to be up by six. I have to be up by seven."

"How can it help to fire a hundred volts of electricity through the brain?"

"Robert!"

BLEEDING. SHE JUST kept bleeding. No matter what he did she kept right on bleeding, from her bowels, from her rectum, from an ulcer somewhere, this old woman lying there, thin hair, tossing head, her bed filling with reeking blood, red-black clots, and he fumbling for a vein, anywhere a vein, to put a new line in because, moaning and squirming, she had ruined each line before it, and now her veins were flat or used up and the blood kept coming. Alone, after midnight, third night in a row, white on white, fresh red and coffee black on white. Angry wishes, fear, life clinging, being sucked away.

This time the top of her foot, and that would hold her for awhile, a number-eighteen cannula, an IV drip and a fresh bag of blood dripping in, dripping in but no faster than it was flowing out and soiling the bed. Her old face registered nothing beneath the oxygen mask, and then terror and open-eyed confusion. So why did she, like all the others, flail and thrash about, and fight against the needle going in her vein, moaning and muttering, so much he wanted to slap her, shout, for Christ's sake, lie still so I can get this done? It was three in the morning and he hadn't slept for more than minutes in the past forty-eight hours, having been up each night with this same woman, keeping her alive, because with no consideration at all she would start to bleed and go into shock after midnight. He fell back in the chair in the small room, green towels and gowns, white curtains and walls, steel poles, a harsh fluorescent light, shut his eyes and drifted immediately into a nervous dreamscape. And this time Martin Luther King was being shot standing on the balcony of a motel somewhere facing down all that anger while Snow was in Sick Children's Hospital doing a failure-to-thrive rotation with kids and babies being brought in undersize and underdeveloped and slow and stupid and they were going through this long elaborate diagnostic process figuring out why the kid in question was not going any place and finding rare liver disease sometimes and neglect and abuse other times, and handing these ones over to the social work department with King bleeding on the balcony of a good motel room in front of a bed the FBI probably had

bugged with the hopes of taping some Commie subversive pillow talk while King lay dying on the balcony, a bullet though
his head or his heart, right through that sonorous rhythmic
passionate voice in the same month Robert Snow watched an
eight-year-old die and felt sick deep inside.

He awakened suddenly but partially, his eyes blurred, his
body itching and unresponsive. She had done it again, moved
in some way to block the drip, and her vein had clotted,
stopped. But she'd still be leaking blood and fluids as if bal-
loon-punctured, her pulse thready, her blood pressure close to
shock. One last hope was to send the Red Cross blood straight
into the central venous line, the plastic tube threaded into a
major vein in her upper arm, through her chest into the big
vein as it entered the heart, a line to take measurements at
the heart of things without the interference of peripheral
events. Good idea if it doesn't kill her. He attached the bag of
blood to this plastic tube, got it going, sat back and watched.

A small room, four in the morning, Snow near hallucinations from sleep deprivation, this woman breathing shallowly,
this woman who might die, or might live, the two of them
alone in this hospital room, in the center of the hospital, in the
center of the city, people asleep, four in the morning, the two
of them bound together, she not knowing his name, seeing him
as what? An angel, an undertaker, a white malevolent blur. He
closed his aching eyes and drifted somewhere to be less alone.
This time the woman he was watching over became his mother, bleeding to death, fading away, dwindling, melting into the
bedsheets, slipping away from his grasp, his hands and arms in
jelly, in glue, unable to fill a syringe, unable to open a valve, his
eyes failing to read the contents of vials, of intravenous bags.
His uncle in the room, slumped in a chair, his uncle, his brother the same, his father in the distance. Light and air being
sucked from the room. He couldn't breathe. He fought to come

awake, to surface. When he finally broke through only half his mind reentered the room and registered that the dripping blood, transfusion, had stopped again. Remnants of the dream intruded.

He pulled himself to his feet, looked at the place the plastic tube entered her body. It was now a large swollen yellow mass streaked with purple, blood under the tissue, the skin stretched, a fucking mess, her whole upper arm, shoulder, breast. Jesus Christ. His eyes itched, his legs crawled. Fluorescent reality. Blood and shit still pouring out the woman's anus, filling the bed, filling the bed, filling the stinking bed. Die, for Christ's sake, please die, die, you bitch, you goddamn bitch, close your eyes so I can sleep, please die, leave me alone, let me go, let me go, let me go. Dear God, please die.

THE NEXT DAY, early morning, after a half hour's sleep, he trailed the small group of students following Harvey Ryan from room to room. In each doorway he leaned against the frame, shuffled his feet, tried standing in different ways, snapping his eyes open when the lids drifted down and took his mind away. In the old woman's room he muttered the case history as required, mentioned he'd been up all night keeping her stabilized with six pints of blood.

Ryan said, "We'll get surgery to look at her this morning." And they all moved on.

Just outside the door a woman caught Snow's eye. Supplicant, frazzled, sleepless. She had a small child with her, maybe four or five years old. "Will she be all right, doctor, my mother, Mrs. Polsky?"

Snow looked at her and tried to reconcile the bruised and swollen object in the bed with the worried living person before him, and the child, her child, Mrs. Polsky's granddaughter.

He told her she was stabilized now, not bleeding for the moment, at least, and the surgeons would consider operating, looking for the stomach ulcer that must be causing this.

The woman thanked him, thanked him profusely for doing everything possible for her mother, a kind wonderful woman who loved her granddaughter, and she couldn't thank him enough for all his care and concern, and Snow slouched there by the doorway, the weight on his shoulders building and the acid in his heart eating at his soul with his mind flipping back to the night before, early that same morning, in the dark hours when he'd wished with all his strength that the old woman would just for Christ's sake die, just fucking die, and now her daughter was here thanking him and he wanted to apologize and cry in her arms and still be strong and kind and survive and most of all he wanted to find a bed to lie on.

A NURSE AT that other hospital tells Robert that his mother has had three treatments so far and is responding well. The lounge television tells him that Surveyor 7, the last of five unmanned modules, has made a soft landing on the moon. Three American deserters have asked for asylum in Sweden. And there is something now called the credibility gap. The people no longer believe their leaders, or so the American press has discovered. Don't trust anyone over thirty. Robert has found the emergency ward to be a good place to study the cutting edge of public opinion, and on this subject one of his patients tells him the whole thing's bullshit. "Trick photography," he says, "stage sets, television networks in on it, little rocket-ship models, papier mâché rocks, nothing landing on the moon, all American show biz. They can do that now," he adds, having far more faith in the technology of illusion than that of space travel.

Snow asks him to hold still while he dips plaster-laden gauze in the bucket of water and wraps it around the man's hand and its fractured metacarpal, a little bone that often breaks when you make a fist and hit someone on the chin with it.

His patient's opinion differs from that of Lyndon Baines Johnson, on the television, regarding Vietnam. "Yanks are taking a shit-kicking over there," he tells Snow. But he also harbors the notion that if the politicians would lay off, give Westy and the others a free hand, they could turn the place into a parking lot. "A fucking parking lot," he says, relishing the idea. Snow tells him to come back to the orthopedics clinic and stay out of fights for a while.

They are defoliating the jungles with Agent Orange in order that they may fight an American kind of war, with high tech, shrapnel, napalm, and not men, at least not American men. But those little pajama-clad Oriental men just keep coming down the Ho Chi Min trail. Boys, not men, reflects Snow. Old Hollywood movies and Bill Mauldin's cartoons of the Second World War always showed men, grizzled and tough, maybe thirty to fifty years old. But this war is live, videotapes transported by jet, pictures and sound by satellite. Those are kids out there, younger than he is, thinks Robert Snow. And probably even more confused about life than he is, dying without having the slightest idea what it's all about.

They can't win this goddamn war. Everybody can see that. It doesn't matter who can win it, says Ann. It's wrong either way. The winners write the history books, Robert tells her. I hate it, she says. I just hate it. Goddamn politicians. Goddamn men.

New euphemisms for killing are being added to the language: to waste, to blow away, to terminate.

Standing over a dying man with Harvey Ryan, realizing it's the medical phrases, wasting away, wasting disease, terminal illness, that have been transformed into new verbs, or old verbs with new meanings, accelerated meanings: to waste, to terminate. "It's all changing," he tells Harvey.

"What is?"

"Everything. Our perceptions."

"What the hell are you on about now?"

"Ah, nothing," he says, and then tells Harvey Ryan about his patient who figures the moon landings, satellites, pictures of the earth are all special effects.

Ryan says, "I wouldn't be fucking surprised if he's right." Closes the dead man's eyes, looks at his watch, takes his stethoscope out of his ears and heads off to chart the time of death. Leaving Robert alone with his thoughts, at the bedside.

Pictures from satellites and moon probes are coming back, of the earth in blues and greens, shrouded in vapors, a single finite orb. Gaining new wonder. Creating new internal images. The fields and streets and mountains do not go on forever, they circle around and come back, finite. And the whole thing sits out there alone. With a billion other bits of matter, sitting out there alone, beyond touching. Each bit attracted to and repelled by the other bits.

"Dust to dust," he mutters to himself, and goes back to the emergency ward.

PAULINE WAS DEALING with one of the regulars. He had observed that drunks and emergency departments have a very special relationship. For the most part it's mutually abusive, but with moments of care and concern, and other moments of shared humanity, usually in the middle of a cold winter night, when the nurse, alone in the night, would let the drunk, also alone in the night, sleep it off in a side room.

"Here comes Charlie again."

"Oh, God. Didn't we have him earlier this week?"

"He's back again."

"What is it this time, Charlie?"

"I got this ankle, keeps swelling up, here, lemme get this shoe off."

"I don't want to see your feet, Charlie."

"Tha's a hell of a note, don' wanna see my feet, I'm a cit'zen y'know, hell of a note, here, can I use this chair here, miss?"

"Has the Mission thrown you out again, Charlie?"

"They say I bin drinkin' but it was that Bill Ribbles, he plants a empty in my bags, goddamn bastard, 'scuze the language."

"I'll get you a coffee and that's it. You gotta go right after."

"You're the most kindest person I ever met, and a good nurse, too."

"Cut the crap, Charlie."

"I mean it."

Snow, coming in at the end, said, "Maybe we oughta X-ray his ankle."

THEY WERE TEARING the American cities apart again, their rage turned back on themselves. Thirty-one dead, the papers said. Parts of Washington reduced to smoldering rubble.

But Johnson signed the Civil Rights Act into law and both McCarthy and Kennedy were promising to end the war. And Trebilcock had told Snow as he left the room, "Snow."

"Yeah?"

"I got it under control."

MOVIE TIME, THEY announced on Friday night, screen in place, projector, everyone told to shut up, drink quietly. And then they showed this home movie they had filmed on Super-8 a few weeks before, a group of residents, three in the morning. Dressed in surgical robes, caftans, hoods, shrouds, togas, they had led a procession through the hospital, the neurosurgery chief resident in the lead carrying a big IV pole in the shape of a cross over his shoulder. He was also wearing a holster and a pair of pistols.

Their destination was the main operating theater. On the way they clowned for the camera, mooned for the camera, strutted for the camera. In the main OR the enemy awaited in the form of other residents dressed in cowboy hats over green cotton gowns. They had as an ally an old yellowed skeleton dangling from a pole, a gruesome marionette. The camera was steadier in the OR, which also had adequate light, until, during the climax, it was knocked to the floor. And what did they do in the operating theater? They had a shoot-out with water pistols, IV tubing turned into water cannons, water-filled condom grenades. One among them, Snow thought it was the chief res. for ENT, tried to keep them from going too far, from wrecking the place, his hands raised in calming protest, and like playground children they all turned on him and strapped him to a table, feet in stirrups, spread apart, and then they poured assorted liquids on his body, naked before the camera.

Snow tried to make sense of this. A morality play? Theater of the confused? The crucifixion? Cattlemen versus sheep men? Foolish disciples doing battle with evil disease? Who was the enemy here? Maybe that was the problem. Nobody knew.

SNOW EXPERIENCED HIS own crystalline ambivalence at three in the morning. During the day the hospital was crowded, chaotic, noisy. The work was endless, distractions unlimited, instruments, papers, teams in white and green, orders, protocols, routines, surprises. At night the hospital was quiet, the lights muted. People spoke in whispers. Patients died in the early morning as if purposely avoiding another long day of bright lights, visitors, intruders, needles, pills, buzzers, bells, loudspeaker calls, bed baths and platitudes.

Robert was walking the long corridors returning from

seeing a man who had died quietly, expectedly, listening a final
time for a heartbeat extinguished, pulling the man's eyelids
down over his sunken eyes, the sheet up to his chin, standing
in the silence of the night looking at him, a nurse quietly
removing the last of the tubes and needles, looking at him
with sorrow and excitement.

Walking back, his feet were light on the marbled floor. In
each of the rooms he passed there were two, three, four
patients, and in the dormitories twenty more, some coughing
in the night, some moaning, some recovering, some dying. He
felt them there. He felt it on his skin. The hospital faintly
hummed. He had yet to sleep that day. He hated this place.
He hated all he did, all he had to do, all he saw, all he heard.
And he loved it, too. God help him, he loved it, too.

AND THEN THEY killed Robert Kennedy. One month after King.
A man with the ridiculous name of Sirhan Sirhan, shown in
the pictures with a harmless smile on his face. In the kitchen
corridor of the Ambassador Hotel.

He stayed in the hospital that night and talked to Ann on
the phone. "They've done it again," he said. "They've fucking
done it again."

"I can't stand it, Robert," she said. "I can't stand it anymore."

"You know where I was when JFK was killed?"

"I remember."

"We were dissecting a cadaver's neck in the anatomy lab."

"And I was serving cinnamon buns to law students in the
cafeteria."

"Those stupid fucking bastards."

"There's nothing much to hold onto, Robert. I feel it slipping away."

"We don't live there, Ann. We live in a very different country."

"No, you're wrong. Everybody lives there."

He didn't know what to say to that. Listened to silence on the phone, her breathing, then her sniffling on the other end.

"Are you all right?"

"No, I'm not. I'm not all right."

"We'll make it. We'll get through this."

"I'm afraid, Robert."

"What about?"

"Everything, Robert. Everything. Us."

TREBILCOCK. THE WORD spread quickly through the hospital. Several slightly different versions. In the bathroom of his parents' home. In a car he rented and drove to Halton Hills. After being caught stealing narcotics from a ward. He had been happy that day, up. He had been down that day. He had been refused a fellowship. He had been using amphetamines and crashed.

"What's the real story?" Snow asked Harvey Ryan.

"Does it matter?"

"No. I guess it doesn't."

"The silly fucker blew his fucking brains out, that's all that matters."

"He wouldn't talk that night."

"Yeah, I know."

"I tried. He just wouldn't talk."

"His old man's a big-shot surgeon up in Scarborough, you know that?"

"No. I didn't know that."

"A war hero, too."

"So he couldn't live up to his old man."

"Don't fucking analyze it. It just is, that's all."

"Christ, what a thing."

"He was married before."

"You mean before residency?"

"Something like that. I don't know the whole story."

"I don't know anything about him."

"Hell of a thing."

"Stupid bastard."

"Silly poor fuck."

That Friday night they didn't dance. They sat in small desultory groups and drank. Snow looked deep into his one bottle of beer and found nothing there. He talked with no one. He lay on his small bed through a sleepless night, aware, viscerally aware of the empty room next to his. He was grateful for the many calls he received to come to the wards.

FIFTY THOUSAND PEOPLE marched on Washington protesting poverty and discrimination. Ralph Abernathy was arrested for unlawful assembly.

"He was badly assembled," Ryan explained.

"Would you believe this?" asked Snow, catching up on old newspapers in the lounge, "the students took over Columbia."

"It's called a sit-in."

"They took over the Sorbonne, too, but the flics threw them out and closed the place down. First time it's been closed in seven hundred years."

"'The sun turned black as a funeral pall and the moon all red as blood.' Revelation."

"Yours?"

"No, no, no. The Bible."

Snow put his paper down. "You can quote the Bible?"

"You guessed it, Snow, with a name like Ryan."

"Choirboy?"

"Uh-huh."

"Separate school?"

"Jesuits."

"And now?"

"It was either become a whiskey priest or a doctor."

"Y'know, in medical school," said Snow, suddenly feeling nostalgic, "we had a prof who said that priests and country doctors are expected to drink too much." He was aware that this was the first time they had spoken about matters not medical without being at least mildly intoxicated. "Not all the time. Sometimes." It had been a harmless memory but he found his eyes pricking. He realized that if he continued talking to Ryan this way he would soon be crying.

Saunders entered the lounge, stood for a moment looking at them, then walked on.

Ryan said, "The funeral's just a family thing. No one else invited."

Snow picked up his paper and made his eyes focus on the print.

Ryan said, "We should have tried harder, something, I don't know." And then he, too, buried himself in a newspaper.

247

CHAPTER SEVENTEEN

And she feeds you tea and oranges
That come all the way from China

And she shows you where to look
Among the garbage and the flowers
— LEONARD COHEN

T HE SURGEONS HAD taken Mrs. Polsky away and opened her up and removed most of her stomach, including the part with the bleeding ulcer that strangely enough looked benign, they said. After surgery she developed all possible complications including septic shock from some source of infection, most likely her severed bowel, and so they kept her on oxygen, antibiotics and cortisone and watched her urine output carefully for a few days but anyway she died.

Thinking about it, Snow realized Trebilcock must have assisted at the operation, held scalpel in hand, forceps, tied off bleeders, sewn up.

He talked to his mother on the phone and told Ann that she sounded much better, brighter, hopeful. I don't know how it works, he said, when she asked. Maybe it just kills the memory, makes it so she can't remember why she's supposed to be so depressed. She sure doesn't remember much of the last few weeks. Maybe we should all get some, said Ann. Not a bad idea, said Robert, not a bad idea.

MRS. GRACE LING was a teacher, newly arrived in Toronto with her engineer husband and four-year-old son. She was petite, soft-spoken, polite, eager to please, and she smiled readily. Her English was limited and very formal, without nuances, and accompanied by almost imperceptible bows and nods. She was close to term the first time Robert met her in the prenatal clinic, having undoubtedly suffered indignities at the hands of other interns before his rotation. Her husband came with her and brought their son during each of her two visits. She introduced them to him, and her husband, not much taller than she, seemed equally pleased and grateful. An immaculately dressed little man, his son clinging to his leg, shaking hands with the tired, rumpled, white-clad and white-skinned, large Dr. Robert Snow, before the five green curtains, the stirrups, the women mounted.

The Red Guards had been unleashed by Mao Tse-tung, a scurry of avenging disciples reclaiming the revolution for which Dr. Norman Bethune had given his life with a slip of the scalpel, pre-penicillin. The Red Guards were reported to be, in the manner of their ancestors, chopping off bits and pieces of the bodies of their foes. When Robert considered the Lings' alternatives, or at least the possibilities were it not for certain migratory decisions, he was no longer quite as surprised at their gratitude for the free clinic, the five cubicles, the stirrups too large for her tiny feet, the big doctor's clumsy hands. And naked and starving Biafrans, the people of Ibo, were dying on the electronic screens in everybody's living room. McLuhan's global village had come to pass. Against these events the hospital prenatal clinic for the indigent and uninsured did not look so bad. Or, Snow wondered, was he simply getting used to it? Inured.

Before her third visit she arrived at the hospital in labor. They took her straight from the emergency department to the delivery room, where, now an old hand at this, Snow delivered her baby smoothly, easily, for only a single heartbeat worrying about the head-shattering tile floor beneath them. It was a tiny little girl baby, already adorned with straight black hair. He placed the baby on her mother's chest, her mother's legs still dead from the epidural block given her by the anesthetist who had arrived on time. He dropped silver nitrate in the baby's eyes and then walked to the cafeteria for a midnight meal.

They were talking about Kennedy, what might happen now. Ryan offering the opinion that the Americans couldn't be so bloody stupid as to elect Nixon, now could they? Tell me if I'm wrong. If I'm wrong, I'm wrong. They didn't talk about Trebilcock. Each of them, Snow knew, wondering what pushed him past the point of no return, and if they would reach that point themselves, each trying to believe that Trebilcock was weaker, more fragile than they. Addicted, depressed, different. Each feeling safer if they avoided talking about him.

HE VISITED MRS. Ling the next day and found her alone in a four-bed room, the infant asleep in the crook of her arm. She grasped his hand in her free hand and thanked him, thanked him as if he alone had done this thing, ordered, created, arranged, delivered this female package, her first being a boy, her husband oh so happy, thank you, thank you, thank you.

It was nothing, really, he said to himself. But he did feel their joy, their hope, eroding the tragic backdrop of the last few weeks.

The next three days he visited each day. On two occasions, her husband, visiting at the same time, left the room quickly, bowing and nodding, in spite of Robert saying, "It's all right, you can stay."

He sat on the edge of her bed in the oversize room, admired the baby, asked the medical questions he had to ask, watched the spring sunlight move about her face, talked with her about this baby, her first Canadian baby, her little boy having been born in Hong Kong. Her husband had a fine job, engineer in a large firm. She had a teaching appointment starting next year. Everything was good.

ON THE FIFTH day after delivering Mrs. Ling, after long hours in the operating room, the prenatal clinic, working up new patients, investigations, rounds, in the evening, during the lull, he was resting on the bed in his room when he received the call from the ward. He was wanted urgently on the floor. What's going on? he asked. Just come over, please.

Sandals on, white coat stuffed with instruments, he walked quickly down the stairs, into the tunnel, across to the main building, up the elevator to the sixth floor. As usual, all possible disasters tramped through his brain: the diabetic waiting for a cesarian gone into hypoglycemia, or pre-eclampsia, hypertensive crisis, ruptured placenta, the ectopic they were watching closely, ruptured. Breaking, bleeding, thrombosing, convulsing, dying. These would be God's doing. He had another list in mind, which might be headed Robert Snow's Doing: too much insulin, too little insulin, wrong diagnosis, wrong pill, something forgotten, something omitted, another story to join Elsa, Mrs. Polsky, the old Greek who stopped producing urine and George Martin, in his permanent file of regret.

The nursing station, midway down the ward, lay in darkness except for the amber cones of several reading lamps. In the shadows there seemed to be a crowd, a group of people standing, whispering to one another. Saunders was standing at the nursing station, and the head nurse, two or three others, and then, as the crowd in the shadows came into better focus, Snow could see it was made up of Oriental faces. And a policeman was there, too.

When he reached the counter the head nurse looked up and Saunders moved a few feet away. She said to Robert, this is what she said, "Mrs. Ling's husband and son were killed this afternoon."

Snow, not taking it in at first, looked over at the Oriental faces, the cop. They had stopped whispering and were all scanning his face. He turned to the nurse. Was about to ask her what's going on when her words reached him.

"He took his boy to see some work on the construction site, he's an engineer."

"Yes, yes, I know that."

"He was holding the boy in his arms and he walked behind a truck, a dump truck, and the driver didn't see him and backed up, and...that..."

"How did it happen?" he heard himself ask, as if his voice, his tongue, had slipped into a rhythm of their own. Then hearing her answer he turned to look at the crowd again. It didn't seem there were so many now, a handful really, and her words settled themselves in his brain.

"Are you sure?" he asked.

She didn't answer this question. She waited for him. Robert, incongruously, remembered this was the same head nurse who had screamed like a schoolgirl and chased Saunders down the hall after Mrs. Didioto's delivery, the same tough lady, and Saunders the same master of the gynecology universe. Mrs. Didioto, who had taken her new baby home many weeks before. He was holding his boy in his arms. The dump truck backed up. Snow could see it now, though he didn't want to. Like *il padre* before him, laying concrete foundations, large holes, red mud, shriek of steel on steel, trucks with enormous double wheels, the little man with child in arms.

The policeman had slipped away. Saunders was looking past Snow, over his left shoulder. The head nurse was still there, on the other side of the counter, watching his face. There was something he did not understand. They had told him, he had pictured it, the words gradually taking on substance, images, causing a large hole to grow in his chest, a strange anxiety to flutter in his throat. They've told him. That's fair. He should know. Saunders, where is your mastery now? Why aren't you taking over and making this fun? His mind tripped along auxiliary paths and he wondered what had happened when the head nurse had finally caught up with him, perhaps in the change room, a linen closet.

What are they waiting for?

And then he understood. "Does she know?" he asked, his voice strangled in his mouth.

The head nurse shook her head. No.

"A relative should tell her," he said.

The handful of Orientals had a whispered discussion in Chinese. Then a taller man in a business suit stepped forward. "I am not a relative. I came with them to translate. They feel it would be better if the doctor tells her." He bowed slightly.

ROBERT SNOW LOOKS at the relatives, acknowledging their eyes. They are small, like Mrs. Ling, and frightened, overwhelmed. He doesn't know in what manner they are related.

He looks to Saunders but Saunders takes a step back into the shadows. And then he hears his own voice saying, "You want me to do it."

He doesn't know how or why these words issue from his mouth. He knows there is an outward calm about himself, a lie of his making, a calming demeanor, calming words, fooling most, transparent only to lovers and mothers, and not always mothers.

The head nurse nods. Yes.

No more words are spoken. He has committed himself.

His knees feel weak when he walks away from the relatives, the nursing station, and down the corridor alone. It is a strange, long, awkward journey. Nothing about his body is working automatically. He must remember, he feels, how to walk. His arms hang without use at his sides. He wonders if this is right, the right way to do this, appropriate, approved. But he knows his performance is not being judged, or if it is, it is an entirely minor event. He tries to be here, now, to focus his thinking, to not let it wander in panic and horror.

Outside the room he finds he has a grin on his face. A smile. A rictus. Why the hell should he have a grin on his face? He is not smiling. He doesn't feel like smiling. His face seems to have a will of its own. He takes a deep breath and calms himself. The grin is still there. He can feel the curl of his lips. It is there, clinging to his face, a foreign thing. It won't leave of its own accord. He places his left hand on his face and feels the grin. He pulls the corners of his mouth down and holds them there. Takes another breath.

The grin is gone. And he understands its purpose now, for his face feels dragged, flat, brittle. But he must do this thing. As brittle as he feels, he must walk in this room and tell her. He opens the door and walks in.

She is sitting up in bed reading, and she greets him with a warm smile. Her smile fades and her eyes question him as he approaches the bed. He sits on the edge and says to her, this is what he says: "I'm sorry, there's only one way to tell you this. Your husband and your son were both killed in an accident this afternoon."

Her face goes blank and drains of color. Her eyes widen in terror and her mouth opens and closes, opens and closes, opens and closes. No voice, no sound. For a long time there is silence. Silence sitting between them in the half-light. Then she asks him something in Chinese, and he nods, yes, somehow knowing she is asking him again and again if it is true, what he said, willing him to take it back and failing. And she asks him something again and he nods, yes, again.

Head back on the pillow, she weeps, letting him see her face. He takes her tiny hand in his and holds it. Her fingers curl around his. His eyes fill with tears as she sobs, lying with her head to one side. He stares out the window at the vaguely outlined rooftops. It is beginning to rain. He wants to hold more of her than her hand, but he can't ask her if that is also what she needs or wants. There are no words to be spoken, no words adequate. She weeps quietly, turning her face into the pillow. She is quiet for a moment, then shudders and weeps again, her hand tightening on his, then quiet again. He has no idea how long they have been like this. The city is dark and silent. Not a sound from the corridor beyond the room. He imagines a construction site equally stilled. She shudders again, sits up, sobs into his chest. He holds her tiny body. She falls back, buries her face in her pillow, holds his hand tightly. He doesn't know, can't know, what she is thinking and feeling.

She releases his hand and he guesses she wants to be alone. He finds nothing he can say to her. He touches her tiny shoulder, holding gently for a moment, and then leaves quietly, wiping his face at the door.

Out in the corridor they are all waiting silently, just a few feet along in the shadows.

"Will she be all right?"

"How did she react?"

"Should I give her the needle now?"

He says to them, "Don't give her anything. Leave her alone."

"But what about a sedative? Surely she'll need..."

"Leave her alone," he says. "Just leave her alone."

They are asking him more questions but Robert isn't listening

255

anymore. He is moving away from them, down the corridor, walking somewhere, faster now, to the exit sign, through the fire door, down five flights of stairs, taking the last flight two steps at a time, accelerating, seeing nothing as he spirals down, thinking nothing as he enters the corridors of the main floor, past offices, into the main hall, men and women in white, cleaning ladies mopping the floor, walking out the main door, into the cold spring night. A block away from the hospital he wonders why he feels so wet, his cotton slacks clinging to his legs, and then becomes aware of the rain on his face. He looks directly into it and lets it wash his eyes and continues walking. The sidewalk is almost empty. The wind picks up and the rain grows cold. Black puddles under street lamps. His feet in white socks and open sandals quickly chilling. He realizes he is on duty this night. He should be in the hospital. The rain washes over him in gusts. He runs across an intersection, hands stuffed in his pockets with his notebook, stethoscope, little red hammer. Headlights cut through the rain. He turns a corner and walks into a residential area. The trees have new spring leaves, sometimes sheltering him, sometimes sending him splashes of cold water.

He slows and looks around and finds himself alone on the street. The houses are brick, two and a half stories, side by side, some with porch lights on, an old neighborhood with large trees, mingling with poles and wires, now silhouetted in the cold domain of mercury lamps.

When he reaches the next corner he looks at street names and recognizes the one Pauline lives on. Old houses. The number he remembers is 482. Quite suddenly 482, and Pauline, and the house she lives in, become his destination, his refuge. He walks a block and a half the wrong way, turns and retraces his steps. His cottons are heavy with water.

In his flight from the hospital, in the moment of his brain

imploding, of his legs carrying him away, he was running from, not to, and now suddenly he is running to, obsessively searching the street for number 482. Very few numbers are visible. Anxious, cold, wet, he finds 486 and then 478. The one between has to be 482. Now what? He stands under a street lamp and then moves into the shadows. He becomes suddenly more aware of himself, his white pants and white jacket now sodden. Wet through and through, and chilled. The rain has stopped, the clouds moved on. Down the street to the west, away from the main city, he can see a few stars blinking between a web of black twigs. He is alive. Elsa is not, Mrs. Polsky, George Martin, his uncle, Trebilcock, King, Kennedy, and now Mr. Ling and his son. But he is.

All at the same time he feels small, weak, cold, vulnerable, tall, strong, invincible. His feet take a step away and then bring him back. He can't stay here forever and yet he can't bring himself to walk away. It is a short, hesitant stray to 482, up three steps onto a porch. He stands before a large oak door, a leaded-glass window in the upper half, revealing, with distorted angles, an entrance hall and an open flight of stairs.

He finds her name beside a buzzer and pushes it. He can stop now and return to the hospital, but the light changes in the hallway and through the panes of leaded glass he sees her descending the staircase, fractured, like Duchamp's painting.

She opens the door and looks at him. He has nothing to say. She says, "I knew you'd come eventually."

"It's very cold," he says.

"You're soaking wet."

"I walked from the hospital."

"I live upstairs."

She leads him up the winding staircase, walking ahead of him, looking over her shoulder once, her eyes smiling at him. He has not seen her without a uniform before. Her legs are bare with an unseasonable tan, a silver miniskirt riding on her hips, her feet in leather toe sandals, her toenails painted, her black hair swinging over her shoulders.

Her apartment is sparsely furnished. As if answering his thoughts she says, "I haven't been here long. I was married for a while."

He moves to the radiator and holds his hands above it, dripping on the floor.

"Here, give me that," she says, pulling his white jacket from him. She takes it to her bathroom and returns with towels, talking him into giving her the rest as he wraps himself in one large beach towel and mops at himself with two others. His underwear, doubly protected, is only damp. His toes ache as the cold leaves them. She calls to him that she is hanging his clothes above the tub for now. There is a dryer in the basement they can use later.

She brings him a cup of tea and he curls into the one big armchair in the angled room, notices leaves brushing against a dormer window. Bookshelves made from bricks and rough pine planks, a stereo system with records scattered beneath it, a mattress on the floor with a paisley spread, incense burning in a small brass cup, an old standard lamp with a Victorian shade, a weaving on the floor, a stone carving of an Indian woman's head, twisted on the neck, mouth open as if screaming.

"I'm Métis," she says, following his eyes. He looks at her, sitting cross-legged on the mattress, black straight hair, olive skin, high cheekbones, dark eyes. "Partly Métis, anyhow, French and Ojibwa. My maiden name was Boucher."

She goes into the kitchen to make more tea and find some biscuits and he looks through her record collection for something to do. When she returns she places the tray on the floor and beckons him to sit beside her on the mattress. Warmer now, still wrapped in towels, he does what she asks.

When he has a warm cup in his hands she asks, "Are you going to tell me about it?"

He begins to tell her about Mrs. Ling and her husband and son, and he does tell her, but finds himself also telling her about his mother, and then it is too late to stop the tears. They roll down his cheeks silently. "I'm sorry," he says. "I'm sorry."

"It's all right," she says, taking his hand in hers.

He is now shamelessly sniffling, weeping, blowing his nose and talking when he can catch his breath. "Oh, Jesus," he says, shaking his head, smiling a little. "I didn't know this was going to happen."

He discovers how much he feared his mother would kill herself, how sad he is for her, for Mrs. Ling, for George Martin, for Trebilcock, for Martin Luther King, how angry he is at his helplessness.

He lies back, no longer sobbing but his eyes still leaking tears. He feels relief, unburdened, the cells of his body suddenly free to breathe again, and now aware of her body next to his, her midnight hair, long legs, the musky perfume of her.

When they make love he feels himself falling off a cliff, plunging into free flight, cut lose, spiraling into her and reclaiming himself.

SAUNDERS CAUGHT HIM in the corridor. "Christ, what happened to you last night? You were on call. I was up all night covering for you."

"I had to get away for a while. I had to get out of here."

"Yeah? You look a mess. I'll buy you a coffee. C'mon."

In the cafeteria, just the two of them, Saunders said, "Look, thanks for, you know, doing it last night, telling her."

"It's okay."

"No, I mean it. I can't do that kind of stuff. I'm no good at it."

Snow looks at him. This is not an easy admission. He's a good-looking man. Blond hair slicked back, straight nose, blue eyes. Soon he'll be a very successful gynecologist, adored by his patients. And he will like them, no doubt about it, girls, gals, ladies. And he will get plenty of loving.

Robert wants to talk with him about Pauline, explain his absence, explain his now dry but very wrinkled jacket. But instead he asks, "Is she going home today?"

"Yeah. Her relatives, the ones there last night, they're picking her up this afternoon."

So Robert would visit her later, after all his scut work, as they called those thousand little duties a technician could do, a high-school dropout for that matter. Scut. Said with familiarity and contempt. And after assisting in the OR. And after doing his new admissions. After lunch, he tells himself.

When he finally looks in her room on the sixth floor she is gone.

A decade later, two decades later, whenever he hears the breep, breep, breep of a truck backing, now a mandatory signal, he thinks of Mrs. Ling and wonders if there is a connection. There might have been an inquest. There might have been recommendations. Maybe.

Chapter Eighteen

No one I think is in my tree
I mean it must be high or low
That is, you know you can't tune in, but it's all right
That is, I think it's not too bad
                 – LENNON/MCCARTNEY

I don't know why you say goodbye, I say hello
                 – LENNON/MCCARTNEY

SNOW WORKED EMERGENCY until midnight on the last day of June. It had been a busy day. Hot humid air had rolled in the door accompanying each new casualty. There had been a three-vehicle accident not far from the hospital, during rush hour, and those that survived were being patched and plastered in several of the emergency rooms. A man had walked in slathered in brown grease, which he had applied to burns he received when an industrial boiler ruptured. Bits of debris removed from eyes, smashed fingernails incised, large boils lanced, the stomachs of suicides pumped, psychotics put back in ambulances and sent to Queen Street.

IN THE EARLY MORNING, while they were sipping tea and waiting for his clothes to dry, she had said, "Will you be coming back?"
    And he had said, "I'm married."

"I know that."

He held his cup in both hands, sipped from it, looked into it. She said, "You don't have to come back, Robert. I'd like you to, but it's up to you."

She had told him how she came from a small town north of Montreal, her father disappearing, her mother putting her in a convent school, to be raised by sisters, silent and ghostly, until she ran away when she was fifteen. Taken into a big house in Montreal by a very large and kind woman who trained her.

Trained her?

"*C'était un bordel*, Robert, a brothel."

"Oh."

"It wasn't so bad. She was like a real mother to me. Are you shocked?"

"Not as long as you don't tell me the details."

"You are such an innocent, Robert."

"I don't feel so innocent."

"Well, eventually I got away from there, too, and lived with an artist and modeled for him, and got pregnant, and the artist dumped me, so I had to give the baby up. Then I was stoned on hash for maybe four months until I met a rich doctor who set me up in a pad, paid the rent and encouraged me to go back to school."

"Why would he do that?"

"Robert..."

"Yeah, okay."

"I finished school and went into nursing."

"Is this the, uh, pad?"

"No. When I finished I decided I had to get away, start a new life in a different city. I wasn't actually married. This is my own place."

"You've been through a lot to get here." Over his cup he

watched her black eyes, thought about how thoroughly they had made love, how easy she had been with it, how expert.

She said, "They're probably dry now."

HE HAD AN urge to tell Ann but managed to bite his tongue, stop the compulsion to confess. And he didn't tell her about Mrs. Ling, her husband and her son, not wanting to see her cry, see her upset. His mother, much better now, for now, had a discharge date. "They're letting me out first of the month," she told him. "I feel so cooped up in here."

"You'll be all right on your own?" he asked. "We might not get back for another six months."

"Of course, I'll be all right. Why shouldn't I be?"

"I'm sorry, forget I asked. We'll get back for a visit as soon as we can. How's Grandma doing?"

"One of these days she really is going to get sick, Robert, and nobody will listen. She's cried wolf so often."

"Well, she is eighty-eight now."

"I worry she'll just drop dead in that damn old house and nobody will know."

"That's not such a bad way to go."

"I still worry about it. I'd feel so damned guilty, if that happened."

Forever, thought Robert, and pass it on, and pass it on, and pass it on. Ah, but it was so much better to have his mother healthy again, even if it sounded slightly strained, fragile, even if it depended on lacunae of memory, topics avoided, filtered perception.

There were days he felt obsessed by Pauline, compelled to run to her dormered apartment, lie on her mattress, listen to the branches brush against the window, let incense and music envelop him, seek her healing arms. His Métis whore. He resisted, and worked, and flew home on the trolley on his few nights off. In the hospital they shared coffee and talked, and he grew to accept that she had offered him an unencumbered gift one dark night, had been a doctor for the doctor. And he hoped that he could learn to be as strong as she, to live, to survive, to love, to give.

A THUNDERSTORM ERUPTED in the early evening and from out of its clutches a very tall and heavy man rushed through the doors and paced up and down the corridor, dripping from the rain and talking incessantly. Snow walked beside him. It was the only thing to do. As they walked in tandem the man talked at Snow, through Snow, around Snow and not to Snow at all. "My name," he said, "is Andrew P for Philip McMurtry, they have it all here on file, address, phone number, social security, the works, the entire snot-green sea, the scrotum-tightening sea. I am experiencing absolute joyicity, Dr. R. Snow, R no doubt for Robert, and you'd be interested of course in what R.D. Laing has recently said on the subject, R, in his case, signifying Ronald. Mr. Laing informs us that" (there was here a pause as they reached the end of the corridor and Andrew P. McMurtry was momentarily distracted by the scene in the last room) "my, oh my, where were we, oh, yes, Mr. Laing informs us that those behaviors that you are no doubt about to label schizophrenia are really a special strategy that I have invented in order to live in an unlivable situation. Quote, unquote. Thumpsday, frightsday, shatterday, everyday and everywhere."

Andrew P. McMurtry was several inches taller than Snow and many pounds heavier. His long hair rampaged above his high forehead. His insect eyes shattered the air before him, and his voice spoke to everyone. Snow had questions he should be asking, but soon gave them up to simple observation. Mr. McMurtry's speech poured forth as if pumped, his ideas moved about like bumper cars, a salad of words and thoughts and a few neologisms, invented words, cascading from his lips. Snow retreated behind the desk to find some old notes on the man.

He discovered that Mr. McMurtry had visited the emergency in roughly the same condition approximately once per year for the past five years. Dr. McMurtry, for the man had a Ph.D. and was, or at least had been, on his last visit, a chief librarian. He reconsidered Mr. McMurtry's neologisms in light of his, probably, protean reading habits. But the rest was clear.

When he caught up with his patient (who had not actually signed in, but Snow decided to worry about that later) he offered him a glass of water and two hundred-milligram tablets of chlorpromazine.

"The nets are holding back my soul from flight," Mr. McMurtry announced to all who might listen. And then specifically to Robert, standing before him with pills in hand, "Let me die a youngman's death, Not a clean and in-between-the-sheets, holy-water death, Not a famous-last-words, Peaceful out-of-breath death."

But to Robert's surprise he took the pills and swallowed them, and then said, "You have sad eyes, but Santayana tells us that the young man who has not wept is a savage, and the old man who will not laugh is a fool." And then off down the corridor once more announcing that he was the limp father of thousands.

He moved on in his discourse through Shakespeare and then Sartre, announcing during a brief pause at the nursing station, *"L'existence précede et commande l'essence,"* and adding with a flourish, *"il buono, il bruta, il cattivo."* Snow, writing notes on his patient, looked up at a nurse with Anna on her name plate and raised his eyebrows.

"That last bit," said Nurse Anna, answering Snow's eyebrows, "is the good, the bad, the ugly."

She must have immediately regretted speaking, for Mr. McMurtry turned on her to announce, theatrically, "O tell me all about Anna Livia! I want to hear all about Anna Livia. Tell me all. Tell me now."

An hour later he was still pacing and talking, though Snow had given him more medication. The chief resident from orthopedics, still dealing with survivors of the car accident, came down to tell Snow, "For God's sake get him under control, will you. He was just in eleven telling me how to put a cast on."

Four hundred, six hundred, eight hundred milligrams and he still walked and talked, sloppily perhaps, but with the same energy. Intrusive, funny, belligerent, expansive. One thousand, twelve hundred. The residents working on the accident victims and now a couple of acute chest pains wanted Snow to put Dr. McMurtry down. Or, as Ryan said, "For God's sake, snow him, Snow."

Snow was the only one who paid any attention to what Andrew P. McMurtry was saying. Ryan told him it was a sign of his own mental state that he should be listening to the ravings of this madman. About twenty minutes after he got his patient to swallow the last two pills to complete a dozen, Anna said, "Here it comes. Watch it." And Snow got there just in time to see McMurtry's eyes snap shut in mid-sentence and his body collapse to the floor in the corridor. One on each limb, they dragged him to a quiet room with a mattress on the floor. Snow took his blood pressure and listened intently to his chest to make sure he hadn't killed the man and then went to finish up his other patients, one eye on the clock.

McMurtry had collapsed just in time. Sirens heralded ambulances approaching. There was no lull this night. Another accident, head injuries, internal injuries. A regular back again, a man who seizured at will, convincingly, until given the medication he craved. Another man with a kitchen knife in his shoulder, brought in by the woman who put it there.

And suddenly in the chaos Pauline appeared. He couldn't leave the woman whose wounds he was suturing, masked and gloved, needle in hand. So Pauline stood on the other side of the table and talked over his patient. Behind a curtain on another gurney in the same room lay a man attached to a BIRD. Robert's patient was drunk and abusive, her expletives flavored with cheap wine, nicotine and vomit.

Glass shattered next door as the recently concerned woman once again tried to kill her lover. The BIRD wheeze-popped, wheeze-popped.

"I'll take over," Pauline said to the nurse assisting Snow.

"Fucking bassard," said the woman. "Watch it, doc. Fucking Jesus that hurts."

"I came to say goodbye," said Pauline, slipping gloves on, handing Robert a new needle and thread.

"Hello," said Robert.

"You'll be a good doctor, Robert."

"Holy shit, doc. Concentrate. This is my face we're working on."

"Maybe."

"And what is this be a good doctor? Are you just a fucking intern?"

"For another twenty minutes," said Robert.

"Robert?"

"Uh-huh?"

"My offer still holds."

"C'mon, doc. I'm thawing out. Get with it."

"I think you saved my life that night."

"Don't be silly. You just needed someone."

"Oh, god. Is this a hospital or a soap opera?"

"It's a hospital, Mrs. Mirksic."

"Ms Mirksic, doc. I'm leaving the bastard."

Robert tying the last knot. Pauline cutting the thread, pulling her gloves off, said, "Good luck, Robert. I really mean it."

She walked to the door, turned for a moment, and he said, "I love you."

"I know," she said, and was gone.

"Are you gonna sew me up, doc, or do I haf' t' do it myself?"

"You're done, Mrs. Mirksic. You can take a look if you want."

She heaved herself off the table to look at her face in the mirror above the sink. As she gingerly fingered her wound she said, "You oughta marry that little girl, doc."

"I'm already married," he told her.

"Fuck, doc. You are a pistol."

"Five days from now you should have your family doctor take those out or come back here."

Buttoning her blouse she said, "You decide to leave your wife, doc, you look me up." And at the door she turned and reconsidered. "Fuck, doc, you stay with her or not, you look me up."

He could hear her laugh all the way down the corridor.

Behind the curtains: wheeze-pop, wheeze-pop.

It was twelve o'clock when he looked. No bells. No sirens. But twelve o'clock. Midnight. The end of his last shift.

SANDY ARRIVED TO take over. Robert led him around from room to room to show him his patients, waiting for X rays, lab results, beds, family members, transportation. In each room he heard himself use the easy shorthand, the confident medical jargon: "Seventeen's a drunk sleeping it off, couple more hours, eighteen's going up to medical, orders are written, the kid in twelve's fever comes down his parents can take him home, the lady in seven's got an L4 compression fracture, the orthopods'll probably admit her for a few days. The quiet room's a manic, a big man, took twelve hundred milligrams of CPZ to snow him." He stopped himself and began introducing Sandy to his patients. "Mr. Fratelli, this is *Dottore* McKenzie. He's taking over for me."

"You off now, *dottore*?"

"Yes, I'm off now."

HE LEFT THE emergency ward. He left the hospital. A thousand loose ends vying for his attention. As he walked away he fought against a surprising tide of the undone, unfinished, unexplored, unexplained. And he realized much of it, especially the worst of it, would come with him, stay with him, travel with him forever. Well, not forever, he said to himself as he stepped into the quadrangle between the hospital and the residence, the air cleansed by the thunderstorm, black puddles multiplying the building's lights. Not forever, only as long as his own heart took oxygen from his lungs and dribbled it in his brain.

He breathed in deeply and splashed his way to the residence, taking a child's delight in the puddles.

He heard the party before he opened the door. Some of them had a two-, three-hour head start in the race to the benediction of bliss consciousness offered by Purple Jesus. It was a good one, spilling into the hallways, music louder than usual, voices raised above it. Ah, and what music. The Who, the Doors, Three Dog Night, Jefferson Airplane, the Mamas and the Papas, the Beachboys, the Beatles, the Rolling Stones, the Byrds, the Lovin' Spoonful, Chicago, Creedence Clearwater Revival, Canned Heat, Janis, Jimi, Otis, Gordon, Bob, Robbie.

The Great Dane searched out each of her boys and gave them big sloppy kisses. Snow was enfolded in her arms and tasted her heavy lips. He had thought of her as, well, a large sexy loose broad. In a flush of benevolence he saw her as more than that now, nurse mother to the surgical residents, and God knows, they needed it. It was crowded, a large hiving ants' nest of activity. He filled his right hand with a cup of Purple Jesus and his left with a beer to wash it down. And found himself searching through the crowd for Pauline.

She wasn't there, not in the middle dancing, not in the corners standing, sitting, moving, talking, not in the hallway. For a moment he thought of chucking the party and seeking her out at 482. But then what? Then what? Tomorrow would come. Hello. Goodbye.

He drained his cup of Purple Jesus and then swallowed cold beer to ease the flame in his throat. He found Harvey Ryan, sitting in a Goodwill of whites and greens, bleary eyes, a grin on his face. He beckoned Snow to come over. "Hey, you made it, Snow."

"Got off at twelve."

"No, no, you stupid fuck. I meant the whole year. You got through the whole year."

"Yeah. I did, didn't I."

Ryan pulled himself out of his chair, put an arm around Snow's shoulder and led him to the food and booze table. "I can see you need more. Let Dr. Ryan fill your prescription."

Snow drank more. The thunderstorm returned with a flash that lit up the lounge. In the thumping bass guitar, the whirling whites and greens, voices shouting out a chorus of "We all live in a yellow submarine," the alcohol hit him quickly. He turned and Ryan was gone. Then he saw him, his heavy, sloppy body dancing sinuously in the center. A surgical resident, caped, capped and booted in green, leaped high and thumped his feet in an energetic solo. And Snow found himself dancing in the crowd, pulled in by a nurse whose face he couldn't bring into focus.

He danced himself into exhaustion, then sat and drank, shouted nonsense into the ear of whoever sat beside him, and then danced some more, and some more, whirling, shouting.

When he looked again the crowd had thinned. Some of the nurses were gone, some of the sober residents on duty in their rooms trying to sleep. The diehard crowd here, the ones still dancing and drinking and whooping, were the ones who were finished the last day of June, and now it was—Snow tried to focus on his watch—about three-thirty in the morning of July 1, 1968.

Rain was blowing in the open windows but nobody moved to shut them. Ryan was still out on the floor, an Irish drunk, singing something in Gaelic, a surprising tenor that reached above a quieter Beatles tune. But he stopped suddenly and looked at the ceiling and shouted. This is what he shouted: "Trebilcock, you stupid bastard, can you see what you're missing?" Snow couldn't decide if the glistening wetness on his face was sweat from his forehead or tears from his eyes.

And then, with far too much Purple Jesus mingling with Labatts and Molsons in his spent body, Snow's mind fractured. They all rushed in on him, overlapping, transposing, Mrs. Ling's husband and son under large double wheels, Elsa saying to him this is a dying place, this is a dying place, the head of the young VC being blown apart, a naked eight-year-old running from napalm, dying from asthma, his own image shouting at Mrs. Polsky, die, please die, just die, and George Martin's no, don't, no, don't, no, don't, a bullet through King and Kennedy, his uncle seizuring with DTs, his mother seizuring with ECT.

He pulled himself to an open window and washed his hot face in the rain. He could hear bottles breaking, and the music punished his ears. He slumped against a wall and still it came in nauseous swirls. Blue nodules everywhere, lines feeding

271

bottles of dark piss, tubing in, tubing out, faces imploring, faces screaming, the BIRD, that simple, clean thing, standing on one leg, wheeze-pop, wheeze-pop, tentacles linking socket, tank and lungs, his mother imploring, and Ann, poor Ann, her face puzzled by this year strangling them both. He heard his voice saying into the void, I only killed two of them, only two, the medical director's mustached grin, a urine bottle shoved up the ass of a nephrologist, and Philip Trebilcock. That stupid goddamn bastard.

They used five-liter bottles as bowling balls, stacks of wine and beer bottles as pins, light bulbs as grenades. They overturned tables and threw chairs out the window. And they washed it all down with a fire hose. And Snow, face wet with beer, rain, tears, did this, too, joined in and collapsed against the wall, laughing, when he realized at least one puzzle was now solved, from exactly twelve months ago, and beer-soaked Harvey Ryan collapsed there with him.

"Feeling better now?" Harvey asked him without turning his head.

But Snow had to pull himself up the wall and grope for the open window from which he tossed once more into the quad, this time Purple Jesus, Molsons, Labatts, cheap wine, egg rolls and bile.

His brain returned to personal ownership about ten that morning when his eyes opened to the ceiling of his closet, his duty room, his cell. His lungs were working, wheeze. His heart was working, if somewhat excessively, pop. He reached for the phone and dialed Ann's number, their number. He was still damp. More than damp, wet in places.

When she answered he said, "I'll try to get there around noon."

"What kind of shape are you in?"

"I dunno. I haven't tried to walk yet."

"Are you hung over?"

"Not yet. Soon. Very soon." He made a mental note to drink a quart of water.

"Robert?"

"Uh-huh."

"I was going to wait till you got here."

"Yeah?" And for just a fraction the voice in his head said, She's leaving you and you deserve it, but instead she told him:

"Remember I went off the pill."

"You went off the pill?"

"We discussed it."

"Yeah, but you used a diaphragm."

"They're not a hundred percent."

Robert, sitting up now, causing a scalpel to slash through his eyes and stick in his forehead. Gasping, easing himself back down. "You know what I think?"

"Robert, were you listening to me?"

"Sure, sure, but let me tell you what I think."

"All right. What do you think?"

"I think we should grow our hair long."

"My hair is already long."

"Well, then, my hair, then. And we should join peace marches, and wear beads."

"Robert."

"Just let me finish. We should join peace marches and smoke a little weed."

"You're impossible."

"And make love and burn incense and sit by the sea."

"Uh-huh."

"And work and earn a little money, too."

"Uh-huh."

"And I'll write poetry and you'll teach children."

273

"Where are you going with this, Robert?"

"And…"

"Robert. I can hear you breathing. Are you all right? Where are you going with this?"

"And I think…"

"What?"

"And I think we should have a baby."